Praise for

Rest Ye Murdered Gentlemen

"Delightful . . . [A] humorous tinsel-covered tale that made me laugh out loud even while keeping me guessing."

—Jenn McKinlay, *New York Times* bestselling author

"Witty writing, an unexpected solution, and truly likable characters ensure that the appeal of this holiday-themed series will last long past the Yule season."

—Kings River Life Magazine

"Delany has given us a story full of holiday cheer, an exciting mystery, wondrous characters all in a place I would love to really visit. Its charm just lit up my day. This is one mystery you shouldn't miss this holiday season."

—Escapc with Dollycas into a Good Book

"I delved right into this story—it grabbed me in and wouldn't let me go."

—Socrates' Book Review

"Vicki Delany does a masterful job of creating an inviting fictional small town that is all about Christmas."

—Open Book Society

"Ms. Delany has started a promising new series with *Rest Ye Murdered Gentlemen*."

—Fresh Fiction

"A fun Yuletide-themed cozy with an appealing amateur sleuth."

—Library Journal

Berkley Prime Crime titles by Vicki Delany

REST YE MURDERED GENTLEMEN
WE WISH YOU A MURDEROUS CHRISTMAS
HARK THE HERALD ANGELS SLAY

Hark the Herald Angels Slay

Vicki Delany

BERKLEY PRIME CRIME
New York

BERKLEY PRIME CRIME
Published by Berkley
An imprint of Penguin Random House LLC
375 Hudson Street, New York, New York 10014

ISBN: 9780425280829

First Edition: November 2017

Printed in the United States of America
1 3 5 7 9 10 8 6 4 2

Cover art by Julia Green
Cover design by Sarah Oberrender
Book design by Tiffany Estreicher

For the happy couple:
Julia and Coleman

Acknowledgments

Thanks to the Ottawa gang, Barbara, Robin, Mary Jane, and Linda, for laughs and fun times and great ideas, and to Cheryl Freedman for her unerring editor's eye and love of Canadian crime (writing).

Chapter 1

In Rudolph, New York, we love Christmas so much, we celebrate it twice a year.

Christmas in July. A time to be silly, enjoy our brief hot summer, have some fun. And attract tourists to our town, of course.

I was in the back room of my shop, Mrs. Claus's Treasures, surrounded by boxes, studying my costume. My Mrs. Claus getup consisted of an ankle-length wool skirt, long-sleeved checked blouse worn under a knitted sweater-vest bearing a decorated Christmas tree design, plain glass spectacles, and a cap with gray curls attached. The forecast for the weekend was for temperatures reaching into the high eighties, and it would be even hotter, taking humidity into account.

Dressed in that outfit, standing in the sun, I might well melt.

I briefly considered going for a seductive Mrs. Claus look, but decided against that for two reasons. I don't do seductive, and Santa is played by none other than my own father.

"Merry!" Jackie, the shop assistant, called. "Someone here to see you."

"Back to work we go," I said to Matterhorn, my ten-month-old Saint Bernard.

I put the costume back on its hanger, left the storage room, and shooed Mattie into my office. He gave me a mournful, pleading look, as if to say, *No! Not the office! Anything but the office*, before doing as he was told. "You are such a ham," I said, heading to the front of the shop. I'd have to decide soon what I was going to wear. Today was Thursday and the big weekend was coming up fast.

I expected the caller would be a salesperson waiting to introduce me to their line of goods that I couldn't possibly live without. But it wasn't.

I stopped dead in the curtained doorway separating the private areas at the rear of the building from the salesrooms. A man stood at the counter with his back to me. Jackie was behind the cash register, smiling broadly at him, head cocked to one side, her light laugh filling the air.

He didn't have to turn around. I knew that stance, the broad shoulders, the slim hips, the long legs, the short dark hair. I started to back away, to run through the storage room, out the back door into the alley, and keep on running, but before I could move Jackie said, "There she is," and he turned. I also knew the high cheekbones, the straight white teeth, the eyes so dark they were almost black, the long lashes, the trace of black stubble on the strong jaw. Jackie widened her eyes, fanned her face, and her mouth formed the word "Wow!"

"Hello, Merry," he said.

"Mmmm." I cleared my throat, feeling a wave of heat as color rushed into my face. "Max."

Even Jackie could sense the tension in the air, and she dropped her comic expression to stare at us. Unfortunatcly, at this moment the shop was empty of customers. There was nothing to distract Jackie's attention or provide me with something I could pretend was in desperate need of my services.

He kept his eyes, those gorgeous black eyes under lashes so long and thick they could be used to string tennis rackets, fixed on my face. "Your shop's very nice, Merry. You have lots of great things. You must be doing well."

"Well enough." I struggled to find my voice. "Can I help you find something, Max?"

"Actually, Merry, you can. I've lost something very precious, and I've come here to get it back."

"I'd be happy to do what I can. What are you looking for?"

"The love of my life," he said.

Jackie gasped. I threw her a look over Max's shoulder. Her eyes threatened to pop right out of her head. She pointed to Max, did the fanning-the-face thing again, and then she pointed at me and mouthed "Wow!" again.

I tried to ignore her. "Max, why are you here?"

"I wanted to see you again, Merry. To talk. But"—he

turned toward Jackie—"as charming as your helper here is, I'd like to go someplace private."

I had a death grip on the curtain. "My office is . . ."

"Not in your office. How about we have dinner tonight? The place across the street looks okay. I'll make a reservation for seven. Shall I pick you up or meet you there?"

"I'll meet you. I mean . . . I don't want to have dinner with you, Max."

"Sure you do," he said. "Seven o'clock it is."

The chimes over the door sounded as the door opened and a woman came in. "There you are. Why aren't you answering your phone?"

Max gave me another long look before turning to face the newcomer. "I'm on a break."

"No time for breaks. Isn't that what you always say, Max? Breaks are for losers." She looked past him for the first time. Her eyes were about to flick over me, but then she did a double take. "Merry, is that you?"

"Willow?" I said. "Good heavens, Willow, what are you doing here?"

She crossed the room, arms outstretched. Max stepped aside, and Willow Rasmon enveloped me in a light hug accompanied by a kiss on the cheek that was more of a peck at the air. At five foot eleven and wearing her customary four-inch stilettos, Willow had to just about fold herself in half to reach me. "Max Folger, you are a naughty boy." She waved a bloodred nail at the end of a long finger. "Getting us to come here under a false pretext so you could see Merry."

"Nothing false about it," he said. "It's still a great story."

"Will one of you tell me what's going on?" I said.

"It was all Max's idea," Willow said, "and for once I have to admit it's a good one. We're going to do a feature on Christmas in July for the new travel section of the magazine. And what better place to celebrate Christmas than America's top year-round Christmas destination."

Jackie squealed. "You're from *Jennifer's Lifestyle*! Oh my gosh. I love that magazine. My mom has a subscription, and she gives me her copy every month when she's finished with it."

"How nice," Willow drawled.

Jackie ran around the counter and almost jumped up and down in front of Willow. "I can help you. I've lived here all my life. I know everyone!"

Willow peered down her long nose. "Goodness, I wouldn't have recognized you for a *small-town girl*."

Jackie beamed. I threw Willow a glare. Now I remembered: beneath the air-kissy façade Willow was nothing but a ruthlessly ambitious, stuck-up Manhattan snob.

Max laughed, and I glared at him, too.

Willow's oversized Michael Kors bag trilled, and she dug into a side pocket for her phone. At least she'd given up wearing one of those ridiculous earpieces that made people look as though they were about to be assimilated into the Borg Collective. "We're at Mrs. Claus's Treasures. Across the street from the library." She hung up and put the phone away.

"Who was that?" I asked.

"Our photographer," Willow said. "He's been scouting out vantage points around town."

Jackie squealed again. I felt the air move as she ran past us heading for the back rooms.

"Is someone going to tell me what's going on?" I said. "Or do I have to guess."

"Guess away, Merry," Max said. "It shouldn't be too hard."

The door opened once again and a man came in. He wore a beige, multi-pocketed vest of the sort last seen in the pages of *National Geographic*, carried a large bag, and had a long-lensed black Nikon slung over his shoulder. "This is going to be rich," he said. "I don't know what to shoot first."

"Jason Kerr, meet Merry Wilkinson," Willow said. "I don't think Jason did any work for us in your day, Merry."

He grinned at me. "I've heard a lot about you, when we were getting ready for this trip. You left big shoes to fill when you quit."

I couldn't help sneaking a peek at Max. Jason, I'm sure, meant when I left my job. Max would have been thinking of something else.

"Welcome to Mrs. Claus's Treasures." The curtain was swept aside, and Jackie stood there, framed in the entrance. She'd been gone for only about one minute, but she'd undone the top two buttons on her blouse, twisted the shirttails into a knot so it rode up to give us a peek at her taut belly, tightened the belt on her short denim skirt, applied a heavy layer of rose blush, and pulled her hair out of its clip so it fell in waves around her shoulders. She struck a pose, hip cocked, one shoulder forward, head tilted.

Max grinned at her. Willow's lip turned up in a sneer and she rolled her eyes. Jason said, "Do you work here?"

"Here? Yes, I'm Jackie O'Reilly. Head of customer service." That title was new to me. Jackie was my only full-time employee. "If you're looking for something *special*, I'd be delighted to assist you." She turned her smile on Max. "Both of you."

"I'm sure," Willow said.

The chimes sounded and a customer, a real live customer, came into the shop.

"If you don't mind," I said, "I have a business to run. Jackie. Jackie!"

"What?"

I jerked my head toward the customer, a middle-aged woman dressed in comfortable, but not inexpensive, clothes.

Jackie pouted prettily. But she knew where her paycheck came from and went to assist the new arrival.

"Since you left, Merry," Max said, "we've started a new regular feature in the magazine called Discover America. It's all about road trips and vacations the reader can find right in their backyard. We're here to do Christmas in July in Rudolph."

As much as I wasn't happy to see Max in my shop, or in Rudolph, I have to admit I was pleased at the idea. We were a tourist town. If there's one thing tourism needs, it's publicity. Good publicity, that is, not the sort we had in the days leading up to last Christmas, which threatened to turn Rudolph into the Ghost of Christmas Towns Past. "Sounds like a great idea."

"It was Max's suggestion," Willow said. "I wonder what made him think of it."

"Don't you have locations to scout, Willow?" Max said.

"I suppose I do. There's a darling little bakery up the street with a display of gingerbread cookies in the window. So charming."

"Victoria's Bake Shoppe," I said. "Their gingerbread is a Rudolph institution."

"I'm thinking we might be able to expand into a piece for the food section. I'll try and pry some of the recipes out of them for our test kitchen." Willow pulled a small notebook out of her bag. It was a real paper notebook, too, with a pen attached. Willow was always jotting down ideas. It was part of what made her a successful style editor.

"Don't get ahead of yourself," Max said. "We're not here for food."

"I thought," Willow said, "we were here to do a good story. Heaven knows, the magazine needs *something*. Anything to get circulation back up."

"Not food," Max said. "That's Adrienne's domain."

"If we run pictures of the bakery window," Willow snapped, "we'll get letters asking for the recipes."

"Then Adrienne can decide if she wants to feature some."

"Gee, you guys are sure making me wish I was back at the magazine," I said. "Not. Find someplace else to do your storyboarding, will you? I have a business to run."

Willow pointedly studied the room. Jackie was showing earrings to the sole customer. As can be guessed by the name of my shop, I sell Christmas things. The earrings in question were gold, formed into the traditional triangle shape representing a Christmas tree, with red and green glass draped from the frame to represent the lights and decorations. "I can see how busy you are," Willow said.

"We'll be busy on the weekend." I rushed to defend my business. In defending Mrs. Claus's Treasures, I was also defending the decision that had me leaving my life and job in Manhattan and returning to my hometown.

"Of course you will, sweetie," Willow said. "That's why we're here."

"The focus of the section will be on Saturday's activities," Max said. "Family-friendly stuff. Right now we're checking things out, looking for a bit of color."

Jason lifted his camera and took a picture of Jackie. Caught unaware, she squeaked and struck a pose. The customer pretended not to notice the camera as she patted her hair, thrust out her chin, and sucked in her stomach.

"You can get a full schedule of the day at the town office," I said. "Santa will be arriving by boat and setting his chair up on the beach to meet children of all ages. We'll have other activities going on throughout the day."

"Say cheese," Jason said, swinging the camera in my direction.

Instinctively, I smiled. Then I remembered myself. "Don't do that. I don't want to be in your magazine."

"Sure you do," Willow said. "Everyone does. I'm going to the bakery now. Jason, come with me. So nice to see you, Merry. I'm sure we'll have lots of time to chat before I leave."

"I'm heading back to the hotel," Max said. "I have calls to make. Willow, stop in at that restaurant across the street and make me a reservation for two for seven o'clock." He kept his eyes fixed on me. I shifted.

"I'm not your secretary," Willow snapped.

"You are if I say you are," he said.

She huffed, but didn't reply, and she and Jason left. "Catch you later," Jackie called after them. "I'll be here all weekend, hard at work. Although, I don't have to be here *all* the time if you need someone to show you around."

Jason gave her a wave, but Willow didn't so much as slow down.

"I'll take these," the customer said, holding the earrings. "Miss, I said, I'll take these."

"Sorry." Jackie tore her eyes away from the window. She went behind the counter to ring up the sale, wrap the jewelry in tissue, and put the packet into a paper bag bearing the Mrs. Claus's Treasures logo.

"See you at seven, Merry," Max said to me.

"I don't . . ."

"It'll be fun to catch up, won't it?" He gave me the grin that once upon a time would have been guaranteed to melt my feeble heart.

No longer.

The bells tinkled as the happy shopper left.

Max crossed the shop floor. "Those earrings you just sold," he said to Jackie, "or ones like them, would be perfect for our article. I plan to do a sidebar on shopping. Maybe you could model them for us."

I thought she was going to faint. "I'd be . . ."

"Good," he said. "Our readers enjoy seeing what ordinary women are buying." He walked out.

She watched him go with a look of pure adoration on her face. Jackie was vain and completely self-absorbed, but she had a kind heart and never a bad word to say about anyone. Poor Jackie didn't even realize how deeply she'd been insulted. "You're having dinner with that gorgeous man," she said with a happy sigh. "You are so lucky, Merry. But what about Alan? What will he think? If you don't want to go to dinner, I'll take your place."

"Jackie," I said. "Stay away from him. From all of them. They are not nice people. Max Folger, most of all."

"Pooh. You're not my mother, Merry. When did you become such an old fogy? You always try to spoil everything for me."

"You're right that I'm not your mother, but I am your boss. And this is your place of employment. Button up your shirt and tuck it in."

She pouted once again, but did as she was told, throwing me poisonous glances all the while.

"I'm going to take Mattie for a walk and grab some lunch on the way back." I tried to make nice. I wasn't an old fogy. I was merely trying to be a responsible businesswoman. My employees' welfare was my concern, whether they wanted my help or not. "Want me to pick up a latte for you?"

"Sure. I've been thinking. Maybe I should wear my elf costume on Saturday after all."

"Whatever," I said. When I'd suggested Jackie and Crystal, my part-time helper, dress in costume on the weekend, Jackie had refused on the perfectly reasonable grounds that their elf getups were winter clothes. But the costume was cute, and after Jackie made a few unauthorized adjustments, playfully sexy. Easy to guess why she'd changed her mind.

The women who read *Jennifer's Lifestyle* were not the type to want to see pictures of pretty, flirty young women posing in skimpy costumes. Max would lead Jackie on, have a good laugh about it, and throw out any pictures they did take.

I opened my office door and was hit full in the chest by a hundred and twenty pounds of happy dog.

"Down," I wheezed, struggling to get my breath back.

Mattie grinned at me, his big pink tongue lolling out one side of his mouth. He was ten months old and was now well enough trained that I could bring him to work with me most days. He knew he didn't belong in the shop (I shudder to think of him among the glass ornaments, delicate jewelry, and china dishes) and was content, if not exactly happy, to stay in the office. My office, not much more than a storage closet with a single visitor's chair and a desk buried under stacks of paper, had been small before Mattie settled himself into the dog bed on the floor.

I reminded him that we didn't leap upon our friends, no matter how pleased we were to see them, and took his leash down from the hook by the door. All winter and spring we'd worked hard at our training—training me as much as him. With an animal of his size good behavior was vitally important. He'd quickly become used to the activity in the shop and never barked when the door opened or people talked. I gave him an affectionate pat and he yipped in reply. We slipped out the back way into the alley and headed toward the park.

It looked as though I'd be having dinner tonight with Max Folger, ex-fiancé and cheating no-good son of a . . . after all. He always did have a way of talking me into doing things I didn't really want to do. I could, of course, simply not show up at the restaurant. But then he'd hunt me down, probably arrive on my doorstep, and I'd feel obliged to invite him in. I needed to find out what he was up to. He might want to spin me a line like "love of my life" but I wasn't going to fall for that again.

I'd enjoy a nice dinner and then tell him to go back to New York and the woman he'd dumped me for.

Chapter 2

The moment Mattie and I stepped out of the building into the alley, the heat hit us full on. Like all Saint Bernards, Mattie suffers dreadfully in the hot weather. Nothing he likes more than a romp in the snow, but no snow was threatening to come our way anytime soon, so at home and in the shop I kept the air-conditioning turned up as high as I dared. Nothing I could do about the great outdoors, though.

The humidity settled on my shoulders like a blanket. A hot, wet, sticky blanket. Mattie panted and his gait was noticeably slower than his usual all-out, enthusiastic gallop. As we walked, I pulled out my phone and called my best friend.

"Can I get back to you?" Vicky Casey said. "Lunch rush is starting." I could hear the background buzz of her busy bakery.

"Just calling with a heads-up. A tall woman in white capris and a blue jacket with white piping, a white collar, and giant white buttons is possibly heading your way. She's a style editor with *Jennifer's Lifestyle*, and they might do a feature on your bakery."

Vicky gasped. "You're kidding? No, I know you, you're not kidding. Hold on. I'm taking a peek. Yup, I think I see the one you mean. Tall is right. I think she's even taller than me."

"That's the shoes," I said. Vicky was five-eleven and a half. A good six inches taller than me. She was also rail thin, which I (not rail thin) thought highly unfair considering the woman baked delicious breads and mouthwatering pastries for a living.

"She's studying the display case. She's writing something in a little notebook. A guy's with her and he has a camera. A heavy-duty camera. What should I do? Should I introduce myself?"

"No. Go out front and look authoritative, in charge. Keep your apron on. Whisper something to one of the staff. Give the visitors a polite nod. Maybe rearrange some pastries or something. Look important."

"Don't I always?" she said.

I refrained from saying, *No, you don't.* With her midnight-black hair cut almost to her scalp, save for the single purple lock that fell over one eye, heavy dark makeup, tattoos, and piercings, Vicky rarely looked like the astute businesswoman she was. I put my phone away, and Mattie and I continued on our walk. Rudolph sits on the southern shores of Lake Ontario, tucked into a small bay. The sandy beach at the park was crowded with colorful umbrellas and folding chairs, and a handful of people were throwing balls in the shallows or swimming farther out. Past them, white sails dotted the sparkling blue water. The lake stretched to the horizon, calm and peaceful. I kept the walk short, not only because I needed to get back to the shop, but because the heat was bothering Mattie. He was panting heavily, leaving a trail of drool on the sidewalk behind him. A squirrel dashed across the grass and ran nimbly up a stately ancient oak. Mattie flicked his tail, took one step toward the creature, and then thought better of engaging in a chase.

"Enough for now, I think," I said, leading him back to town. I tied the dog to a bike rack on a shady patch of sidewalk outside Cranberry Coffee Bar, next to a bowl of water they kindly kept refreshed for passing dogs, and went in to get my lunch, knowing Mattie would soon attract a circle of admirers. Despite his size, he was a gentle animal, as were all members of his breed, and he was particularly great with children. More than once I've had to ask parents to, please, not let their child try to ride the dog. He's not a pony. He never seemed to mind, but I did think some people were inclined to take liberties.

We hadn't had pets in my family when I was growing up, because my mom said fur stuck to everything. When I left home, first for college and then for a minuscule third-floor walk-up in Manhattan, a dog wasn't possible. I wasn't even thinking of getting a pet when I returned to Rudolph last year, but Vicky Casey had other plans, and somehow Mattie, born on the wrong side of the doggy blanket to a purebred, reams of papers, kennel-show-star mother and a father with a wandering eye, came into my life. And, I have to say, into my heart.

I ordered a bran muffin and a small green salad with an iced coffee for me and a superlarge full-fat latte for Jackie. I carried my purchases outside and found, as well as the expected crowd of dog admirers, my parents. I was pleased to see them; I'd been wondering how I was going to manage untying the dog while carrying two cups and a paper bag. "Hold these," I said, thrusting the cups at Mom. She looked wonderful, as she always did, in a white dress cut exactly at her knees, with short sleeves, a scooped neck, a thin pink belt, and matching pink sandals. My dad looked . . .

"Are you Santa Claus?" a small girl was brave enough to ask.

Dad tapped the side of his nose. "I might be. I might not be. Although, I am here checking to see if children have been naughty or nice. Have you?" His round belly shook and his blue eyes twinkled above his red nose and curly white beard. He wore red and green striped Bermuda shorts with a green checked shirt and white socks thrust into heavy brown sandals.

"Yes, Santa," she said, giving him a huge grin that showed two missing front teeth.

My mom took a step backward in case some overly bold child would dare to ask if she was Santa's helper. My parents are a strange pair. Totally mismatched in every way, but completely devoted to each other.

"I hear," Dad said, "Santa is coming to town on Saturday for his summer vacation. He'll be arriving around one, at the boat dock."

"We'll be there, Santa," the child's mother said, smothering a giggle.

"Is that a reindeer disguised as a dog, Mom?" I heard the girl say as her mother led her away.

I untied Mattie. "Don't even think it," I said to Dad.

"Think what, honeybunch?" he said innocently.

"Mattie is not going to put antlers on his head and a red ball on his nose and pretend to be Rudolph."

"Perish the thought," Dad said.

"He has his dignity, you know." I gave the dog a hearty pat. One advantage of owning a giant dog—I didn't have to bend over to reach him.

My parents fell into step beside me and we walked down the block to the alley.

"We were coming to see you," Dad said, "and saw your dog. I hear a magazine's in town wanting to write about the weekend."

"Not just a magazine," Mom said. "*Jennifer's Lifestyle*. Your old colleagues."

"I know. They came into the shop earlier. Max is with them."

"I hadn't heard that," Mom said. "Are you all right, dear?"

"Of course I am. Why wouldn't I be?" I didn't miss the look that passed between my parents. "I have no problem seeing Max, none at all. The publicity will be good for the town."

"Yes, it will," Dad said. "Be sure and tell Max about the boat parade."

"If they want information," Mom said, "they can get it from the town publicity office, like anyone else."

"I'm okay with it, Mom. Listening to them sniping away at each other made me realize I made the right decision in leaving the magazine and coming back to Rudolph." Mom touched my shoulder and I gave her a smile. "Here, the only person I have to snipe at is Jackie, and she's no challenge."

Dad laughed. "With them in town, all the more reason to hope the boat thing goes off okay."

"I still think it's a wonderful idea," I said. "Are you having doubts?"

"No more than the usual misgivings before implementing any new idea." One of the major Rudolph traditions is the semiannual Santa Claus parade. As well as the main event the first Saturday in December, we also have one on the Saturday before July 25th. This year the town council decided to shake things up a bit and have Santa arrive by boat at the rear of a gaily decorated flotilla. Traditionalists grumbled, as traditionalists always do, but most people liked the idea. It was a lot less work for one thing, sticking a bit of tinsel and some baubles onto a boat, than doing up a flatbed float to be pulled by a truck or tractor. Some people worried that we wouldn't be able to find sufficient boats for everyone who wanted to participate, but with our perfect small-boat harbor, plenty of Rudolphites own some sort of watercraft, and that turned out not to be a problem.

We reached the back of my shop. I dug in my pocket and pulled out the key.

"I haven't seen Alan around much lately. Will he be helping you on Saturday, Noel?" Mom spoke to my dad but her eyes were on me. I lowered my head and fiddled with putting the key into the lock.

"Of course," Dad said. "Why wouldn't he?"

Alan Anderson was a local artisan, specializing in woodwork. He created many of the beautiful handcrafted things I sell in the shop. He also served as Santa's head toymaker at official functions.

"Merry?" Mom said.

"Yes, Mom?"

"Alan hasn't been around much since he got back from Florida."

"He's been busy. I've been busy. We've all been busy." I shoved the door open, and Mattie dashed inside. I dropped the leash and took the cups from Mom. "Thanks."

"If you need to talk, dcar."

"I don't. Catch you later." I didn't *quite* slam the door in my parents' faces.

Alan Anderson. I didn't know what was going on between Alan and me, and my parents were starting to give me questioning looks (Dad) and dropping hints (Mom). Alan and I had dated in high school and broke up on graduation when we went our separate ways. Now that I was back in town, we'd discovered that the old spark hadn't died, and over Christmas we realized we wanted to pick up where we'd left off. After that, things had gone nowhere fast. I didn't know who to blame. If anyone.

Alan's parents had moved to Florida for their retirement, and in February his dad broke a leg while golfing.

That seems like a joke, but Mr. Anderson stepped into a hole in search of his ball buried in the weeds and fell hard. Alan had gone to Tampa to help out. His dad was also a woodworker, which is how Alan had learned his craft, and he'd set up a fully equipped woodworking shop at the new house. Spring is quiet in Rudolph, so Alan stayed in Florida, where he could keep working while he helped his mom look after his dad. He'd come home in May, but we'd scarcely seen each other since. Somehow our schedules hadn't seemed to mesh. Maybe that was my fault. I'd had a hard time when Max left me for another woman with no warning. One day I'd been expecting a ring in a little box with a big ribbon and obsessing over wedding magazines, and the next I was packing my bags and heading out of town. That had been less than a year ago, and my heart still shied away from the possibility of hurt.

"I have never stopped loving you, Merry Wilkinson."

"Please. No."

"It's why I'm here. I want you back. I want you back in New York and back in my life. Where you belong."

"I have a life here," I said.

"A small town in Upstate New York, owning a one-employee store? That's not a life for you. I saw your parents earlier. Your mom looks great. She says she misses her old life sometimes but she's happy in retirement. That's your *mother*, Merry. It can be you in forty years. Not now."

I twisted the stem of the wineglass in my fingers and studied the deep red liquid. I looked up, into the face of the man sitting across from me, and I realized I wasn't tempted in the least.

I'd moved on. I'd seen Max Folger for the shallow, money-grubbing, ruthlessly ambitious man he was, and I wanted no part of him. "Are we going to order? I'm looking forward to a nice meal, but this conversation is over."

"Have you found someone else?"

An image of Alan flashed through my mind. I shook my head. "None of your business if I have or have not."

"Okay. I'll drop it. For now, but don't expect me to give up, Merry. I'll never give up on you."

"What about Erica? What about your engagement to her? I thought you were getting married next month. Isn't it going to be the social event of the season?"

He grimaced and ran his fingers through his hair. "It's turned into a nightmare. I was desperate to get the heck out of town, so when I remembered you talking about this quirky place you came from, I grabbed at the idea. I was lucky to be able to drag a couple of the staff with me. Everyone else is all tied up in *wedding* preparations. It's complicated."

"I bet it is." Trust Max. He hadn't broken off with Erica yet, not until he was sure I wanted to come back to him.

Erica was the granddaughter of Jennifer Johnstone, founder of the *Jennifer's Lifestyle* empire, which included, as well as the magazine, a TV show, a restaurant chain, and stores selling deck furniture, patio accessories, and supplies for alfresco cooking. Jennifer was the doyenne of anything and everything to do with casual, outdoor, modern American entertaining. Max and I had worked together at the magazine. I'd loved every minute of it. The exciting job, being part of the fashionable New York world, living in the heart of Manhattan. I'd loved Max, too, and my life had been perfect. Then Jennifer retired and handed control of the magazine to her granddaughter. And we were all reminded of the old saying: rags to riches to rags in three generations. Erica had not an ounce of business sense, along with no desire to accumulate any, nor did she feel the need to accept any advice. She clearly hadn't inherited her grandmother's excellent taste and eye for the next big thing.

She did, however, have an eye for a handsome man, and as her grandmother was pushing her to produce great-grandchildren, Erica settled that eye on Max Folger.

I don't know if Max had ever loved her, and I didn't really care. She had enough money to convince an ambitious man that he was in love. And so Max was promoted to executive editorial director, given a big corner office with a fabulous view of the East River, and I was told I was surplus to requirements, in the romance department anyway. I wasn't actually fired, but I could hardly continue working there any longer. I quit and came home to Rudolph with my tail between my legs.

Which turned out to have been a marvelous thing to do, and I hadn't regretted it for a moment. As far as I was concerned, Erica could have not only Max but the heartless, shallow world in which they lived and worked. I'd had a lucky escape.

I hadn't picked up a copy of *Jennifer's Lifestyle* since, but the business news, as well as my friends who'd found new jobs rather than work under Erica's imperious management style, reported that circulation was dropping fast and advertisers were stampeding to pull out. Erica, quite simply, didn't know her audience and wouldn't let anyone tell her. She wanted stories on makeup and clothes and features on celebrities, not articles on how to throw a casual alfresco dinner party, prepare a perfect picnic for twelve on the beach, or decorate a woodland getaway. It was rumored that Jennifer was considering coming out of retirement. The new travel section sounded like a good idea to me, and I wondered if that was Jennifer, who I'd adored, trying to get back in the saddle before her empire collapsed into ruins.

"Isn't your wedding going to be a big story in the magazine?" I said. "And the honeymoon?"

Max growled. "You see my problem, Merry. It's not just a wedding, it's a *special edition*. The whole magazine has been tied in knots all year getting ready for the big event. I'm nothing but a prop. They might as well get a store mannequin to fill in as the groom for all the input I have into this. I don't want to do it. I can't do it."

I studied the menu. "I'm going to have the seafood pasta and an heirloom tomato salad to start. All the produce used here will have been sourced directly from local farmers. What about you?"

"Merry, I . . ."

The waiter arrived at our table, pencil poised. He'd rattled off the specials when he took the drink requests.

"Order, Max," I said.

He didn't even open his menu. "Steak and frites. Rare. Caesar salad."

I placed my order, and the waiter collected the menus and left us alone.

"You'll want lots of pictures of Santa arriving by boat," I said. "The weather forecast is for a hot sunny day with only a light wind. The kids are going to love it."

Max always did have a way of not paying any attention when I was talking. Funny how I never realized that when we were together, but in retrospect it became perfectly clear. Now he was looking over my shoulder into the dining room. An unpleasant half grin turned up the corner of his mouth. "Well, well, I wouldn't have taken her for a fast mover."

"Who?" I turned to see what was happening behind me.

"She's new since your time. Amber Newhouse, junior props assistant. So junior she was the only one I could drag away from the wedding plans"—Max made quotation marks in the air with his fingers—"to bring out here to the back of beyond. You know what they say about still waters running deep. You never can tell with the plain, quiet ones, can you?"

A man and a woman were being shown to a table for two. A Touch of Holly was the nicest (and most expensive) restaurant in the town of Rudolph. Each place was set with a stiff, ironed white napkin with a small cluster of red berries embroidered in the corner. The tables had starched white tablecloths, a tiny votive candle in a glass holder, and a small vase containing a few sprigs of fresh summer flowers accented by a clipping from a holly bush. The big fireplace was unlit, of course, and the space had been filled with giant vases piled high with colorful glass balls, most of them from my shop. The room glowed with subdued lighting and the flickering glow of candles shining off crystal glassware. Conversation and laughter swirled around us.

My heart stuck in my throat. Somewhere in the deep recesses of my mind, Max's sneering comments droned on.

The woman was attractive enough, never mind Max's scorn. She was in her late twenties, but I thought her hairstyle—a shoulder-length blond flip—was seriously out of date as was her too-short pink skirt. She walked awkwardly on pink sandals with miles of lacing and four-inch heels. The man following her across the crowded room was none other than Alan Anderson, woodworker, toymaker, and . . . I didn't know what he was to me anymore.

The woman saw us watching and lifted a hand to wave. Alan followed her gaze and his brilliant blue eyes settled on me. She said something to the waiter and changed direction. They headed toward us. Max got to his feet.

"Amber! So nice to see you." He thrust his hand at Alan. "Max Folger."

Alan's expression shifted when he heard the name, but I doubt Max noticed. "Alan Anderson."

"Alan's an old family friend." Amber's voice was so

high-pitched it was heading toward the grating end of the scale. "When I heard we were coming to Rudolph, I knew I had to look him up." She giggled and smiled at me. "Hi."

"Merry Wilkinson," Max said. "A local businesswoman. Merry's giving me the inside scoop about what we need to be on the lookout for on Saturday."

"Oh, Max." Amber giggled. "You're always working."

Alan smiled at me. I smiled back. "Merry and I are old friends," he said. *Old friends? Is that what we'd become?* I continued smiling.

"Why don't you join us? We've only just ordered." Max apparently hadn't noticed that we were at a table for two, and the tables on either side of us were taken.

"That would be great." Amber looked around for the waiter. "Let's see if we can get a bigger table." Max's smile cracked, and I smothered a laugh. As awkward as this was, it was funny to see Max's New York fake politeness taken seriously.

"We wouldn't want to disturb you," Alan said. "Have a nice evening. Nice meeting you, Max. Merry." He led Amber to their waiting table. She wiggled her fingers at us over her shoulder.

Max sat back down and picked up his glass.

"She seems nice," I said.

"Way out of her league," he said. "We'll see how long she lasts. Not long, I expect. The first small-town hick to offer her a house with a white picket fence and two-point-three kids and she'll be gone. Speaking of small-town hicks, he fits the bill. Judging by those hands, I'd say he's a pig farmer." Max laughed and took a swig of his wine.

"You know what I've just realized, Max?" I said.

"That you can't live without me?"

"You're not a very nice person. Were you born mean, or did New York make you that way?" My blood was rising and flames shot through my face. My hands shook. Alan's hands were scarred and calloused because they were the hands of a man who earned his living with them. He made stunning things that filled homes with beauty and children with delight. Things even people with limited funds could own and cherish. His wasn't a fake world of garden parties for one hundred, picnic boats, morning horseback rides through fog-draped woods, meals prepared and rooms scrubbed and polished by an army of invisible servants before the photography team arrived.

I pushed back my chair. "This was a bad idea. Good night, Max."

"Wow," he said, "you really have got the small-town bug, don't you, Merry? Or is it that guy? I'll admit, he scrubs up well."

I reached under my chair for my purse.

"Don't move."

"I'm leaving. Enjoy your dinner."

"I mean it. Don't move and don't turn around. I can't believe this." He was staring over my shoulder with a look of absolute horror on his chiseled face. I started to turn, to see what dreadful event was going on behind me. "I said, don't look," he snapped. Then he swore. "Too late. She's seen us." He planted a smile on his face and stood up. I swiveled in my chair, thinking that it couldn't be all that bad.

But it was. It was worse.

An excessively thin woman dressed in a blue and white striped summer dress and sky-high stilettos was bearing down on us. Her heels tapped a furious rhythm on the hardwood floor, carefully colored brown hair with caramel highlights swung around her shoulders, and her perfectly made-up black eyes threw thunderbolts around the room.

The hostess skipped along behind her, waving a menu, mouth flapping open and shut.

I heard one of the women at the table to my right say, "Isn't that . . ." and to the left someone said, "I think that's Erica Johnstone. My, but she's thin."

Erica stopped at our table. She put her hands on her nonexistent hips and said, "I should have known."

"Hey, babe. Isn't this a pleasant surprise? Won't you join us? Bring another chair," he ordered the hostess. "And a wineglass." She scurried away to do his bidding.

Women tended to do that for Max.

I'd once done that for Max.

"When I heard about your idea to run a feature on some stupid summer Santa Claus parade, I figured it would do you good to get out of town and out from underfoot. Looks like I was too busy planning my *wedding* to worry about what my *fiancé* was up to." She looked at me for the first time, but continued speaking to Max. "Some people are loyal to me. Jason phoned and told me *she* was here."

"Gee, thanks, Jason," Max mumbled.

"You can't admit defeat, can you?" Erica pointed a

sharp red fingernail in my direction. "You had to lure *my man* back into your web by dangling a story in front of him." The light from the candle on our table caught the ring on the third finger of her left hand and white fire flashed. The square-cut diamond at the center of the ring was enormous, and a row of smaller diamonds was inset into the band. That ring would have cost far more than Max could afford on his salary from the magazine.

"Hey," I said, tearing my eyes away from the diamonds. "This has nothing to do with me. I didn't even know . . ."

A waiter arrived with a chair, and another held a wineglass. Everyone in the restaurant had stopped what they were doing to gape. The only one not watching was Amber, who had buried her face in her napkin, no doubt not wanting her boss to see her. Alan had risen to his feet, his eyes fixed on me.

"Why don't you sit down and have a drink, babe?" Max said, his voice low and soothing. "It's all a misunderstanding. Merry and I were discussing the best location for the photo shoot on Saturday. Santa Claus will be coming by boat, so I'm wondering if we should rent a boat for ourselves, to get the best perspective. What do you think?"

"What do I think!" Erica's voice rose. "I don't *think* my fiancé takes a woman to dinner behind my back to talk about photo angles."

I glanced around the room. People were pulling iPhones out of jackets and bags. Oh dear. I put my hands over my face and peeked out from between my fingers.

"No need to be concerned," Max said. I was surprised at how calm he sounded. He must have had a lot of experience trying to control this spoiled drama queen. His hand was steady as he poured wine into the fresh glass and held it out to Erica. "Another bottle," he said to the waiter. "This is nothing but a business meeting. Merry used to be one of our top style editors. You remember, don't you, babe?"

Erica accepted the glass and took a deep drink. "Oh yes. I remember her. I fired her because her taste hadn't evolved since she left the rust belt on the back of a turnip truck."

"Hey," I said. "That's not true. I quit."

She threw the contents of her glass into my face. The entire room let out a collective gasp. Lights flashed as cameras clicked. Wine stung my eyes and liquid dripped down my face. I felt a hand on my arm and I was lifted to my feet.

"Let's go, Merry," Alan said.

"That's enough," Max said. "Sit down, Erica."

She dropped into a chair.

"You folks can go back to minding your own business now," Max said in a voice just loud enough to be heard in a restaurant that had gone deathly quiet. He snapped his fingers and shouted, "Muriel!"

"Oh my gosh, Erica, are you all right?" A woman rushed past us. "Can I get you anything? A glass of water, more wine?" It was Muriel Fraser, Erica's personal assistant. The one the employees called the Unfriendly Ghost.

When Max first started seeing Erica, I'd wondered if Muriel went along on their dates. I guess she did.

Alan pressed a napkin into my hand, and I was still blinking tears and wiping wine out of my eyes when we left the chilly air-conditioned restaurant and walked into the fresh night air. A light breeze carrying the scent of flowers from the huge pots on either side of the door ruffled the hair on my arms.

"You don't think she saw me, do you?" Amber said. "Oh my gosh, if she saw me watching, I'm finished."

"I suspect she had her mind on other things." I opened my eyes cautiously. I blinked rapidly, trying to focus.

"That'll be all over Twitter in about half a minute," Alan said. "If not sooner."

"She won't care," I said. "Not unless her grandmother sees it, and she probably will. Jennifer keeps herself up to date." Erica would be called and a lecture given. She'd be contrite and tearful. And nothing, I knew, would change.

For the first time, I felt very sorry for Max.

Chapter 3

I live only a couple of blocks from the center of Rudolph, so Alan and Amber walked me home. At eight o'clock it was still daylight, and shades of soft pink and gray streaked the clouds in the west. As we passed the park, the lights of the town's year-round Christmas tree in the bandstand came on. Lights bobbed on boats moored in the harbor, and the park was crowded with picnickers and walkers. Tomorrow, the weekend festivities would open with a family BBQ hosted by the mayor and town councilors, followed by a teenage dance party at the bandstand.

Amber moaned a few more times that if Erica had seen her in the restaurant, watching, she'd be fired, but at last she stopped talking. We walked on in blessed silence. Alan didn't talk much, and never if he had nothing to say. I suspected he had a lot to say tonight, but he could tell I wasn't up to making idle chatter. Activity on the street died as we left the shopping district and then the park. A few people were out walking their dogs and the occasional car drove past. The lower level of my house was a blaze of light, and that, I knew, was not a good thing. I live on the top floor of a grand old Victorian in a charming apartment with use of the spacious backyard for Mattie. The only thing I didn't like about where I lived was my landlady, Mrs. D'Angelo, the fastest gossip in the East.

The curtains in the front room moved as we turned up the path. The door flew open before I could dash for safety, and Mrs. D'Angelo came onto the porch. She wore a lime green T-shirt and matching shorts secured by a wide belt. The purpose of the belt was to hold her cell phone on the odd occasion she didn't have it firmly in hand. She'd updated her technology recently, and blue earbuds trailed from her ears into the pouch on her belt.

"Merry Wilkinson! Janet Lawrence, whose daughter works at A Touch of Holly, called to tell me you were attacked by Erica Johnstone. Imagine! Erica Johnstone here in Rudolph. I knew, of course, that a team from her magazine was here, but not Erica herself."

Mrs. D'Angelo seemed far more excited about the presence of Erica than the supposed assault on me. "Don't worry, Mrs. D'Angelo," I said, "I am unharmed."

"I read that magazine all the time. They did a lovely piece on historic homes of Cape Cod a couple of years ago. Perhaps they'd be interested in doing the same thing again, this time here in Rudolph. We do, of course, have some marvelous examples of eighteenth-century colonial architecture, many with beautiful gardens to match. I might even be convinced to open my own house for a photo spread." This property did have a lovely garden. Eight months of the year, Mrs. D'Angelo could be found out front, digging, planting, weeding, trimming. All the better to keep an eye on activity on our street. In the winter, she spread salt, chipped ice, and shoveled snow, whether we had any or not. "Perhaps you could suggest that to her, Merry."

"Suggest what?"

"The article on my house and garden, of course. I mean, the houses and gardens of Rudolph."

"I don't think Erica will be seeking my advice anytime soon."

Mrs. D'Angelo glared at me, clearly disappointed that I had allowed Erica to fight with me. Her phone rang and she pushed the button on the blue cord. "Yes, I heard. Here in Rudolph!"

"Thanks for coming to my aid," I said to Alan. "I'm okay now. You'll want to go back and finish your dinner."

"I can't show my face there," Amber said. "If she sees me, I'll be done for. I really need this job. It's all I've ever dreamed of."

"You didn't get any dinner, either," Alan said to me.

"I seem to have lost my appetite." That was certainly true. My stomach was only now beginning to stop churning. "I'm going to get Mattie and go for a nice long walk."

"Need company?" he asked.

I flushed and glanced away.

"I'm starving," Amber said.

"You two go and have your dinner. I'll be fine."

"Okay," Alan said. "If you're sure."

"I don't think she saw me, do you?" Amber said. "She was focused on Max. She doesn't usually notice the staff much. I was at her house for a few days when we did the story on her engagement party. She barely even looked at me the whole time. Except to tell me I was doing everything wrong. Right now she's like totally occupied with her wedding."

They walked away, into the deepening dusk. I headed upstairs.

I'd turned my phone off before going into dinner, and I turned it on as I climbed the stairs. It immediately started beeping to tell me I had voice mail messages. I ignored them all and switched the phone off again.

I couldn't ignore the messages forever. When I got up the next morning, my voice mailbox was full and I had received numerous text messages telling me to check Twitter.

Reluctantly, fearing the worst, I did so.

It wasn't as bad as I'd feared. Under the label #richgirlmeltdown there were unflattering (to say the least) pictures of Erica screaming. Max could be seen in some of the shots, looking perfectly calm and quite handsome. Of me, only the back of my head or my outstretched fingers were visible. If my mom saw the pictures, and she probably would, she'd recognize the ring I was wearing on my right hand as one made for me by a local jewelry designer. But for anyone else, the ring wasn't enough for a positive identification. The crux of the stories was that Erica had discovered her fiancé in a "compromising situation" with an "unidentified woman."

Never have I been so happy to be unidentified.

I brewed coffee and popped a bagel into the toaster. When it was ready, I prepared a tray and carried my breakfast downstairs to sit at the picnic table in the yard while Mattie sniffed under bushes and verified that no overnight intruders remained in our yard. The top floor of the house is divided into two apartments, and we share the use of the back garden. My neighbors, Steve and Wendy and their baby, Tina, were away on vacation. The property's surrounded by giant old oaks and maples, and bird song filled the air. It was delightfully cool in the dappled morning shade, but I knew the heat was on its way. I finished my coffee, called Mattie in, and got ready for work.

I settled Mattie into the office with a big bowl of water and promises to return soon, opened the shop, and settled down to do some paperwork before the (I hoped) rush of customers descended. The first person through the doors was Vicky.

"I heard what happened," she said.

"Is there anyone who didn't?"

"Probably not." She put a bakery bag on the counter. "I figured you required sustenance."

I didn't need to open the bag to know it contained one of Vicky's justifiably famous cinnamon buns. The scent of warm pastry, melting white icing, and lavishly applied cinnamon was intoxicating. I'd once told her she should charge people for sniffing the air outside the bakery on cinnamon bun–baking day.

"I can't stay," she said. "I have to get back. I'll be making molasses spice cookies all day for the town cook-out tonight."

"Does it look as though we're going to get a good crowd?"

"Mark says they're fully booked for the weekend, and I've heard that the other B&Bs and hotels are the same." Mark Grosse was Vicky's boyfriend, the executive chef at the Yuletide Inn. "Mark also says, by the way, that Erica Johnstone checked in last night."

"Better tell the staff to beware of small explosions and flying ornamentation. If they were fully booked, how'd she get a room?"

Vicky shrugged. "She's Erica Johnstone. I assume she gets whatever she wants. She's in one of the outbuildings. Two bedrooms, a small kitchen, a living room. She needed the extra space for her entourage."

"I don't suppose Mark told you if Max Folger is . . . ahem . . . part of the entourage."

Vicky shook her head and brushed the long purple lock out of her eyes. "Do you need to talk, sweetie?"

"I'm fine. I'm long past Max Folger, and as far as I'm concerned I made a lucky escape."

"You were engaged to him, Merry. You were in love with him, and he threw you over for another woman. How'd he go about breaking the news to you again? Oh yes. He sent you a text five minutes before you went into a staff meeting where it was announced that he was going to marry Erica. At least," she added dryly, "he had the courtesy to send a text, so it wasn't a *total* surprise. Your head knows you're better off without him, but does your heart?"

"Yes," I said, emphatically. And I knew, even deep down, that it was true.

"Glad to hear it."

"Although . . ." I remembered Alan, out last night with Amber. Nothing wrong with that, of course. Dinner with an old family friend, whatever could be more innocent?

"What?" Vicky, who knew me so well, said.

"Nothing. Nothing at all."

"If you want to talk to me about nothing, anytime, feel free."

"Thanks. How's Mark?"

"Perfect, absolutely perfect in every way." She sailed out of the shop on a cloud of love, the scent of fresh baking floating behind her.

Love. Who needs it?

On the other hand we all need cinnamon buns. I pulled the still-warm pastry out of the bag and took that first marvelous bite. My taste buds did a happy dance.

But love, in another way, was next through my doors. My dad. He gave me a kiss on the cheek and went straight to the point, as he usually did. "I hope you didn't agree to go back to the city with Max Folger?"

"You may rest assured that I didn't," I mumbled around a mouthful of pastry. I wiped my sticky fingers on a napkin. After licking off the last of the icing and sugary goodness, of course.

"I know you have more sense than that, honeybunch. I never did like that man, although your mother told me I wasn't to say so. I'm saying so now. She ran into him yesterday afternoon in town and had a few choice things to say about him when she got home. It's good that the magazine is doing a story about the town, but not good what happened last night at A Touch of Holly. Everyone's talking about it."

"Look on the bright side," I said. "It might increase the number of visitors. People will be coming to Rudolph hoping to get a look at Erica. Celebrity sells."

"In these shallow times in which we live," he said. As he talked, Dad wandered through the shop, picking up things here, putting them down there. I'd brought my iPad to the counter so I could work on the accounts while keeping an eye on the shop, and my business e-mail beeped with incoming. When I next looked up, Dad was taking the display of white and gold dishes and matching linens off the center table. "Hey! What are you doing? I worked hard arranging that. We're featuring table settings for the weekend."

"You need tree decorations."

"I do not. It's July. People aren't thinking about decorating their tree, but they're always thinking about entertaining."

He took the dishes into an alcove and came back with a box containing Alan's eight-foot-long strings made of wooden cranberries and another of multicolored glass ornaments the size of marbles, each with a thin red ribbon for the hook. He arranged the decorations on the live rosemary plant trimmed into a triangle shape that was the centerpiece of the table.

"I don't want those there," I said, feeling the need to keep arguing in the face of overwhelming odds, probably in the same way the passengers on the *Titanic* kept treading water long after the great ship had gone down. "We have a tree. In case you didn't notice."

I kept a real tree in the shop all year round, draped with ornaments for sale. This month it was a beautiful Douglas fir. It had only gone up a few days ago, and the powerful scent still lingered in the air. Inspiring, I hoped, shoppers into a frenzy of advance holiday buying.

"These small ornaments will get lost in that tree. This one is better." He stepped back to admire his handiwork before fetching boxes of larger ornaments and scattering them around the rosemary bush.

When the table was arranged to his satisfaction, I admitted defeat. "Are you going to the park tonight?"

"No. Your mother and I are having dinner at the inn with Grace and Jack." The owners of the Yuletide were close friends of my parents. "Santa is staying out of sight until his big arrival tomorrow. You are still planning to be on the boat with me, I trust?"

"Yes, Dad. Although I have absolutely no idea what I'm going to wear. I'll die in my Mrs. Claus costume."

"You'll think of something, honeybunch," he said.

"Come to think of it, what are you going to do? Your costume is even heavier than mine."

He winked at me. "It's a surprise. I've had my breakfast, but that bun you were eating has made me awfully hungry. I think I'll pop over to Vicky's before going home. Don't tell your mother." He gave me a kiss on the cheek and left.

Jackie arrived spot on time for work. I didn't have to wonder what had prompted this unusual circumstance. "You had a fight with Erica Johnstone over that man who was here yesterday! That's so romantic. I wish I'd seen it, Merry."

"I didn't fight with anyone and it wasn't romantic in the least. I hope you're not gossiping about me, Jackie."

She tried to look innocent. It was not a good look on her. Jackie's boyfriend, Kyle Lambert, drifted into the store behind her. "I'd fight for Kyle," she said. The man in question puffed up his skinny chest.

I rolled my eyes.

"So, are you going back to him?" she asked.

"Back to Kyle? I've never been with Kyle." *Perish the thought.*

"Ha-ha. You're so funny, Merry. Max Folger. He's soooo handsome. A real dreamboat. That chiseled jaw, those dark eyes—a woman could drown in them. And then she could use his eyelashes to save herself." Jackie was an eager reader of Regency romance novels. I cringed at the image. Kyle scowled. Kyle was a good-looking guy in his own way, but it was unlikely anyone ever called him a dreamboat.

The chimes over the door tinkled, a group of women came in, and I was saved from continuing with that conversation. Kyle breezed out. Jackie put on her professional smile and went to help the new arrivals.

We kept busy all morning. The town had advertised the Rudolph Christmas in July family weekend extensively throughout New York State as well as Pennsylvania and Ohio and even into Canada. Rudolph was filling with families here to watch Santa Claus begin his vacation. Toys, including Alan's wooden train sets, sold briskly as did our jewelry to those people wanting to get a start on their holiday shopping.

The decorations Dad had arranged, however, were not selling. I considered putting them back in the alcove and getting the dishes and linens out.

Shortly before noon, I was thinking it was time for me to slip out in search of a coffee when coffee arrived for me. Russ Durham, the editor in chief of the *Rudolph Gazette* handed me a tall latte. "I hear our little town's about to hit the big time, publicity-wise. Thought you might need this."

"Perfect," I said, accepting the offering. "Thanks."

"And what about me?" Jackie said. "I could use a drink, too, you know."

"Sorry," he replied. "Things are so tough in the newspaper business these days my salary only stretches to one extra treat a day."

Jackie huffed and continued replenishing the decorations on the big tree to replace the ones that had been picked over. A few customers were browsing, but no one seemed in need of my attention. I slipped onto the stool behind the counter. "It's going to be a big coup, all right," I said to Russ. "Having a magazine with the circulation of *Jennifer's Lifestyle* doing a segment on us."

"Particularly after what happened at Christmas with *World Journey* magazine."

We sipped our drinks in silence, remembering what a disaster that had been. "I've just come from town hall," Russ drawled in his deep Louisiana accent. "Sue-Anne, they tell me, is in Rochester today for a meeting of local mayors. I think that's code for getting her hair done and shopping for a dress to wear for the cameras."

I laughed. Russ was a handsome man, charming, flirtatious, and overflowing with Southern grace. He'd begun spinning that magic on me, and for a while I'd teetered at the edge of falling under his spell. But then I realized that charming and flirty were simply the way he was, and his feelings for me had no depth. I'd pulled back from the edge of the cliff in time, and I was pleased we'd remained friends. Although, he still did drop the occasional little hint that he'd like to be more than friends.

"Having Erica Johnstone herself in town," I said, "is only going to create more interest."

"Erica's here!" The blood drained out of his face.

"I'm surprised you didn't hear. She showed up last night. Quite the social media event, it turned out to be."

"I was in budget meetings all morning. I wonder," he said in a low voice, "what she wants."

I didn't tell him that I knew full well what she wanted. "When you were at town hall, did they say if everything's on track for the boat parade? I don't know what I'm going to wear. My Mrs. Claus costume . . ."

I broke off at a gasp from Jackie. Her eyes were open wide and her jaw had dropped to her toes. I spun around as Erica Johnstone strolled into my shop. As one, the customers stepped back, taking themselves to the wings and giving Erica center stage. She was accompanied by her ever-present assistant Muriel; the young props assistant Amber; Jason, the photographer; and Willow, the style editor. Last of all came Max, strolling casually, hands in his pockets.

"Gotta run," Russ said. "I forgot about an important meeting."

And the editor in chief of our local newspaper ran out of the shop in the face of the biggest story to hit town all year. I didn't have time to wonder what that meant. I hopped off my stool and came around the counter.

"Isn't this positively delightful?" Erica trilled, extending her long thin arms to take in the entire shop. "Max, darling, look at what our Marie has done here."

I stepped forward. "Merry."

She waved her hand. Her diamond ring flashed. "Of course you are. So lovely to see you." She bent her head and we exchanged the required air kisses. Her floral perfume was strong and spicy, overlaying, but not able to hide, the scent of tobacco.

More people began to arrive, pushing themselves into the already crowded shop. Erica held out her hand, and Max came up behind her and took it. He looked me straight in the face with no sign of contrition or embarrassment. "You simply must do a story on this shop, Max darling," Erica said.

"That's a great idea, babe," he said.

"I think an entire article on miniature Christmas trees

to run in December. That one there"—she pointed to the rosemary bush on the center table—"is perfect. Look at those delightful decorations. Don't you just love love love the teeny balls and the red wooden beads on a string? They look exactly like cranberries."

"I love them, Erica," Muriel gushed. As usual Muriel was dressed in shades of gray. A plain gray skirt, a button-down shirt with gray and white stripes, flat gray shoes. In this heat, she had panty hose on her legs and a gray scarf around her neck. She was a short, thin woman, black hair streaked with gray pulled into a tight bun. With her choice of colors, her size, and her constant nervous twitching, she put me in mind of a mouse. I wondered if the effect was deliberate. If she'd been ordered to dress that way, to ensure that Erica—bright colors, expensive fabrics, stiletto heels, lots of flashy jewelry—would stand out.

At Erica's words, whispers of approval ran through the shop. I was thinking I'd have to lock the doors before the room burst apart under the strain of all these people crowding in.

"Merry has excellent taste." Max, still holding Erica's hand, gave me a big wink. *What was he playing at?*

"That's settled, then." Erica snapped the fingers of her free hand. "Who's in charge of props here?"

Amber leapt forward, blushing to the roots of her fair hair. "Me. I mean, I am." She'd discarded the retro look and today had dressed casually in distressed jeans, a T-shirt, and sneakers. Her hair fell loosely around her face.

"Get whatever we need. Oh, Max, isn't that darling?"

"Perfectly lovely," he said, not much caring what had caught her eye. Erica dragged him across the room to the jewelry display. She picked up a necklace, a long chain of interlocked gold rings with a center wreath bejeweled with beads of green and red glass. "Isn't it beautiful, Max darling? It would be perfect for me to wear to Christmas parties."

He took the necklace from her and ran it through his fingers like a golden waterfall. "Let me buy it for you, babe. A pre-wedding gift."

"Oh, Max. Would you?" Erica sighed happily. The watching women whispered to one another. Max walked up to the main counter, making a big display of taking out his wallet. Jackie tripped over her own feet getting herself to the cash register in record time.

Once it was paid for, wrapped in tissue, and popped into a store bag, Max presented his purchase to Erica. She kissed him on the lips with a loud smack. "My darling Max, you spoil me so much." The watchers tittered. Tonight, husbands and boyfriends all across New York would be treated to the story of this shining example of how a man should behave toward the woman he loves. Erica pulled Max to her, smiled widely, and struck a pose. Max grinned, a man with nothing but a wedding on his mind. Bright lights flashed and the camera clicked repeatedly as Jason snapped a series of pictures with his enormous black Nikon.

Erica spun around. Her eye was caught by a shelf near the counter, which displayed a choir of singing angels. Carved out of wood, ranging in height from about two inches to three feet, wearing gold-painted halos and white robes, they either sang from carol sheets held in their hands or blew trumpets. "How charming. Max, be sure you get those in our story."

Willow wrote in her notebook.

"Now," Erica said, "I know you people must have work to do, so I'll take myself out of your way. Muriel!"

"Yes, Erica?"

Erica thrust the bag containing the necklace at Muriel, who slipped it into her cavernous tote bag. "I don't want to go back to the hotel for lunch. Find us something nice but not too fancy."

I stepped forward and raised my voice to be heard at the very back of the packed room. "I can recommend Victoria's Bake Shoppe. Excellent breads and pastries, everything homemade from scratch, fresh every day." I eyed Erica's frame, all jutting bones, sharp angles, and shadowy hollows. "And, uh, they serve organic salads and light soups, too."

"That should do. You have a lovely shop here, Marie. Perhaps I'll be back later." Once more Erica leaned forward and air-kissed my cheek, drowning me in the scents of French perfume and American tobacco.

The crowd parted—Erica playing the role of Moses at the Red Sea—and she sailed out of the shop, while Muriel scurried along behind clutching the tote with the gift from Max. Jason and his camera followed.

Half of the watchers rushed after them to see where Erica went next, and the other half surged forward. In seconds every last one of the decorations had been snatched off the display table, the rosemary bush itself had been snapped up, the singing angels were gone, the jewelry had been picked down to the bones of black cloth and display frame, and Jackie was fighting her way to the storage room in a hunt for more stock.

I staffed the cash register, ringing up purchases, running credit cards, and accepting money. Jackie staggered back laden with boxes; the goods were grabbed before she'd so much as finished laying the items out.

Max leaned against the back wall, a smile on his face, watching. Amber picked her way through the store, taking pictures with her phone and talking quietly to Willow, who jotted down notes.

Finally, the mass of shoppers left. I surveyed the wreck of my store. In the main room scarcely an item remained, although some goods were still on the shelves in the alcoves.

"Wow!" Jackie smiled at Max. "You're good for business."

He shrugged. She cleared her throat, tossed her hair, and wiggled her hips. "I just so happen to be personal friends with the girl who made that necklace you bought for Erica. I'd be happy to introduce you to her and you could maybe get Erica a surprise present. I'll model some pieces for you, if you'd like to see what they look like on."

"I don't think so," he said. He turned to me. "Merry, I . . ."

"Let me know if you change your mind," Jackie said. "It's no trouble."

"I'm sure it's not," he said. "Amber, Willow, did you get what you need?"

"We have pictures, at least, of the merchandise," Willow said. "Merry, can you order more of whatever got sold out?"

"It shouldn't take long to get more stock. Most of my pieces are hand-made by local artisans. The cranberry strings are by Alan Anderson, who Amber knows, and the necklace Erica liked was made by a teenager named Crystal Wong, who works here part-time. She's very talented and is heading to New York for jewelry design in the fall."

"That would make a story in itself," Willow said. "What do you think, Max? Our readers absolutely adore handcrafted goods."

"I know Crystal really well," Jackie repeated, trying to force herself into the conversation. "We're great friends." I refrained from pointing out that as far as I knew they couldn't stand each other. "I'll go around to her house right now if you like, and see what she's working on. Hey, I've an even better idea! I can bring her stock down to New York City myself. It's no trouble."

"Unlikely Erica will let us run another story on a jewelry maker," Max said, ignoring Jackie. "We're doing that woman in North Carolina in November."

Willow snorted. "You mean that talentless hack who strings colored beads and shells she buys by the truckload on a string and sells them for a thousand bucks a pop—I mean offers them for sale, there's a difference. The one who got into the magazine because she went to college with Erica?"

"That one," Max said dryly. "Merry, we'll do the photo shoot on Saturday, after closing."

"What photo shoot?"

"Of the shop. Didn't you hear Erica? She wants to feature you and your shop."

Jackie squealed.

"I don't have a lot of stock at the moment." I pointed to the almost-empty shelves.

Max shrugged. "Get stock, then. Willow, arrange it, will you?"

While we talked a few customers continued browsing. The flapping of their ears was creating quite a wind.

"Merry," Max said. "Can we talk privately?"

I didn't want to. I didn't want to hear what couldn't be said in front of a roomful of people. But, it had to be done. Last night he was telling me he was going to call off the wedding, and today he was all adoring fiancé. Either he'd changed his mind, or Erica had refused to listen. Wouldn't hurt to hear what he had to say, I decided. Perhaps he intended to apologize.

I wanted to take him to my office. I'd sit behind my desk; he'd take the visitor's chair. We'd have an intelligent conversation in a calm business environment as befits two mature adults.

Unfortunately, my office was occupied by a giant, slobbering, very friendly dog, and the chaos of invoices, packing slips, accounts receivable, accounts payable, company catalogs, sample products, and boxes of stock (if any were left) didn't make for calm.

"This way." I led Max through the curtain into the back. I opened the door to my office. Mattie leapt to his feet, all doggie smiles, flapping tongue, and drooling jaws.

"Whoa!" Max said. "Is that a dog or a . . ."

"No, he is not a pony. That's Matterhorn." I gave him a hearty scratch behind the ears as a reward for not jumping on us.

"Are you babysitting him?" an incredulous Max asked.

"Nope. He's all mine. And I'm all his."

Max, never an animal lover, suppressed a shudder. Once again, I wondered why I thought I'd loved this man.

"Mattie needs a stretch." I took down the leash and snapped it onto his collar. "We can talk in the back alley."

As soon as we stepped outside, I thought this might not have been the best idea. If Vicky's ovens broke down she could use the pavement out here to bake bread. I let the extendable leash out to its full length, and Mattie sniffed at corners and under trash cans. In the recessed doorway of Cranberry Coffee Bar, a few doors down, something rustled. Mattie strained at the leash to check it out, but I held on tightly. I didn't want him chasing mice.

"Erica seemed happy this morning," I said. "I assume the nuptials are back on. Congratulations."

"Actually, Merry." Max rubbed at his head. "I want to talk to you about that."

"What has it to do with me?"

"After you . . . uh . . . left the restaurant, Erica and I went back to her hotel. We had a walk in the garden, and I told her the truth. I told her I am very uh . . . fond of her, but you're the woman I love."

"What? Max, this conversation is over. I'm going back inside." Max had dropped that bombshell on Erica last night, and she was huggy-kissy with me this morning? Good thing I didn't have anything to drink when she was in the shop. I wouldn't put it past her to wear a ring with a secret compartment containing poison.

"Wait, Merry. Hear me out. I love you. I want to be with you. It can still work out. Erica did some talking, too. She told me she doesn't much care what I get up to, but the wedding's all planned, and Jennifer's pushing her for great-grandchildren. Erica's parents died in a car crash when she was small and Erica's Jennifer's only grandchild."

"I know that. But I don't understand."

"The wedding can't be canceled. The magazine's done so much on it already. Erica shopping for gowns, selecting a florist, going to bridal shows. They even ran a piece on me hunting for the perfect ring. If it doesn't happen, she'll be humiliated and Jennifer furious." Max took a deep breath. "Erica's promised me five million dollars six months after the wedding, with another ten million as soon as she gets pregnant. And five million more on the birth of a second child. That'll be my own money, to use as I like. In addition to the normal living expenses associated with being with her, of course."

Of course. All I could say was, "Wow!" Then I said, "How nice for you. Now, if you'll excuse me, I have work to do."

"Don't you see, Merry? That means we can be together."

"It means nothing of the sort!"

"It won't be a real marriage, except in the eyes of the law. She wants to be married, she wants children. I'll be the prop so she can play happy families. The rest of the time, I can do what I want. And what I want is to be with you. She was only angry last night because you and I were out in public."

Mattie pressed his nose up against the leg of Max's immaculate dark jeans. He looked very New York, I thought, in a white button-down shirt tucked into a belt with an unadorned buckle, worn under a lightweight, but perfectly tailored, gray jacket. He shoved Mattie's head aside. "Think about it, Merry. We can live together most of the time. You can even bring your dog, if you want." He smiled.

I did not smile back. I was horrified. *What kind of sick world did Erica live in? What kind of sick world did Max want me to be part of?*

"Mattie, here!" I gathered up the leash. "Good-bye, Max," I said, and went inside.

Chapter 4

Jackie complained bitterly, but I put my foot firmly down. I had to be on the boat with Santa, therefore she had to be in the shop. I was not going to close on Saturday afternoon. So there!

"Why can't Crystal work? She doesn't have to sing."

"Jackie, stop arguing. Crystal is not only part of the choir, she has a solo."

"Not fair. I was going to ride behind Kyle's friend Sam on his Jet Ski. How about if I make up a banner advertising Mrs. Claus's Treasures and I can pull it along behind?"

"No!" If she'd told me a week ago she wanted to be part of the water parade, I might have been able to arrange something. One of Vicky's many cousins is always ready to help out in the shop if I'm desperate. But it was nine o'clock the night before the big event, and everyone in town would have an assigned role to play. I briefly considered just giving in, closing the shop for a couple of hours, and letting Jackie have the time off. If she was here, she'd be so sullen, she'd chase whatever customers we had away.

Instead, I decided to take a page out of Erica Johnstone's book and pay for loyalty. "Because I need you here, and because you're such a good employee, I'll give you a bonus of an extra fifty dollars."

She sniffed. "Only fifty? We pretty much sold out earlier, and *you're* going to be part of a photo shoot for *Jennifer's Lifestyle*."

"We're going to be the photo shoot," I said. "The store. I won't even be in the pictures. One hundred."

Max hadn't come back inside after our little discussion in the alley earlier, but Willow arranged that they'd come to the store tomorrow after closing to take the required photos. I'd spent the remainder of the day on the phone and on the road, having managed to get Crystal to put in a few extra hours helping Jackie at the shop, trying to pry additional stock out of my suppliers, and if needed driving to pick the stuff up myself. Most of the artisans I regularly bought from were thrilled when I said their work might be part of a *Jennifer's Lifestyle* feature. Alan told me he'd be working all through the night making more cranberry strings and the choir of wooden angels that had proved to be so popular. Crystal, fortunately, had been busy in her jewelry studio now that it was summer vacation. As for the rosemary bush, I remembered that my mom had one in her herb garden and called to beg her to give it to me. She agreed to drop it off later.

By closing time, if the shelves weren't exactly overflowing, at least there were no gaping spaces, and extra boxes were stacked in the back. Thank heavens, I thought, not for the first time, for locally sourced goods.

Not yet entirely mollified, Jackie didn't know to quit when she was ahead. "It's bad enough that I'm missing the start of the dance party at the bandstand because you made me work late."

"You always work until nine on Friday. You wanted to go to a teenage dance party?"

"Kyle's there."

"Jackie, grow up. Do you want the hundred dollars or not?"

"Okay."

Sometimes I wondered why I put up with hcr, but then I always remembered. She was an excellent sales clerk. Polite, friendly, borderline flirty when it suited, serious when it didn't. Some of the staffing horror stories I heard from my fellow shop owners would curl the hair on my head, if it wasn't a mass of unruly dark curls already.

"Time to close up," I said. "Tomorrow's going to be a busy day."

As usual, Jackie was determined to get in the last word. "I've decided not to wear my costume. Not if I'm not going to be in the pictures. So there."

"That will be fine," I said.

Jackie left. I locked the door behind her and flipped the sign to "Closed." I went into the back to get Mattie, and we left the shop by the back door. The sun was almost down and the alley was wrapped in dusky gloom, but the heat of the day still lingered in the pavement and the concrete walls, and the humidity was intense.

The door to the shop next to mine opened, and Margie Thatcher, owner of Rudolph's Gift Nook, came out carrying a bag of trash. "What are you doing hanging around the alley?" she asked me.

"Good evening, B . . . I mean, Margie," I said as sweetly as I could manage. "Lovely evening."

She harrumphed. Margie was the sister of Betty Thatcher, previous owner of the Nook. When Betty left town shortly before Christmas last year, Margie stepped in to take over. The women were twins, identical looks as well as identical—meaning foul—temperament. "You had quite the fuss and bother earlier today." Margie sniffed. "It seems to me there were a good many more people in your store than fire regulations would allow."

"We were busy. Don't you ever get busy?"

"When some people couldn't get into your shop, they came into mine. I simply didn't have time to call the authorities to come and investigate. You should make sure you comply with all safety regulations at all times, Merry. I wouldn't want to file a complaint, but I know my civic duty."

"I'm sure you do."

Mattie sniffed at Margie's sensible shoes. Her lips pursed into a tight pucker of disapproval and she recoiled. "Keep that vicious creature under control." He'd moved on to check out the garbage bag she'd tossed into the bin. I ground my teeth. As much as I didn't like her, I had to keep things reasonably pleasant between us. Or who knows what damage she might try to do to me and my business, not to mention my dog?

My phone beeped with an incoming text, and I reached gratefully for it. Margie tossed her head and went back inside. The door slammed behind her.

It was Vicky. She'd called me earlier to say that not only had the café filled with people wanting to have lunch where Erica Johnstone was eating, but crowds were gathering on the sidewalk, peering in the windows. She'd sent one of her waiters into the crowd with trays of samples and the bakery brochure advertising catering services and wedding cakes. The implication being that Erica was considering asking Vicky to make the cake for her wedding.

Vicky: *Finished here. What U doing?*

Me: *Going home.*

Vicky: *No Alan?*

Me: *No.*

Alan was working, making more cranberry strings and singing angels to satisfy the hordes of eager Jennifer fans. Word had gotten out on social media that Erica was in town. Frankly, I wished she'd leave. Never mind anything personal between us—this weekend was supposed to be about Santa Claus and kids, not a skinny, spoiled diva.

Vicky: *Pizza and wine. I can pick up.*

Me: *You're on.*

Vicky: *Saved you a cookie.*

Me: ☺

The sound of a live band filled the night air long before

I reached the park. A good-sized crowd had turned out. The butcher shop had set up a barbeque and was grilling hamburgers and hot dogs, and a line stretched out the door of the North Pole Ice Cream Parlor. Young people spilled out of the park, moving to the music, smiling and laughing. An almost-full moon hung over the lake, casting a long white streak across the dark water.

A young couple, walking close, holding hands, smiling up at each other, approached me. "What a beautiful dog," the girl said. "Can I pat him?"

"Sure," I said. "He's friendly."

She crouched down and touched her nose to Mattie's, letting him lick her face. She giggled and her boyfriend smiled. *Alan.* Yes, I knew Alan was working tonight. He was working because I'd asked him to. But if not, would it have been another excuse not to get together on a Friday night? The excuses, I realized, were coming from me, not him.

Mattie and I went home.

The first day of Santa's vacation was another hot, humid, sunny day. Perfect for a boat parade.

The parade organizers, including my dad, had ordered that anyone on a boat had to wear a life jacket, so I decided that the clothes part of my costume didn't matter all that much. Shortly before we'd broken up, Max and I had vacationed in the Turks and Caicos islands. I'd forgotten to pack a beach wrap and grabbed the first thing I saw in the hotel's massively overpriced gift shop. A flowing, one-size-fits-all, ankle-length wrap in lime green with Pepto-Bismol pink trim. It was hideous. Meaning absolutely perfect for Christmas in July.

I planned to top off the ensemble with a wide-brimmed straw hat on which I'd tied a pink ribbon, and massive dollar-store sunglasses. I tossed everything into a tote bag. Once the parade was over and Santa was greeting kids on the beach, my task would be to help keep the lineup organized. To that end, I'd bought a giant bag of small candy canes and a wicker basket.

"Sorry, buddy, but no work for you today," I said to Mattie. "I'll be in and out of the shop all day." I collected the beach bag and candy basket and left the broken-hearted dog staring mournfully after me.

I'd need my car to get to the parade assembly ground later, so today I drove to work and parked in the back alley. Alan was waiting outside with boxes piled at his feet: two boxes of cranberry strings and another of the singing angels. Stubble was thick on his jaw and shadows like smudged makeup were under his blue eyes.

"I really appreciate this," I said as I unlocked the door. "Were you up all night?"

"Most of it." He gave me a smile that went a long way toward taking some of the tiredness out of his face. "You know I'm happy to do it for you, Merry."

"Thanks."

"I'd do just about anything for you," he said, so quietly I barely heard him.

My tongue wrapped itself into knots. "How's Amber?" I blurted out.

"Amber? I guess she's okay. I haven't heard otherwise. Oh. Merry, I was only having dinner with her the other night because her mother's a good friend of my mom's. She heard Amber was coming to Rudolph, so asked me to give her a call."

"You don't have to explain anything to me," I said.

He gave me a look I couldn't decipher. "No, it sounds as though I don't."

I wanted to say something, anything, to make the awkward silence that had fallen between us go away. But before I could apologize, try to explain, he began carrying the boxes inside, deposited them on the floor in front of the main display table, and began taking the goods out. I put down my beach bag and the basket of candy canes so I could help. He passed things to me to arrange. "Alan," I said. "I . . ."

"Anyone here?" Crystal, coming in the back.

"We're out front," I called.

She also carried a box. "This is the absolute last of my stuff, Merry. I hope it's okay."

"I know it will be," I said.

"I hear one of your necklaces will be gracing the thin neck of none other than Erica Johnstone," Alan said. "Congratulations."

Crystal flushed. "I can't say I'm not thrilled. But let's wait and see if she actually wears it. I bet she has closets and jewelry cases full of stuff she buys but never so much as looks at again."

I thought of the way Erica'd tossed the bag containing

the necklace to Muriel. I wondered if she'd only wanted it so as to make a big show of Max's devotion in public.

"The photographer and the other people from the magazine will be here after closing tonight," I said. "That's at six. Why don't you two come by? Maybe they'll want to talk to you about your stuff."

Crystal beamed. Alan said, "Okay."

"What are you wearing for the parade?" Crystal asked.

"Secret," I said.

"The usual," Alan said.

"The usual?" she said. "You're going to roast in that getup."

"I'm sure a breeze will be coming off the water."

"Let's hope. Gotta run." She opened her mouth and sang a scale. "Practice, practice."

"You'll be great." I gave her a hug for good luck. Not that she needed it.

Alan walked out with her. I quickly arranged the new arrivals on the shelves, and then I took the bag containing my costume into the office before flipping the sign on the front door to "Open." Minutes later, two women came in. I guessed they were mother and daughter, as they looked remarkably alike despite the thirty-year age difference. They glanced around the shop, and the older one asked me to show her the necklace Erica's fiancé had bought.

"I'm sorry, but I don't have one exactly the same because that piece was individually crafted. But many other examples of the artist's work are in stock." I held up a brooch designed to look like a holiday wreath in one hand

and a silver chain with a reindeer pendant in the other. "These arrived only a few minutes ago. The artist delivered them herself."

"I cannot believe our luck," the older woman said. "Imagine, we booked at the Yuletide Inn months ago as a special treat for the children, and who do we find staying there but Erica Johnstone!"

"Mom's a big fan of Jennifer Johnstone," the younger woman said.

"I don't know that I'd say I'm a fan. But I do admire her taste and her business smarts. She built that company up from nothing, you know, after her husband died. He owned a little magazine for the furniture business, and she turned it into a billion-dollar company all on her own. I can't say I'm happy about the direction the magazine's taken since Erica was put in charge. I don't need makeup tips using face cream at a thousand dollars a jar, thank you very much. I don't suppose Erica said anything about getting a gift for her grandmother?"

"Sorry, no." I was still holding the jewelry. The daughter had wandered off to look at the toys. If I was a shady sort of businesswoman, I'd tell this woman that Erica had said her grandmother would adore the brooch. But I wasn't, and so I didn't.

My honesty was rewarded when she said, "Too bad. I'll take those pieces. They'll make nice gifts." I put them on the counter.

"Mom saw her last night," the daughter said, adding two stuffed reindeer to the purchases. "At the hotel. In the garden."

"We'd fed the children early so we could have a nice adult dinner in the restaurant. It was marvelous, wasn't it, dear? I had the lamb chops. Delicious. After dinner, I said to Jim, that's my husband, that I wanted a stroll in the garden. So romantic." She looked at her daughter. "It's important, dear, to keep the romance alive. Particularly when children start to arrive and so many other things seem to take precedence."

"Yes, Mom."

"There she was. None other than Erica Johnstone. I can't say I'd recognize her if I saw her walking down the street, but of course everyone in the hotel was talking about her. She was with her fiancé. *They* have time for romance." Another side glance at her daughter. "The gardens at the inn are so beautifully done."

"They certainly are," I said. "They're a popular wedding destination."

Last night, over pizza and a glass of wine in front of the TV, Vicky had told me that, according to Mark, ever since Erica had been observed walking in the Yuletide gardens, bookings for the inn's outdoor wedding space had started flooding in. They were almost fully booked for the next three years. If this woman—and all the brides looking for the perfect wedding venue—knew what Max and Erica had been talking about on their supposedly romantic walk (her paying him to marry her and father her children; him plotting to set up a second household) she might not be pushing her daughter so hard to emulate them.

"A photographer from the magazine was following

them," she said. "He was taking some pre-wedding pictures. Imagine, I might see them in the magazine."

I reminded myself that whenever I found myself thinking it would be nice to be rich, I'd think about what it must be like living a life of people peering into restaurant windows watching you eat, or tiptoeing through the bushes to see what type of flowers you admired.

The parade was scheduled to begin at one. Shortly after noon I went into the back and changed into my costume. When I emerged, Jackie peered at me through lowered eyelashes and said nothing. Which was just as well. She was still annoyed at having to work and making sure I knew it.

"I'm off," I said. "I expect to be back around three, depending on the size of the crowd."

"Harrumph," she said.

I went out the back. I pulled the door shut behind me, checked the lock had secured as I always did, got into my car, and drove out of town.

When I passed the park and the beach, I could see that a good-sized crowd had gathered.

The flotilla assembled at a small boat launch near a rocky shoreline and a patch of scrub about two miles past the park. Mattie and I came here regularly so I could let him enjoy a swim and a run off the leash.

Every sort of watercraft from thirty-foot sailboats to canoes to Jet Skis would be taking part in the parade, and most of them had been decorated with a heavy hand.

Extravagantly trimmed Christmas trees stood on decks, lights draped all visible surfaces, excited children in colorful clothes and elf hats or reindeer antlers (and life jackets) lined the gunwales or sat in the bow. A fishing boat carried the high school band and another had been commandeered to bring some of the town dignitaries. Vicky, who usually won best of parade twice a year, had declined to participate this year. She didn't, she told me with a sniff, *do* boats. Instead, she'd decorated her bakery's tent and table in the park.

Santa's boat was a big pontoon, conveniently painted red and white. A thronelike chair had been set up in the back for Dad to sit in, and younger kids from my mom's vocal school had been recruited to be elves. They looked adorable in white shorts, turquoise T-shirts under their life jackets, and matching turquoise ball caps. Parents loaded them onboard with last-minute instructions about not leaning over the side and not removing their life jackets.

I was looking around, wondering where my dad was—we couldn't start without him—when an excited murmur stirred near the parking lot.

Santa was coming. Even though we all, except for the youngest children, knew it was only Noel Wilkinson, the excitement began to build. I stood on my tiptoes to see better. I laughed.

Dad was dressed in a 1900s-style men's bathing suit with short sleeves and buttons at the throat. It had wide horizontal black and white stripes and came to midthigh. His big round belly made the midsection look like a soccer ball. He wore a red ball cap with a white pom-pom sewn onto the top and rimless sunglasses. His curly gray hair and full white beard needed no augmentation.

"Absolutely perfect." Alan stood beside me. He was in his head toymaker costume of knee-length britches, wool stockings, heavy jacket, gray wig, stuck-on gray sideburns, and plain spectacles. He wiped his brow. "I'm beginning to regret not dressing for the season. You look great, Merry."

The wig made me feel as though I had a pizza oven on my head. "Thanks." I smiled at him. He smiled back, and I hoped I'd be able to make everything okay between us.

"Let's not keep the kiddies waiting," Dad said. "I drove past the park on my way here, and there's quite a crowd. The chair and umbrella are set up on the beach, and some of the elves are in position. You have your pen ready, Alan?"

"Sure do. It's on the boat." At the beach, Alan would stand beside Santa, writing the children's wishes down with a feather-topped pen onto a long paper scroll while I gave candy canes to those waiting in line.

Candy canes!

"Shoot! I left the candy and basket at the shop. Forgot all about them." I tried to remember where I'd last seen them. I'd put them down to help Alan arrange his goods. I'd taken my bag into the office but I didn't think about the candy again.

"That won't do, Merry," Dad said sternly.

"When we dock, I'll run and get them," Alan said.

"No," Dad said. "I need you with me. I'll phone Aline

and get her to send Crystal. No, they'll have begun the concert by now, and she'll have switched her phone off."

I briefly considered calling Jackie and asking her to bring the needed items. But I feared that if she closed the shop for ten minutes, she'd hang around at the park and make excuses not to go back. And still expect the hundred dollars. "I'll go," I said. "I can run to the store in a couple of minutes and be back almost as soon as you've made your way to your chair."

That settled, we climbed onto the boat and set sail.

The parade was great fun. Nothing is quite as marvelous as being out on the water on a hot summer's day. At the houses lining the lakefront, people had brought out chairs and blankets to sit on. They cheered and waved as we passed while excited children ran along the shoreline. A good number of the properties had Christmas or Santa Claus flags flapping cheerfully in thc light wind, and the park itself was festively draped with more flags and bunting.

On the bandstand, my mom's vocal class sang the last notes of "We Wish You a Merry Christmas" as we came into sight. The park was a mass of people and color. A great cheer rose up from the crowd as they caught sight of Santa, bringing up the end of the flotilla. I turned to look at Dad, smiling and waving from his throne, and caught Alan's eye over his head. Santa's head toymaker smiled at me.

I was a fool. I couldn't let this wonderful man go just because a shallow, ambitious one had betrayed the entire meaning of love and broken my heart in the process. After I'd gotten the candy canes and we'd fulfilled our roles of Mrs. Claus and toymaker in chief, I'd invite Alan to my house for dinner. It was time to tell him that I wanted to be with him.

I could only hope he still wanted to be with me.

Santa's boat maneuvered close to the small dock at the park while the rest of the parade bobbed on the water offshore. Some of the restaurants and coffee shops had set up refreshment stands on the lawn, including Vicky's bakery, and local farmers were selling fresh eggs and produce. The service clubs and local charities were handing out brochures and accepting donations. The town of Rudolph had a big booth with tourist information. Next to it was the stand from the nearby town of Muddle Harbor's parks and recreation department. I wondered if they chose a tent in that shade of muddy brown deliberately. I also wondered if Muddle Harbor actually had any parks, never mind recreation. They were a dour lot. Closer to the water, the stretch of sandy beach was covered with beach umbrellas, chairs and blankets, picnic baskets, and happy families.

As arranged, Sue-Anne Morrow, the mayor, was waiting on the dock to greet Santa. Dad was first off the boat, and Sue-Anne made a big show of presenting him with a foot-long plastic key on a red ribbon while Russ Durham snapped photos for the paper. Sue-Anne had wanted Dad to come up onto the bandstand to receive the key to the city. He, wisely, refused. Give Sue-Anne a microphone and she'd talk all day. He'd also instructed my mom to resume the concert exactly thirty seconds after Sue-Anne approached him.

I slipped away. Russ raised one eyebrow as I passed, and I said, "Forgot something. Be right back."

A uniformed police officer stood at the bottom of the dock, keeping the eager fans at bay. "Love the look, Merry," she said. "Those colors are so you. Leaving already?" It was Officer Candice Campbell. I'd known Candy, as she'd been called in school, for a long time. We had never been friends.

"Be right back," I repeated, swallowing a return barb. It might be the middle of summer, a big yellow sun was beating down on my hat and wig, and the air was so thick with humidity I could almost swim in it, but it was Christmas in Rudolph, and I was full of the holiday spirit.

The small building housing the North Pole Ice Cream Parlor sits next to the dock, with a front wall that rolls up so the shop opens directly onto the park. For what would probably be the only time today, there was no lineup, and I could see Kyle Lambert, dressed in a pink and white striped shirt with a big red bow tie and a round white hat, wiping down the counter.

I pulled my wrap up to my knees and galloped through the park and down the street, accompanied by the sound of my mom's preteen class singing "Hark, the Herald Angels Sing." Not being in the company of Santa Claus, I looked like an eccentric woman with a severe phobia against the sun, and no one paid me any attention. Not that there were many people around in any event. Even Jingle Bell Lane was deserted; everyone had gone to the park to watch Santa arrive. Some of my fellow shop owners stood in their doorways, wondering where everyone was. I threw open the door to Mrs. Claus's Treasures, and the bells tinkled in greeting. "Just me! I forgot something."

The basket containing the little red and white striped candy canes was sitting on a side table. I headed for it, calling, "Jackie. It's me."

The shop was quiet and empty.

I stopped and listened. If she was in the storage room or the tiny restroom, I'd expect her to call out. "Jackie?"

Leaving the basket where it was, I checked the alcoves first and then slipped through the curtain to the back. The restroom door stood open, and the storage room, usually piled high with boxes, was almost empty. My office door was closed. If Jackie had gone in there looking for something, surely she'd let me know where she was. I checked the back door, wondering if she'd gone out for some air, although today the air in the shop was a good deal more pleasant than the hot sticky stuff outdoors. The door was locked, as I'd left it, so I didn't venture into the alley.

Enough was enough. No matter how good a salesperson she was, if she'd skipped off work, expecting me to be busy down at the park, leaving the store unstaffed and the door unlocked, I'd fire her.

I pushed on the door to my office, but it didn't open very far. Something was blocking it. I shoved harder at it, all thoughts of firing gone. Jackie was young and healthy, but sudden illness could happen to anyone. "Jackie!" I yelled. No sounds came from within. Something shifted, and inch by inch the door opened until I could squeeze in.

My heart leapt into my throat.

Not Jackie.

Max Folger was sprawled across the floor, a string of red wooden balls crafted to look like cranberries wrapped around his neck. He did not move.

Chapter 5

I dropped to my knees beside Max. I gave him a good shove, thinking, hoping, he was playing silly games. His head rolled back. His eyes were open, and I knew no one could hold that look. I fumbled to untie the cranberry string from around his neck, but the end was wrapped over and over itself, and it was too tight for me to get my fingers under it to snap it. It would have to be cut off.

I scrambled across the room on my hands and knees and grabbed for the scissors I keep on my desk in the clay pencil holder I'd made in middle school. The theme of the school project was supposed to be, as it sometimes seemed everything in Rudolph was, Christmas. I'd tried to fasten a pair of antlers onto the blob of clay. Rather than a reindeer, it resembled a *Star Trek* Ferengi. I'd rescued it from my mother's trash when I came home from college after my first semester. Now, in my fumbling haste, I knocked the holder over. Pens and pencils, markers, rulers, paper clips, even a nail file, scattered across the desk and rolled onto the floor. But I had hold of the scissors. I sliced the string around Max's neck. In a burst of color, cranberries flew around the room.

But Max did not attempt to sit up, coughing and struggling for breath.

I touched the side of his neck and felt nothing move.

"Oh, Max," I said. "Poor Max." I pulled my phone out of the pocket of my beach wrap and called 911. I stayed on the line, as instructed, as I got to my feet and went to the street door to wait for the police. Before leaving the office, I glanced back. Max lay on the floor, surrounded by small red wooden balls, office detritus, and my footprints. My feet had been in the water as I clambered in and out of the boat, and my shoes had picked up sand and gravel on the beach. The police would not be pleased at me for disturbing the crime scene, but I had to try to save him. Hadn't I?

That it was a crime scene, I had no doubt, and I'd told the 911 dispatcher so. Max hadn't been casually playing with a cranberry string, and he hadn't accidentally tied it around his neck.

Someone had killed him, and my first thought was *who.* My second thought was, what was Max doing here—in my shop—anyway?

Jackie! All thoughts of what happened to Max fled. Where was Jackie? When I'd been calling for her, I hadn't considered she might be hiding from me, so I'd simply peeked into the rooms.

"Sorry, gotta check something out," I said to the 911 operator, hanging up over her protests. I called Jackie, straining my ears for the sound of her phone ringing in answer. Nothing. A deadly silence lay over the shop. I shivered, thinking the air-conditioning was turned up too high. The phone rang three times, and then Jackie's surprisingly formal voice mail answered. "Jackie O'Reilly speaking. Please leave me a message, and I will return your call."

"Jackie, it's me, Merry. It is absolutely vital that you call me the moment you get this. Please."

I ran into the restroom and the storage room. I peeked behind doors and over boxes. I ventured back into my office and, trying not to look at Max, checked under my desk. In the alcoves, I searched under tables, and I looked behind the sales counter in the main room.

Not a sign of her.

There was also no sign of a fight or a struggle. Had she been overcome before realizing she was in danger and carried off? Was she in the back alley? Unconscious, or worse?

I started toward the back once again, when I heard the sound of sirens approaching. I threw open the door as a cruiser doubled-parked in front of my shop. A male officer got out. In the distance I could see Candice Campbell heading our way at a rapid trot.

Not everyone was at the park. Heads popped out of

shops, cars slowed to see what was going on, and people on the sidewalk stopped walking to gape.

"He's in the back. My office. I'll show you," I said to the officer. "Has someone called Detective Simmonds?"

He grunted in reply. Candy ran into the shop, weapon in hand, and the older cop said, "Search the premises."

"That's not necessary," I said, "I've checked everywhere. No one's hiding."

"Do it," he said.

"Can't you keep yourself out of trouble, Merry?" Candy said with a barely controlled sneer. "Soon as they said possible homicide, I knew it had to be you." Officer Campbell and I, as I have said, have a history. And it's not a good one.

"Hey," I protested. "I had nothing to do with it, Candy." The use of her nickname was a retaliatory shot. She hated to be called Candy. It was not a good name for a cop.

She glared at me.

"I said," the man snapped, "search the premises."

I stepped forward. "I'll show you where . . ."

He lifted his hand. "Stay here. Tell me."

"First door on the right. It's the office. He . . ." I swallowed. "He's in there."

The front door opened once again. Detective Diane Simmonds came in. She'd probably been at the beach, too. She wore white shorts that showed off long, tanned legs, a loose blue and yellow striped T-shirt, and a Chicago White Sox ball cap. "You called this in, Merry?" she asked me.

I nodded.

"I saw you on the boat with Santa not more than a few minutes ago. Did you finish up there?"

I shook my head. "Forgot something."

Candy came out of the back, putting her gun in its holster. "All's clear."

"In here, Detective," the man shouted.

"Take the door, Campbell," Simmonds said. "No one comes in unless they're with us. Log everyone in and out."

"My assistant, Jackie. I can't find her. Can someone look for her, please? She would have been here when . . . when it happened. I'm worried. You should, maybe, check the alley."

Simmonds spoke quickly into her radio. More cruisers were pulling up outside, the crowd beginning to build. "Stay here, Merry. I'll want to talk to you."

"I have to get back to the beach." I pointed to the basket of candy canes on the side table. "Santa Claus is waiting for me." As soon as the words were out of my mouth, I knew how ridiculous I must sound.

Clearly, Simmonds thought so, too. "I think Santa can manage on his own for a little while." She pushed her way through the curtain, and I was alone in my shop. I ordered myself to calm down. People were searching for Jackie. She would have run for safety when Max and his killer came in. *Soon as she sees the police are here, she'll come back.*

I know every inch of this shop and the location of every piece of merchandise. Not a thing seemed out of place. Business would have been slow to nonexistent. Jackie might not have made any sales since I left.

Sales! Money!

I ran behind the counter and pushed buttons to open the cash register. The bills were tidily stacked in their compartments. I wouldn't know for sure until I counted, but it certainly didn't look as though any money had been taken. Someone, person or persons unknown, must have come in, planning to hold up the store. Then Max arrived and disturbed him, Jackie fled, and poor Max ended up dead. I tried Jackie's phone again. Still no answer. I left the same message as before.

Simmonds came back. "I don't recognize him. Do you know who he is, Merry?" Candy opened the door for two men dressed in jackets and sunglasses. They looked all business. They gave Simmonds a curt nod. One of them said something to the other before they headed toward the back.

"His name's Max Folger," I said. "He's with a magazine that's here to do a feature on Rudolph. *Jennifer's Lifestyle*. The whole crew was in here yesterday. They planned to do a photo shoot tonight after closing." For some reason, I didn't mention that Max was . . . had been . . . far more to me than a visiting magazine editor. The death of Max had nothing to do with me. It had to be a random incident. *Didn't it?*

"I'll have to contact his coworkers. Do you have any phone numbers?"

"No. But I heard some of them are staying at the Yuletide."

"Were you in here this morning? Before joining the parade? I know you were there, I saw you myself."

"I opened up at the usual time. I left shortly after noon to get down to the boat, because the parade was scheduled to begin at one. Jackie was here when I left. She was going to staff the store until I got back."

"Did Mr. Folger come in while you were here?"

I shook my head. "No. And he would have had absolutely no reason to go into my office. Even for the photo shoot, he wouldn't go in there. No one wants to see a picture of my messy desk or the dog's bed."

"It looks like there was some sort of a struggle in there."

I hadn't noticed any signs of a struggle. In fact, I'd thought the opposite. I guess that's why I'm not a detective. Then I understood. "Oh, you mean the pencil holder, the cranberries. That was me. Sorry."

"You?"

"I didn't know he was dead. I tried to help. I was . . . too late. Sorry."

"And the footprints?" She glanced at my feet. I was wearing sports sandals. The type with thick treads, which pick up all sorts of sand and gravel, particularly when wet. "Sorry," I said again.

"It would appear, on first look, that Mr. Folger was strangled by a thin rope or a wire."

"A cranberry string was around his neck. I cut it off."

"Why don't you have a seat?" Simmonds said to me. "I need to talk to you, might as well do it now. Can I send Campbell to get you a coffee? Water?"

Normally, I'd like nothing more than for Candy Campbell to be sent on errands on my behalf, but I shook my head. “Nothing, thanks.” I dropped into a comfortable, well-worn wingback chair we keep on the shop floor for a husband (or wife) to get off their feet while their partner engages in an orgy of shopping.

The door opened once again, and several men and women came in. They carried bags of equipment. Simmonds directed them to the back. “Reynolds is waiting.”

“I’d tell you not to touch anything, Merry,” Simmonds said to me, “but I assume your prints and DNA are all over this shop.”

“Every single inch, probably.” I thought of my office in particular. They’d not only have to deal with evidence of my presence, but the forensics people would have to sift through mountains of dog hair and buckets of drool.

“We might as well stay here and be comfortable for our interview.” Simmonds smiled at me. It wasn’t easy, but I smiled back. The detective was in her early forties, attractive beneath a stiff, always professional façade. Even in street clothes no one would mistake her for anything but a cop. She had red hair, kept carefully under control, and penetrating green eyes. I’d had reason to deal with Detective Diane Simmonds before, and I found her to be highly efficient. She also didn’t suffer fools. She didn’t take a seat, but leaned casually against a display case.

“Were you at the beach with Charlotte?” I asked, referring to Simmonds’s young daughter.

“Yes. She was excited about Santa having his summer vacation in the very town where she lives.” Simmonds smiled to herself. “I have to agree with her. This is the most amazing town. You people really can't get enough of Christmas, can you?"

"That's why we're called Christmas Town."

"Look at me, saying 'you people.' I like to think that Charlotte and I are Rudolphites now, too."

"Did she have to leave before she got to speak to Santa?" I asked. "If so, I can arrange for him to pay her a special visit. I do have inside pull, you know."

She laughed. "Thanks, but no. My mom's with her and they scarcely noticed me slip away." The smile and the lines of laughter faded from her face. "You were with Santa on the boat. Tell me why you left so soon after landing."

"I'm supposed to be handing out candy canes, those ones over there, to the children in the lineup. I forgot them, so I ran back." My phone buzzed. I pulled it out and glanced at the screen.

Alan: *What's taking so long?*

"Leave it," Simmonds said. Her voice had completely changed. We were no longer two women chatting about a little girl's excitement at seeing Santa.

"They would have heard the sirens at the park," I said. "Can I just tell them I'm okay?

She nodded. I quickly typed: *Delayed. Won't be back for a while. Sorry to Dad. Gotta go.*

A cryptic message, and not one that would assuage anyone's worries as to what was happening, but I didn't have time to tell the whole story. And part of the story would be worse than nothing at all.

"Can you turn that off now, please," Simmonds said.

I muted the sound and put the phone away. "I left Jackie to staff the store while I was with Santa. I'm dreadfully worried about her."

"The alley's been checked. No sign of her. No signs of a struggle or any injuries, either. Her name's Jackie O'Reilly, right?"

I nodded.

"She's well known around town. We're looking for her. I've met her before, but only here, in your store. Would you say she's trustworthy, Merry?"

"Trustworthy? She's not likely to strangle a difficult customer, if that's what you're asking." Then again, I thought, but didn't say, Max wasn't exactly a customer. Had he finally insulted Jackie so obviously that she noticed? She had, as I well knew, quite the temper. I shoved the thought away.

"Does she usually bring a purse to work?"

"Always."

"Did you see it when you searched for her?"

I tried to remember. "I don't think so."

"Can you describe it?"

"She brings the same one to work most days. I'm pretty sure she had it when she came in this morning. A small black thing with tons of metal hoops and studs. She keeps it in the storage room."

Simmonds made a quick phone call and asked the person on the other end to have a look for it. Then she said to me, "Tell me what happened from the time you left the park to get these candy canes."

I did. I told her how I was initially angry at Jackie for leaving the store, then my momentary worry that she'd collapsed in my office. Finding Max, and trying to get the beads off him.

"The door was unlocked when you got here?"

"Yes. I assumed Jackie had popped into the back for a moment. I checked the cash register. All seems present and accounted for, and none of my stock's missing. Not as far as I can see, anyway, and I keep nothing of any value that's not out on display."

Simmonds glanced toward the center table. The rosemary bush that had been snapped up had been replaced by one that had been in my mother's garden until yesterday evening. This one wasn't trimmed into a perfect triangle shape of thick greenery, but somewhat lopsided with gaping holes I'd done my best to fill with ornaments. "Thc string that had been around Mr. Folger's neck appears to be the same as those on the table."

"It is. They're proving to be very popular." I sucked in a breath.

"What?" Simmonds said.

The strings of wooden beads, painted to look like cranberries, were individually wrapped in a clear plastic bag. The bags had labels with Alan's logo and a Mrs. Claus's Treasures price sticker on them. This morning, when I'd dressed the bush, I'd opened one bag and used the contents for decoration.

That one string was gone. I told Simmonds and she nodded grimly.

"You said Mr. Folger and his team planned to come

here after closing, for their photo shoot. Any idea why he came earlier? I would have thought they'd be interested in the action down at the beach this afternoon."

"Not a clue," I said. *Had Max come back hoping to find me here? Did he intend to make another plea for me to go to New York with him?* I should have told Detective Simmonds about the relationship between Max and me. But I simply couldn't get the words out. I didn't want this to look to her like it might be something personal.

Simmonds lifted one eyebrow. I spoke quickly. "There might be some dissent among the magazine crew. They were squabbling all the time. Minor stuff, but you never know. Oh, you probably should be aware that Max Folger is engaged to Erica Johnstone."

"Who's she?" Simmonds asked.

"I'm guessing you don't follow the celebrity news. Her grandmother, Jennifer Johnstone, owns the magazine Max worked for, and she's super famous and mega rich. Jennifer is all business and not one for the limelight. Her granddaughter, on the other hand, loves nothing more than the limelight. Jennifer is also a super nice person. Her granddaughter is not."

"How do you know this mega rich Jennifer is nice?"

Ooops. Oh well, I wouldn't be able to keep it a secret for long. "I worked for *Jennifer's Lifestyle* until about a year ago."

She didn't look surprised. "So you know these people?"

"Some of them." As we'd talked, a steady stream of uniformed officers and men and women in plain clothes walked in and out of the shop. Every time the door opened, I could hear voices clamoring to know what was going on. I'd put my phone on vibrate, and it had been shaking as though Santa's sleigh had been caught in a hurricane over Florida. "A word to the wise, Detective. Erica Johnstone is major celebrity news. There was an incident Thursday night, when she, uh, had a hissy fit at the restaurant across the street." (No need to tell the good detective what, or rather who, the fit was about.) "Gossip reporters as well as Jennifer fans are already pouring into town."

For the first time, ever, Simmonds's calm façade cracked. She groaned. "I. Absolutely. Hate. That."

The door opened once again, and Candy Campbell came in. Her eyes were wide. "I . . . I . . ." she said.

"Spit it out," Simmonds snapped.

"She's here. She wants to come in."

"Who's here, and why do I care what she wants?"

This time the door flew open with so much force it hit the wall. Jason Kerr came first, ever-present camera around his neck, followed by Erica Johnstone. Muriel brought up the rear, using her small body to keep the press of onlookers away from Erica.

"Good job on the door, Officer Campbell," Simmonds said.

"I . . . I . . ."

"Get back outside, and next time you might want to lock the door before leaving it unguarded."

Candy slunk away.

Simmonds hadn't taken a seat while we talked, and now she seemed to stretch every vertebra in her body. I swear she gained two inches while I watched. I got out of my chair and ducked behind a display of porcelain, silk, and velvet Santa and Mrs. Claus dolls, where I tried to melt into the walls. "I am Detective Simmonds, Rudolph police. This is a crime scene, and you will have to leave."

Erica's face was streaked with black rivers of makeup, her nose and her eyes red and wet. She lifted a tissue to her face and blew. Muriel carried an open box of tissues. Jason crossed the room, fists clenched. "Do you know who you're talking to?"

"I would if you tell me," Simmonds replied calmly.

"Erica Johnstone."

"Your name is Erica?" Simmonds asked.

Jason's face turned as red as Erica's. "You watch your step, lady, or we'll sue this two-bit town for everything it has. And you, too."

"Be that as it may, you have to leave. Officer Reynolds!"

Erica stepped forward. She placed a quivering hand on the photographer's sleeve. "It's all right, Jason. The detective is simply doing her job." She lifted her round, tear-filled eyes to Simmonds's face. "I want to see Max. Please. They tell me he's dead, but I don't believe it. I can't believe it. I won't believe it. You have to let me see him."

Simmonds's face relaxed into an almost sympathetic expression. "Where did you hear about this, ma'am? What's your relationship to this Max?" Reynolds, the officer who'd been first to answer my call for help, came through from the back of the shop. Simmonds gave him a *hold on* gesture.

We don't have any curtains on the windows of the shop. I could see faces pressed up against the glass, Candy Campbell trying to get people to move away. *As if.* Other officers were arriving to give her a hand. The buzz of excitement spilled into the shop even with the door closed.

The news had traveled mighty fast. I knew Max was dead, but I hadn't told anyone other than Detective Simmonds. Three other people had overheard Simmonds asking me if I knew who the dead man was, and me giving his name. Candy Campbell and the two men in jackets who I'd guessed were investigators from the state police. Unlikely even Candy would squeal to the press so soon, but I'd lay odds she'd let the name slip over the radio. And with Erica Johnstone in town, who knows who's listening to the police radio.

"Max. Maxwell Edgar Folger," Erica said. She looked very small and frail standing between Jason and Muriel, both of whom had their arms around her now. "He's my fiancé. We're getting married in . . ." She burst into tears.

"The wedding is scheduled for next month," Muriel added.

"Please," Erica said, "I have to see him. I have to know!"

"One moment," Simmonds said. "Officer Reynolds, will you stay with these people, please. I'll be right back."

Jason patted Erica's back, and Muriel said, "There, there. I'm sure there's been a dreadful mistake. You'll see."

Simmonds soon returned. "You can come with me,

Ms. Johnstone. I'm afraid there isn't room for your friends to accompany you."

Erica lifted her head. She took a deep breath and steadied herself. Then she walked behind the curtain.

Jason and Muriel exchanged looks. "So brave," Muriel said.

All fell silent.

But not for long. A moan of Shakespearean proportions burst through the shop. "Noooooo," Erica cried.

Jason ran for the back rooms. He returned almost immediately, half carrying a weeping Erica. A grim-faced Simmonds followed.

"She has to sit down," Jason said.

"Let's get her back to the hotel," Muriel said. "She needs to rest."

Erica pushed Jason away. I thought she hadn't noticed me, cowering behind the pretty dolls. I was wrong.

She pointed one sharp red nail at me. "You! It was you!"

"Me?" I squeaked, venturing out of hiding.

"He told me you wouldn't leave him alone. He told me you were after him, always after him to make up with you. He tried to be kind, didn't he? To let you down gently. He told you it was over. That he loved me! Me, not you. You pathetic little creature. Look at you. I can't imagine what you think you're wearing."

Everyone was watching us. I didn't care for the look of interest on Detective Simmonds's face. "I never . . ."

"Only this morning, he told me he was going to offer to pay you off. A million dollars not to bother him again."

"Bother him?" I said. "He came to my town. My shop. Not the other way around."

"My poor, naïve, innocent Max. Finally, finally, he made you understand that he didn't love you. And you killed him."

"That's ridiculous."

The tears had dried on her face. Erica swung her finger toward Simmonds. "Officer, I demand you arrest that woman."

Chapter 6

I was not arrested. Although Simmonds was mighty angry that I hadn't told her I'd once had a romantic relationship with the deceased, not to mention he left me for another woman.

"Sorry," I said, once Erica, Jason, and Muriel had been escorted out of the building in the company of an officer who was told to take them to their hotel. And see that they didn't leave. They went out the back to avoid the crowds.

"It's not true, what she said. Yes, I was hurt, dreadfully, when he dumped me for her, but I soon came to realize I'm better off without him. I didn't want Max back, and I don't want to return to New York City. I'm happy here in Rudolph in my little shop. You can search my phone and computer records if you want. You won't find any evidence that I've been calling him or writing him letters.

Because I haven't. He came here to Rudolph, to my place of business. He wouldn't have done that if I'd been such a nuisance, would he? We went out to dinner Thursday night, to A Touch of Holly. It didn't go well. I walked out before our food arrived. You can ask anyone."

"I believe you, Merry," Simmonds said.

"You do?"

"I do. For the reasons you've stated. He was here, where you live. You were not there, where he lives, being a nuisance. Plus, I saw you myself not more than a quarter of an hour before the 911 call, in the presence of Santa Claus and a substantial part of the population of Upstate New York. An autopsy will determine the time of death, but as an educated guess, I'd say it was more than fifteen minutes ago. Ms. Johnstone is in shock. She lashed out at the first available person, which is quite normal. That person happened to be you. If I can play amateur psychologist, I'd say she might carry some guilt at stealing your boyfriend."

"I doubt it. Erica doesn't do guilt."

"I need to talk to the folks in the back and then interview Ms. Johnstone and the other people with the magazine. I shouldn't have to tell you that you can't open the shop today, and maybe not tomorrow, either. You can leave now. I'll call you later to let you know about tomorrow, and any further questions I might have."

"Thanks," I said.

"Are you going back to the beach?"

"Might as well. Things should be almost over by now, but I can help Santa for a while yet." And, I realized, I wanted to be with Alan. "But first, there is one thing you need to know. Far from me begging him to take me back, yesterday Max asked me to start our relationship again."

She raised one eyebrow. "Is that so?"

I told her everything. About the deal Max said he'd made with Erica and the deal he wanted to make with me. It sounded so dirty, so sordid, I didn't know if Simmonds would even believe it.

"Thanks for telling me, Merry," she said. "I'll be in touch soon."

I walked back to the park deep in thought. My main concern right now was Jackie. What had happened to Jackie? Was she even now being held captive by a crazed killer? Or, I couldn't bear to think, was she already dead, so she couldn't be a witness to the killing of Max? She annoyed the heck out of me sometimes—okay, she annoyed the heck out of me most of the time—but there was no malice in her. She was impulsive, and spoke and acted before thinking. I'd always thought she was a bit spoiled, indulged by her family the way small-town girls can be if they're pretty, but on the scale of spoiled, Jackie was nothing compared to Erica Johnstone.

I was pleased to see a good-sized crowd still at the beach; not everyone had rushed off to see the excitement in town. A red and green umbrella had been set up close to the water, with a chair beneath it for Dad. Not a flimsy beach chair, but a solid armchair, lugged down from the abandoned factory where the town stored Santa's sleigh, the stuffed reindeer, and all the other seasonal necessities. Couldn't have Santa collapsing into the sand if a hefty kid jumped on his lap. Alan stood beside him, pretending to jot children's wishes on a long scroll of paper, using a pen topped with a feather. The line was kept organized by high school kids dressed in bathing suits, green elf hats, and sandals with papier-mâché curly toes attached. All that was missing was Mrs. Claus and her candy canes. When I reached for the basket before leaving the store, a watching cop had snarled at me not to remove anything.

I'd checked my phone on leaving the shop and been inundated with calls and texts. News that police cars filled the street in front of Mrs. Claus's Treasures, and that vast numbers of officers had been seen coming and going, had spread rapidly. I'd replied to Mom and to Vicky, saying simply that I was fine, and ignored the rest.

Mom's concert had finished, and on the bandstand a magician was performing to a sparse crowd. At the lake, toddlers splashed in the shallows, watched over by attentive parents, while older kids and a handful of adults swam farther out. Onshore, families built sand castles, men kicked beach balls to each other, and women spread picnics out on blankets. Flags and banners fluttered in the breeze.

It was all so absolutely perfect, I started to cry.

Max. Despite how things had ended between us, I had loved him once, and we'd had many happy moments together.

Alan was the first to see me picking my way across

the sand. He bent over and whispered something to my dad and then slipped away from Santa.

"Merry." He laid a hand lightly on my arm. "Are you all right? You look like you've been crying. What's going on? They say the police are crawling all over your shop." Despite my mood and the shock of what had happened, I had to smile. Alan's strong young voice was a startling contrast to his ancient master-toymaker getup.

"Max Folger. Dead in my office. Jackie's missing."

"Dead? What happened? Was he ill? He looked well enough on Thursday night. And what do you mean, Jackie's missing?"

"He was killed, Alan. Murdered. No one can find Jackie."

He put his arms around me and held me close while I wept. He kissed the top of my head. The sight of a crying Mrs. Claus wrapped in the embrace of the head toymaker would scar some kids for life. Right now I didn't care. I just let him hold me. Eventually I pulled away. I found a tissue in my skirt pocket and blew my nose. "How's it been down here? How's Dad?"

"Great. Noel has loved every minute, as he always does." Alan wiped sweat off his forehead. "Although, I have to say, I cannot wait to get out of this getup. We're just about finished here."

"Ho, ho, ho," Dad bellowed. "Thanks for coming, everyone. Now, who's for a swim?" He got up from his chair and dashed for the water. Elves kicked off their shoes and ran after him, pursued by screaming children of all ages.

Dad loved to swim, but he wouldn't go any deeper than his ankles with a pack of eager children after him.

"Give me a minute, Alan. I want to check something and then I'll join you."

"Sure," he said. "Next year I'm wearing a bathing suit under all this."

The ice cream parlor was busy, Kyle still serving up cones and cups of frosty goodness. I studied him. He didn't look like he was particularly enjoying his job, but he didn't look anxious or worried, either. I headed for the booth. A little girl clutching a cone dripping chocolate ice cream down her fingers said, "Are you Mrs. Claus?" I realized I was still in my wig and glasses.

I gave her a smile. "Sure am. Did you speak to Santa?"

She nodded, wide-eyed. "I told him I don't want a new baby brother, but he said he can't do anything about that." Her voice was firm, her mind made up. "Can you?"

Her mother, enormous round belly protruding from under her tentlike maternity bathing suit, sighed. "For heaven's sake, Sylvie. I told you, you're going to love your little brother."

"Am not," Sylvie said.

At the ice cream booth, I skirted the lineup and leaned over the counter. "Sorry," I said to the father next to be served. "Won't be a minute. Kyle, can I talk to you for a sec?"

He looked up from the tubs of ice cream. The most popular flavors were reaching the bottom. "I'm kinda busy here, Merry."

"I need to know if you've heard from Jackie recently. Say, in the past two, three hours?"

He shrugged. "She's at the store. You told her she can't use her phone when she's working." He made it sound as though that were some great hardship. Perhaps to Jackie it was. "I'm working, too, in case you didn't notice. Whatcha havin', buddy?"

"One small cookies and cream and a large triple chocolate delight," the customer said.

I walked down to the shoreline. Dad was standing ankle deep in the water, surrounded by kids while a circle of adults snapped pictures. For a brief moment his big smile collapsed as he studied my face.

I gave him a nod and a thumbs-up, and he turned his attention back to the children. He splashed about for a few more minutes and then said, "Ho ho ho! There's Mrs. Claus come to take me home. Bye, kids!"

"Bye, Santa," they chorused while delighted parents beamed. Dcspite all that had happened, I realized I was also smiling.

That Christmas magic. July or December—there's nothing like it.

The entourage—Alan, me, and the elves—walked with Santa to the dock. Our boat was waiting; we climbed in and it pulled away to cheering crowds.

"Merry," Dad said, every trace of Jolly Old Saint Nick gone in a flash, "what is going on?"

I explained.

He groaned. "That's dreadful. Are you okay, honeybunch?"

"It was a shock, but I'm fine. Max and I were long finished, Dad, if that's what you're worried about. Right now, I'm more concerned about what's happened to Jackie than who might have wanted Max dead."

Once my dad was sure I wasn't about to collapse into a weepy, muddled heap, he switched his concern to the town. "I don't suppose there's any chance we can keep this hushed up?"

"Not with Erica Johnstone involved. It's going to be a media frenzy."

"I'm going to call an emergency meeting of the town council tonight. We'll need to issue a statement. The usual: unfortunate incident, Rudolph is a safe place to bring your family, etc. etc."

"Were any of the *Jennifer's Lifestyle* people at the beach today?" I asked.

Alan pulled off his wig with a grateful sigh and peeled the sideburns and excess nose away. "I talked to Amber for a few minutes. She introduced me to one of her co-workers, but I don't remember the woman's name."

"Willow?"

"Yes, that was it. A photographer guy was with them, snapping away. He took lots of pictures of your mom's kids in concert and the lineup to talk to Santa."

"I don't suppose you can say what time they arrived. Or left?"

Alan shook his head. "Amber came over when Noel was settled into his chair, but I don't know how long she'd been there. I don't know if they came together, and I didn't see them leave."

"Dad?" I asked.

"Nope. Aline might know. She's observant about that

sort of thing. Journalists, I mean. Photographers in particular."

My mother had been an opera star of some repute. She'd sung major roles at the Met and in some of the best opera houses in Europe. She had a sharp eye for publicity and an instinct as to when to look her best for the camera. She might have retired to Rudolph, New York, where she taught vocal lessons, but she remained every inch the diva.

"You think Max was killed by someone from the magazine?" Alan asked.

"I don't know what I think," I said. "But it's a possibility. I can't imagine a stranger wandered in off the street, found him alone in my shop, and killed him." I shuddered.

"What was he doing in the store anyway, do you suppose?" Dad asked.

I didn't answer. I could think only that Max had returned to Mrs. Claus's Treasures to try to, once again, convince me to come back to New York with him. I didn't want to talk about that to my dad or Alan.

We pulled up to the boat ramp. Alan, Dad, and I had stood in the back, talking quietly, while the elves laughed and chattered in the bow.

"Thanks, Dave," Dad said to the boat captain, as one of the girls nimbly leapt onto the small wooden dock to secure the boat.

"See you in a few months, Santa," Dave said with a laugh.

"Are you going back to the shop, Merry?" Dad asked when we were safely onshore.

"I can't. It's been ordered closed for the rest of the day. Maybe even tomorrow."

"I'll see Merry home," Alan said.

"Good." Dad gave me a hug and told me to phone if I needed to talk.

"I came in my own car," I said to Alan after Dad had left. "I assume you did, too?"

He nodded. As we talked he'd taken off his woolen shirt, to reveal a sweat-drenched tee underneath.

"Then we have an excess of vehicles here. Plus, both of us need to change before we do anything else. You look as though you've had a dip in the lake fully clad, and I need to get out of this escapee-from-the-old-folks-home getup."

"If you're sure you're okay?"

"I am." I gave him a smile. "See?"

Alan shuffled his feet. "You were engaged to that guy, Max. No matter how things between you stood, you have stuff to deal with here, Merry."

"Why don't you come around to my place tonight for dinner? I have a feeling I won't want to be alone."

"I'd like that." The boat ramp wasn't far from town, but it was in an undeveloped patch of land consisting of a rocky beach, a circle of small trees and scruffy shrubs, the boat ramp, a rickety dock, a circular gravel road, and a rough parking lot. Most people had left, although a few of the teenage elves still stood about, waiting for parents to collect them, or perhaps not wanting the day's fun to end. We were standing beside my Honda Civic. Alan's battered pickup truck, which he used to haul raw wood and finished furniture, wasn't far away. I got into my car, started up the engine, gave Alan a wave, and drove home.

"Ecstatic" is the best word to describe Mattie whenever I arrive home after leaving him all day. I have to confess, I'm pretty pleased to see the big guy myself. After we exchanged sloppy, effusive greetings, I took him into the backyard for a romp. He really needed a long walk, but that would have to wait. I tried calling Jackie again, and once again I got voice mail. By now, I was seriously worried. Jackie's the sort of modern young woman for whom her phone is a physical appendage. She would no sooner leave it someplace than she'd forget to take her arm. Mattie galloped about the yard, sniffing under bushes, around the equipment shed, and at the bottom of the fence. I'm not much of a gardener, to put it mildly, and my patch of garden was starting to look more like an Amazon jungle than a New York State backyard. I share property duties with Wendy and Steve, who have the apartment on the other half of the top floor. They both had busy jobs and a baby, and even less free time than I did. We'd had a lot of rain over the past weeks, intermixed with hot weather, and the grass and weeds were reveling in it. I made a mental note to cut the grass later, but right now I had more important things on my mind. I found a well-chewed tennis ball in a patch of weeds and threw it across the yard. Mattie galloped after it, grabbed it, and dropped it, soaking wet, at my feet. I picked it up, threw it again, and the game was on.

Deep within my pocket, my phone rang. I checked the display before answering. Mom.

"Hi, Mom," I said. "I'm fine."

"I didn't ask how you are doing, dear."

"No, but you will." Mattie dropped the ball at my feet. When I didn't immediately pick it up, he nudged it with his nose.

"Yes, I will. I heard about Max, of course. Everyone's talking about it. Are you sure you're fine? Where are you now?"

"I'm home. I'm playing with Mattie in the backyard. No one can be sad when they're throwing a ball for a dog."

"A dog is well and good, dear. But if you need to talk . . ."

"Thanks, Mom." My mother and I had never been particularly close. I've always been much closer to my dad. Mom had had a big opera career that saw her traveling the world and spending a lot of time in New York City, where she kept an apartment. My dad stayed in Rudolph, and he did most of the raising of me and my three younger siblings. Mom came home between gigs. Dad is spontaneous, fun-loving, affectionate, full of fun. Mom is much more reserved. As a child, I'd found her intimidating with her big voice and flamboyant clothes and wide gestures. Now that for the first time Mom and I were living in the same town, I was enjoying a renewed relationship with her.

"They say you found him in your shop. Do you have any idea what he might have been doing there on his own?"

I scooped up the ball and threw it. Mattie dashed in pursuit, tongue lolling, tail wagging. "It's possible he wanted to talk to me without everyone else around. He said we had unfinished business between us. I didn't agree."

"Is that why you were out for dinner with him the other night?"

Mom might not be a longtime Rudolphite, but she had connected to the gossip mill fast enough.

"If you heard about that, you also probably heard that I walked out when Erica showed up."

"Good for you, I must say. It does no one's reputation any good to be caught in the middle of a public fracas between two prima donnas." And *that* was something Aline Steiner Wilkinson would know all about.

"I'm fine, Mom," I repeated. "I'm sad about Max's death, but I'm not broken up about it."

"I'm here if you need me, dear."

"Thanks, Mom." Wc hung up.

I called a disappointed Mattie back inside and hopped into the shower. Then I dressed in capri-length jeans, T-shirt, and sneakers, and headed out. Mattie looked mournful at my leaving him *again*, but this wasn't a job I could do with the dog in tow. It's a short walk from my place into town so I didn't take my car, but I walked quickly.

As I walked, I placed a phone call.

It was answered before the first ring died. "Jeez, Merry. What the heck is going on?"

"Did you get my text?"

"Yeah," Vicky said. "Letting me know you're still alive, that's about all. The cops are all over your store. People say Max Folger's dead. Your Max?"

"He is not my Max, but yes. Someone killed him in the back of Mrs. Claus's Treasures."

Vicky let out a long breath. "You okay, sweetie?"

"I'm sad about Max, yes, but right now I'm worried about Jackie. She was working at the time it happened, alone in the store while I was on the boat with Dad, and she's gone missing."

Vicky let out a whistle. "Look, it's almost five. We're closed here and cleanup is just about finished. Can I meet you somewhere?"

"I'd like that," I said. "I'm almost into town now. I'm going to Jackie's place."

"See you in a sec." Vicky hung up.

Jackie lives in a small walk-up apartment above Candy Cane Sweets, not far from my store. I've never been there, but as her employer, I know her address. Vicky was waiting on the bakery steps, and she ran across the street when she saw me approaching. Cars screeched to a halt to avoid running her over, and she gave them a cheerful wave.

"I know you and Max were long finished," she said, "but that doesn't change the fact that you were in love with each other once. If you need help dealing with this, I'm here for you."

"I know that." I gave her a big hug, blinking away tears. Vicky and I had been close since the first day of kindergarten when she marched up to me in the playground and announced that I was going to be her best friend. Even over the years we were apart, at college and then when I lived in the city, the bond had remained strong. When I stepped away from the hug, she patted the top of my head. I still hate that as much as I did when we were in junior high and she sped past me, height-wise.

I peeked into the window of Candy Cane Sweets as we passed. The cheerfully decorated shop was crowded. "How'd you do down at the beach earlier?" I asked Vicky.

"Great. The town's got to be pleased with the turnout. Everyone says the boat parade was a huge success. They're already talking about doing it again next year, instead of the more traditional Santa Claus parade."

"Did the . . . uh . . . excitement in town draw people away?"

"Not so as you'd notice. Today was all about kids and families. Most parents with children and babies aren't going to drag them away from the beach in hopes of seeing the police in action."

"It was crowded enough outside my shop."

"Celebrity junkies," Vicky said with a disapproving sniff.

A small door was set into the wall between Candy Cane Sweets and the butcher shop. I tried the knob and it opened easily, admitting us into a dark, musty stairwell. We climbed the steep steps. Two doors led off the landing, presumably to two apartments.

I approached the door marked *A*. I wasn't sure what I hoped for. Best case would be to have Jackie answer my knock, red-nosed and sneezing into a well-worn tissue, having "forgotten" to tell me she was going home sick. If she didn't answer the door, I was prepared to break it down. Not that I know how to do that, but judging by TV, all it needed was a good strong kick. I am her employer, and I did have a valid reason to be worried about her.

I hammered on the door. "Jackie! It's Merry. Open up!"

To my considerable surprise the door swung open immediately.

Not my employee, red-faced or otherwise, but Detective Diane Simmonds.

"What are you doing here?" Vicky and I said in unison.

"Have you heard from Jackie O'Reilly since we last spoke?" Simmonds asked.

"No. I've been phoning but no one answers. I thought I'd better come around. See if she's sick or something."

Simmonds spoke over her shoulder. "Back in a minute, Roger." She stepped into the hallway. Vicky, taller than I, craned her neck trying to see what was going on inside the apartment. Simmonds shut the door firmly. Vicky tried not to look disappointed.

I noticed the detective was wearing thin blue gloves. Acid rose into my throat. "Jackie. She's not . . ."

"We have not yet located Ms. O'Reilly," Simmonds said.

I let out a long breath. For a moment there, I'd feared they'd found a second murder scene.

"We've searched your store thoroughly and can't find her purse. Are you sure she brought it to work this morning?"

"Positive. One day pretty much blends into the next sometimes, but not today. She was not happy at having to work, because she wanted to join the parade. When she came in she made a big deal of huffing and puffing, and I remember that she slung her purse over her shoulder. Is that important?"

"If Ms. O'Reilly's purse was in a cupboard in the back, and she took it with her, then we can assume she didn't flee the scene in a panic when the killer of Max Folger came in. Did Ms. O'Reilly normally carry her phone on her person when she was working?"

"No. I've forbidden it after I caught her sneaking some texts while we had customers on the floor. She had to keep it in her purse, tucked away in the back." Of course, every time I left the premises, I was pretty sure she made a dash for it.

"She's been kidnapped," Vicky said.

"We can find no signs of a struggle anywhere in the shop or the immediate vicinity, which indicates she was not taken by force."

"Maybe she was drugged or knocked unconscious and that's why she wasn't able to put up a fight," I said.

"I shouldn't have to explain my thought process to you, Merry, but I will. If Ms. O'Reilly was a witness to the killing of Max Folger, it is highly improbable the killer went to the trouble of subduing her and carrying her off. He, or she, did, as you noticed, make no attempt to hide Mr. Folger's body."

"Unless he was killed someplace else and dumped in my office for some reason."

"There is no evidence of that."

"It's still possible though, right?"

"At this time, anything is possible."

Simmonds was, of course, right. If Jackie had seen the

person who killed Max, either in my office or before, that person surely would have killed her, and left her where she fell.

"You said she wasn't happy about working today," Simmonds said. "How angry was she?"

"Not angry. Just unhappy. It happens to everyone. Haven't you ever not wanted to work when you had to?"

Simmonds gave me a long look.

"Jackie didn't take out her anger, I mean her annoyance, at me or on an innocent customer," I said firmly. I was glad Vicky was standing beside me. I've always been the shy and timid one, while Vicky rushed where the brave fear to tread. It made us a good pair. I calmed her down—sometimes—and sometimes she made me bold.

"So you keep saying," Simmonds said. "Ms. O'Reilly had time to collect her purse and apparently walk calmly out the door. You told me the front door wasn't locked when you got there, Merry. Is that correct?"

"Yes. I mean, no, it wasn't locked. That's why I was sure Jackie was inside."

"Does she have a key?"

I nodded. "She often opens or closes the store."

"As far as you are aware, had Jackie met Mr. Folger before Thursday?"

"No. They didn't know each other. I'm positive of that."

"How did they seem to get on when they did meet?"

"Fine. Jackie was thrilled that they were here. *Jennifer's Lifestyle* is a major publication, and here they were in our town taking pictures. It's always been Jackie's dream to be discovered." I put quotes around the word.

"Is that so? Were Mr. Folger and his magazine interested in discovering her?"

"No. It's not a fashion mag and has no use for models. They feature things mostly, people only rarely, and then farmers, artisans, landscape architects. Max was dismissive of Jackie. Insulting almost. He wasn't a nice man. I . . ." Too late, I realized that I'd stepped right into a trap.

"Not," Vicky said quickly, "that that means anything. Small-town people take that sort of thing in stride, don't we, Merry?"

"Uh, yes. We do. Jackie did. I mean she would have. When she realized what was happening. We'd better be going. Let you get back to work."

"If you know anything, Merry, you are required to tell me."

"I don't. Know anything, I mean."

"What do you think happened, Detective?" Vicky asked.

Simmonds didn't speak for a long time. In the silence I could hear someone moving around in Jackie's apartment, and cars passing on the street. Then the detective said, "We are presently acting on the assumption that, for reasons unknown, Jackie O'Reilly murdered Max Folger, collected her phone and purse, and calmly walked away from the scene."

Chapter 7

Vicky laughed. I did not. Detective Diane Simmonds was not one for making jokes.

"You must be joking," I said.

"I never joke," she replied calmly.

"You can't possibly believe that in reaction to an offhand dismissal, Jackie killed Max?"

"Fortunately, it's not my job to worry about motive. I was about to pay a call on you, but now that you're here, let me ask. Where would Ms. O'Reilly be likely to go if she wanted to hide?"

The very idea of Jackie being a killer was preposterous. But then, where was she? By now, everyone in Rudolph knew Max Folger had been murdered in the back of Mrs. Claus's Treasures. Even if, for some reason, she'd not seen the killer or the killing, she had to know the police would want to talk to her. I shoved down the question of *why* and turned to *where*. Where she might be. "Her parents live in Rudolph. Her mom's phone number is in my files as the emergency contact if you can't find it."

"I've spoken to Mrs. O'Reilly. She says she hasn't heard from her daughter in several days."

"They're not close," I said. "There's Kyle, I guess."

"Kyle?"

"Kyle Lambert is Jackie's boyfriend," Vicky said.

Simmonds pulled out her notebook and pen. "Do you have an address for him?"

"I do," I said. "I've been to his place once, to visit him after the exploding hot dog cart incident."

"Oh yes," Simmonds said. "That."

I told her where Kyle lived. "He was down at the park most of the day. At least he was when I was there." Which, admittedly, wasn't much. "He was working at the ice cream parlor. I asked him if he'd heard from Jackie, and he said no."

"Anyone else you can think of. Girlfriends?"

"Jackie and I aren't friends. We don't socialize. She's just my employee. I don't know anything about her private life." And when she did chatter about this friend or that, her plans for tonight, or what she'd done over the weekend, I usually tuned her out.

"Her mom's good friends with my aunt Marjorie," Vicky said. "And I think my cousin Paula hangs around with Jackie sometimes. That's Marjorie Brewster. She works at my bakery. She left after closing, so she's probably home now."

"Thanks," Simmonds said. She made no move to go back into the apartment, and I realized she was waiting to see us leave.

"Have you spoken to the people from *Jennifer's Lifestyle* yet?" I said. "There was certainly dissent in the ranks there. I think they should be your prime suspects. And Erica was mighty quick to accuse me, don't you think?"

"Erica accused you of killing Max?" Vicky said. "Wow. The nerve of the woman."

"Thank you so much for your suggestions, Merry," Simmonds said. "But I am capable of conducting an investigation. If you must know, Erica Johnstone and her assistant are waiting for me at their hotel under instructions not to leave the premises. The rest of the magazine crew are similarly locked down, as they say on TV, at the Carolers Motel."

"They have to stay at a motel? Standards sure have slipped since my day."

"Is that so?" Simmonds said. "Reason perhaps for discontent. Go home, Merry. I shouldn't have to advise you not to interfere in my investigation, but I will anyway. I don't want you putting your nose where it doesn't belong. And that goes for you as well, Ms. Casey."

"Perish the thought," said Vicky, all wide-eyed innocence. Somehow the look didn't match the cropped black hair, the purple lock falling over her right eye, the multiple piercings in her ears and one through her left eyebrow, and the tattoo of a gingerbread cookie on her wrist.

"Just one thing before we go," I said. "My shop? This

is a busy weekend, and I'm losing money every minute it's closed."

"You should be able to open tomorrow. We were lucky that the forensics people with the state police didn't have anything pressing on their plates so could send extra help. Phone me in the morning to check."

"Thanks," I said.

"You handled that really well, Merry," Vicky said when we were once again standing on the sidewalk in the heat. "You might as well have accused Jackie outright."

"She gets me to say things that I don't even know I'm thinking until out they pop."

"Where to now?"

"You heard the detective," I replied. "Home."

She snorted. "Hardly."

I glanced down the street. All the police cars were gone from the front of Mrs. Claus's Treasures, and the yellow tape had been taken down. I assumed Max had been taken away.

I crossed the street. Vicky followed. There's a nice patch of grass with a bench and a flower bed overflowing with red and white impatiens in front of the library. I dropped into the seat, and Vicky joined me.

"Simmonds must be desperate, if she thinks Jackie killed Max," Vicky said.

I didn't reply, and she said, "Merry? What are you thinking?"

"You know Jackie. She's totally convinced that all she needs is a lucky break and then she'll be the next big thing in Hollywood or the fashion world."

"That's just talk. If she really wanted fame and fortune she'd have left Rudolph years ago."

"She's lazy. I don't mean lazy in her work, although she can be that, but generally she's a good employee. She's a lazy thinker. She'd rather wait for things to come to her than go out and chase them."

"So?"

"Max Folger wasn't a nice man. I don't know how I could have been so blind all the time we were together."

"His looks might have had something to do with that."

"Whatever, but he had a mean streak. He was rude and insulting to Jackie in my presence. He laughed at her small-town pretensions, but she's too naïve to notice. Maybe too innocent to take offense. As I said, Simmonds gets me to say things I don't even know I'm thinking. But now I am thinking them. Suppose he'd been more than just rude when I wasn't there? Suppose he mocked her outright; told her he was way out of her league. Would she have lashed out? Maybe she was decorating the rosemary bush and happened to have a cranberry string in hand."

"What's a cranberry string got to do with it?"

"Forget I said that." I'd been told not to discuss what I'd found in the shop. First chance I got and I blurted it out.

"That's put my imagination into overdrive," Vicky said. "It's going to give me nightmares."

"I'm not supposed to say, but Max was strangled with one of Alan's wooden cranberry strings."

"All the more reason Jackie didn't do it. Can you imagine her having not only the strength to hold it in place, but the determination to keep holding it while he struggled?"

"Vicky, I can't imagine anyone killing anyone. But people do. I don't know what to believe. Simmonds is putting a lot of stock into Jackie's purse missing, but it's entirely possible she had it with her when whatever happened, happened. She's not allowed to use her phone at work, which only means she uses it when I'm not around."

"Maybe she saw the killer and thinks he's after her next. She had her purse with her, grabbed it, and ran. She's afraid to come out of hiding."

"You might have something there. Perhaps she's afraid the police won't be able to protect her."

Vicky's eyes opened wide. "That could only be because the killer's rich and powerful."

I got to my feet. "It's time to pay a call on Erica Johnstone. You said she's taken one of the outbuildings at the Yuletide. I can't just walk into reception and ask for her room number. Call Mark. I bet he knows. She'll be ordering room service. She's got to be the number one topic among the staff."

"Will do." Vicky sent a quick text. "We can take the van." We leapt off the bench, but before we could take a step we were stopped by a shout. Russ Durham was jogging toward us. "I've been calling you all afternoon, Merry."

"So has half the town. I'm not answering."

"Max Folger was found dead in your shop. Do you want to make a statement for the paper?"

"No, I do not."

"How about talking to a friend, then? You dated Folger for a while, didn't you? I hear you found him. Are you all right?"

"I'm fine, Russ." I smiled at Vicky. "I have the support of my friends." Vicky put her arm around me.

"You have me, too," Russ said. "I'm on your side and don't you forget that."

"Thanks."

"What are you hearing?" Vicky asked.

"Not much. Diane Simmonds is giving a press conference at seven thirty. I'm sure Sue-Anne will have a few words to contribute also. It's going to be a crowded affair. Erica Johnstone's fiancé? I hear the major papers and national networks are sending people."

At that very moment a satellite van bearing the logo of the Rochester ABC station lumbered past.

"This won't reflect badly on Rudolph, will it?" Vicky said.

"Not this time, thank heavens," Russ said. "So far it's being presented as more a case of big-city vice and lack of morals among the rich and famous corrupting our innocent small town. If anything, we're getting more visitors because of it. Anyway, I've got to run. I'm hoping Simmonds will give me, as the local press, a bit of a heads-up. If I can find her."

"She's . . ." Vicky began.

I gave her a poke in the ribs. "Really busy," I said. Although Russ was a newcomer he was rapidly turning into a loyal Rudolphite, but he was also a newspaper reporter. If he found Simmonds searching Jackie's apartment, and she told him why, he'd put in his paper that Jackie was the prime suspect.

Vicky and I were facing the street; Russ, the tiny park and the library. At that moment the door next to Candy Cane Sweets opened and none other than Detective Simmonds herself walked out. She hopped into a waiting car and drove away as Vicky and I watched.

"What are y'all looking at?" Russ asked, half turning.

"Nothing," I said.

"We're going to talk to Erica Johnstone," Vicky said. "She might know something about who would want Max dead."

Russ's head snapped back around. "Erica? Good luck with that. Gotta run." He dashed off.

"That's odd," Vicky said. "I guessed that you didn't want him talking to Simmonds about what she was doing in Jackie's apartment, so I thought I'd distract him with mention of Erica. I would have expected him to want to come with us. Try to wrangle an exclusive."

"It is odd," I said. "But right now that's the least of my worries. Let's go. You can be my bodyguard. Erica will be less inclined to try to kill me if you're there. I hope."

Vicky's bakery van, the one she uses to make her deliveries, smells like I imagine heaven might. Even this late in the day, the scent of bread, fresh and warm from the oven, sweet rolls, and sugary pastry filled the air. I took a deep sniff as I put on my seat belt. Vicky drove to the Yuletide, while I pulled up Google. I typed "Erica Johnstone" into the search engine and the little screen immediately filled with far more hits than I could go through. I added "Russ Durham" to the search string, and bingo, the screen refreshed with different results. "Russ was in the shop on Friday when Erica and her entourage came in," I said. "Rather than taking her picture, as a good reporter should, he bolted. I thought nothing at all of it, until just now when, as you said, he bolted again at the mere mention of her name. That made me curious. Listen to this. According to our reliable friend Mr. Google, Russ Durham and Erica Johnstone were a hot item for a while."

"Wow! Our Russ?"

"Plenty of pictures of the happy couple. Of course, they're mostly of her, but it's him in the background, all right. I know he'd spent time in New York City working for a paper there. Looks like he was doing other things, too."

"When was that?"

I checked the dates of the articles. "Around twelve to eighteen months ago." I read quickly. "Here it is. According to Perez Hilton . . ."

"You mean Paris Hilton?"

"No. Perez Hilton is a gossip columnist. Anyway, Russ and Erica had a giant fight in a restaurant. She seems to do a lot of that. It says they were with a small, intimate party celebrating Erica's birthday, and Russ upped and walked out. I don't see any later mention of his name linked with hers. That happened about one month before Jennifer announced that Erica was taking over the magazine." Whereupon she took over my boyfriend as well, but that wasn't what we were talking about here. "Whispers in the office were that Jennifer had finally put her foot down and told Erica to smarten up and settle down. She offered Erica control of the magazine as an incentive. I wonder if this scene with Russ was the deciding factor."

"Check it out!" Vicky yelled.

I looked up from my phone. The road outside the Yuletide Inn was lined with cars and satellite vans. Well-groomed people smiled as less-well-groomed people aimed giant cameras at them. A makeshift barrier had been lowered across the driveway leading to the inn, and two security guards stood firmly against the onslaught of the press.

Cameras flashed as Vicky turned into the driveway and stopped at the barrier. "Good thing we brought the van. Never hurts to get my logo on TV." She rolled down her window. "What's going on?" she said, all sweet innocence.

"Some celebrity's staying here," the guard grunted. "And they're all clamoring for a look. Boss's orders to keep them off the property."

"I'm Vicky Casey from Victoria's Bake Shoppe in Rudolph. I deliver here daily."

He flicked through the papers attached to a clipboard. "Yup. You're on the list. Go ahead." He signaled to his partner, and the barrier arm rose slowly. Vicky drove through.

"Sweet," I said.

Vicky's phone buzzed as we drove down the long driveway. She tossed it to me. "Might be Mark. See what he says."

"He says, *Why do you want to know.*"

She pulled into the parking lot. "Give me that."

The spacious, perfectly maintained formal gardens of the Yuletide Inn are one of the chief tourist attractions of Rudolph. Even in late July, when other gardens are gasping in the heat, these grounds boasted immaculate green grass, lush flower beds, and neatly trimmed bushes. Sections were marked off by tall, stately hedges of American holly or neat rows of boxwood. A large kitchen garden provided fresh vegetables and herbs for Mark Grosse's kitchens. Fountains and statues were tucked away in secret gardens, and all the paths led to a large pond at the center of the property. In winter, the gardens were lovely in their stark, sculptural beauty, the trees draped with fairy lights, and the pond turned into a skating rink. I admired the flowers and foliage while Vicky talked to Mark. Or rather, listened to Mark. Eventually, she put her phone away with a smile. "Cabin C. Mark also says that so far Her Highness, his words not mine, has returned a steak, which was ordered well-done, as not being pink inside; complained about the bottle of 1984 Château Margaux that was delivered to her, because she had asked for the 1985. Although, according to Mark, the restaurant does not stock the 1985 vintage, because it's one of the best years so it's hard to get, and thus it is not on the wine list. It seems that she likes her boiled eggs done for three and a half minutes, not three. Apparently, she can tell the difference. Mark says if that mousy-faced woman . . . Who might that be?"

"Probably Muriel, the PA."

"Well, if this Muriel puts a foot in his kitchen once more, he'll have it off with his meat cleaver. Oh, and

Erica wants her strawberries from California, not the local ones, because they're too small."

I laughed heartily for the first time since I'd seen Max Folger in my store. "And she thinks she can run a magazine that believes in the importance of locally sourced produce and American-made goods. Heaven help them all." I undid my seat belt. "Let's beard the lioness in her den."

"How are we going to play this?"

"Condolence call. Two of Max's close friends comforting each other. It's not out of line. I know Erica and I knew Max well. She might want to throw me out, and if she does, we'll go calmly." Earlier, she'd accused me of killing Max, but I was hoping she'd have calmed down by now. Her moods were mercurial, to say the least. I was prepared to duck if ornaments started flying, but figured it was worth a try.

Cabin C was tucked into a copse of tall oaks and stately maple trees at the end of a neat brick walkway. Because of the gorgeous gardens, the inn's a popular site for weddings, winter and summer. The cabins were mainly rented to honeymooners or newly married couples for their wedding night, and offered complete privacy. Giant terra-cotta pots overflowing with yellow and purple petunias guarded either side of the door, and matching flowers had been planted in boxes lining every window. The cabin resembled a fairy-tale cottage with its fresh white paint, black roof, cheerful yellow door and shutters, and tall brick chimney. A private parking area is tucked in at the side of the building, and a freshly washed silver Lexus SUV with New York plates was parked there.

I knocked while Vicky stood beside me. Muriel opened the door. She was dressed in her usual shades of gray, dark gray slacks and a lighter gray shirt, but today she'd ventured to add a touch of color with a few red threads in the gray scarf. She didn't appear to be overjoyed to see me. "Oh, it's you. We were expecting room service."

"Is Erica in?" I asked.

"Tell them to go away," the diva herself called.

Muriel flapped her hands, but I pushed my way past her. Vicky followed. The small main room was beautifully decorated in shades of pale yellow and cream. A genuine wood-burning fireplace, thankfully not in use at the moment, lined one wall, and wide windows overlooked a small deck and a patch of secluded woodland. Erica was lying on the couch, a white cloth draped over her eyes, a glass of red wine on the coffee table next to her. A half-smoked cigarette lay in an ashtray. The inn was nonsmoking, but I assumed Erica considered that didn't apply to her.

A desk was against one wall. A man sat there, talking on the phone while he typed on the laptop in front of him. He eyed us as we came in but made no move to end his conversation. He was in late middle age, with expensively cut silver hair, a chiseled jaw, and dark penetrating eyes. He wore a blue suit that I guessed might be Armani, white shirt, and a pink silk tie. I hadn't seen clothes like that since I left Manhattan.

He ignored me, so I ignored him.

"Hi, Erica," I said.

She peeled the cloth away and blinked at me. "Come to gloat?"

"I'd never do that," I said. "I'm sorry for your loss."

"My condolences, Ms. Johnstone," Vicky said.

Erica looked at Vicky. "Who are you?"

"Vicky Casey from Victoria's Bake Shoppe. Where you had lunch on Friday?"

Erica swung her legs off the couch and sat up. She'd washed all the makeup off, and her eyes and nose were red and puffy. Her hair was pulled back into a high ponytail. She had changed into black yoga pants and a comfortable blue golf shirt. Her feet were bare, giving her a girlish, innocent look. She looked, I thought as my heart went out to her, truly grieving.

"I am so sorry," I said. "You must be devastated."

She reached for a tissue and blew her nose. "I am. Totally. My wedding is ruined!"

My sympathy dissolved into dust.

"My grandmother gave me one chance to get the magazine profitable again. She'll never forgive me."

"If there's anything I can do . . ." I said, my voice trailing away.

"What could *you* do for me?" She tossed the tissue onto the floor, stood up, and walked toward me. I braced myself, wondering if she was going to attack. To my considerable shock, she enveloped me in a fierce hug. "There's nothing anyone can do for me now. Max!" she wailed. "Oh, Max!"

I patted her back and made cooing noises. She smelled of the usual tobacco scent, but overlaid with vanilla bath products and good soap. Neither Vicky nor Muriel nor the watching man said a word. I held Erica Johnstone as she wept.

At last she pulled back. "You loved him, too, didn't you, Merry?"

"Once," I said.

Wet, red eyes studied my face. "He left you for me. I'm sorry."

"It all turned out for the better." I felt tears behind my own eyes. It obviously hadn't turned out okay for Max.

"If you want your job back, you're welcome. I mean it. Max said you were really good."

"He did?"

"I think introductions are in order." The man put his phone away, closed the lid of his computer, and got to his feet. He walked across the room, hand outstretched. I took it, and we shook. His grip was firm, firmer than it needed to be, and I wondered if he was making a statement.

"This is Merry, James," Erica said. "She owns a charming little store in town. She used to work for me, didn't you, Merry? What happy times." I remembered no such happy times, but I wasn't about to correct her. "Merry and Max dated briefly before he met me."

"Pleased to meet you, Merry," he said.

"Don't mind me," Vicky said. "I'm just a baker. Although I do make the best molasses spice cookies in New York State, if I do say so myself. Possibly in all the United States."

He grinned at her. The smile made him look almost human. Mention of Vicky's baking did tend to have that effect on people. "I'll have to try one someday soon. I'm James Claymore."

"James is Grandma's lawyer," Erica said. I'm sure that came as no surprise to anyone. "He's here to look out for me while the police ask their questions."

"And to that end, I thank you both for coming, but Erica isn't in the mood for company. Muriel, can you show these ladies out?"

Muriel bustled over. "Erica needs to rest." She tucked in the edge of Erica's collar. Erica swatted at her as though she were a pesky fly. "Get your hands off me."

"I'm only trying to help," Muriel puffed.

"Do you plan on staying in Rudolph for long?" Vicky asked.

Erica walked to the window. James watched her, but he didn't make another attempt to tell us to leave. The sun streamed through the trees, casting dappled shadows onto the deck at the back. "It's nice here," she said softly. "Quiet, peaceful. That horrid policewoman told me I can't leave until she says I can. James asked her when I can take Max home, but she said she didn't know. Will you speak to her for me, Merry? Tell her I want to lay my beloved Max to rest."

I shoved away a horrible image of a *Jennifer's Lifestyle* special edition funeral issue. "She doesn't listen to me. Sorry."

"I hope you enjoyed your time in Rudolph," Vicky said, with what I thought a shocking lack of taste. "Did you get down to the beach earlier to see the Santa Claus parade?"

"No," Erica said. "Max and the rest of the crew had their work to do. I try to stay out of their way as much as possible."

Respectfully, I didn't laugh.

"The press were arriving, and they're always *such* a nuisance. I decided to stay in the room and rest. Muriel and I were here together until we got that phone call." Her voice broke. "That terrible phone call."

Good job, Vicky! She'd been prodding Erica for the details of where she'd been when Max was in my shop.

James suddenly realized that Vicky wasn't simply making polite conversation. "Now, I must insist . . ."

"It turns out we have a mutual friend," I said. "Russell Durham?"

Erica turned with a genuine smile that made her almost pretty. "Darling Russell? I thought I saw him yesterday, but he disappeared before I could talk to him. You remember Russell, don't you, James?"

The expression on James's face indicated that he remembered Russ all too well.

"Is he living here now?" Erica said with a light laugh. "How charming. Imagine, fleeing to this hole-in-the-wall town to recover."

"Recover?" I asked.

"I've always adored the name Russell. It puts me in mind of trees in fall. Autumn at my grandmother's country house has always been my favorite time of the year. You must get wonderful fall foliage up here. Do you, Merry?"

"Uh, yeah," I said.

"I'd like to come back then." She sighed.

At a signal from James, Muriel moved in. She slid up to me and attempted to herd me toward the door. I moved a fraction of an inch. She followed.

Erica continued talking. "The poor dear was absolutely devastated when I told him it was over between us. I'd met Max, you see, and I knew right away that he was my one true love. I thought it best to make a clean break with Russell. He was furious. He said so many horrid things, made such terrible threats." Her eyes opened wide. "You don't think he had anything to do with what happened to Max? I couldn't bear to think that Max died because of me."

"I must insist that you ladies leave," James said. "Erica is very tired." He didn't quite grab my arm, but the intention was clear.

We all jumped at a loud knock on the door. "Ms. Johnstone. Police."

James stepped back and put his impassive lawyer face on. Muriel rushed to let the police in. Vicky and I switched on friendly, welcoming smiles.

Detective Diane Simmonds did not look happy to see us. "What are you two doing here?"

"Paying a condolence call," I said.

"Being supportive," Vicky said.

"Out," she said.

"We're leaving," I said. "Any news on Jackie?"

"No."

"If you need anything, Erica," I said, "feel free to ask. Anytime."

She enveloped me in another huge hug. "You are such a darling, Merry. I'm so glad we're friends again."

Again?

"She's certifiable," Vicky said as we walked up the Hansel and Gretel path back to the bakery van.

"Just spoiled and confused, I think. I'm starting to feel sorry for her, if you must know. She loves the press attention and everything her grandmother's fame and fortune can bring her, but she's having trouble realizing that attention can't be turned off when she wants it to be."

"You're too nice sometimes. She's loony tunes." Vicky twirled her index finger in the air beside her right ear. "What do you think of the fact that her lawyer arrived lickety-split?"

"Nothing to think. It's not significant. Press attention's going to be ferocious, never mind the police's questions. Jennifer, Erica's grandmother, has a team of lawyers on standby waiting to spring into action."

"I hope you noticed the way I got her to reveal her alibi."

"Lack of alibi, rather."

"She was with Muriel," Vicky said. "And isn't she the creepy one? I expected her to rub her hands together and walk backward out of the room, bowing all the while."

"Exactly. Muriel is no alibi. Muriel will say they were making plans for an expedition to the North Pole to discover if there really is a Santa Claus, if Erica tells her to."

"Still, I can't see Erica strangling anyone, Merry. She

might have hit him over the head with a frying pan in a fit of rage. But then she'd run straight to the press to whine that it wasn't her fault, dragging her lawyer along behind."

That made a lot of sense, but I wasn't entirely convinced, and I was silent as we drove back to town. Erica had been raised by Jennifer Johnstone, after all, whom I admired and respected, not only for her business acumen but her people smarts. That must have had *some* influence on her. Erica played the fun-loving celebrity and ditzy party girl to the hilt, but how much of an act might that be?

How much of her real self did Erica show to the world? Or even to her so-called friends? Was there more depth to her than there appeared? Max had told me Erica didn't love him and wanted him only to play a part, to give her a big flashy "fairy-tale" wedding and future children. Was Max lying to me? Wouldn't have been the first time, and he'd fooled me before. Perhaps he wanted to have his cake and eat it, too. Maybe there had been no agreement between Max and Erica that he could live his own life separate from hers after their wedding. Maybe she really did love him and was looking forward to their life together, as any bride should be.

She certainly seemed to be grieving. I didn't think it was all an act. But what was she grieving for? The man or the end of her plans? Did it matter? Not if they were one and the same in Erica's mind.

Had he told her he didn't love her, expecting her not to care, and found out that she did care? That she cared enough to kill him. Did he tell her he wanted to set me up as some sort of Victorian-era mistress? Did she follow him to my shop, where they argued? If anyone would have been able to get close to Max while holding a string of red wooden beads painted to look like cranberries, it would have been Erica.

While all that was happening, where was Jackie? I might believe Erica capable of killing Max in a fit of rage, but I couldn't believe she kidnapped Jackie and was holding her hostage someplace. Then again, Erica had a heck of a lot of money. I didn't know if she had her own money or if her grandmother gave her an allowance, but regardless, it would be infinitely more than I, and certainly Jackie, could imagine. Had Erica bribed Jackie to disappear? I wished I'd thought to ask her if she'd seen Jackie today. If she had, she might have let something slip.

"What do you think about what she said about Russ?" Vicky put on the breaks as the van pulled into Jingle Bell Lane. Traffic was stop-and-go all through town.

"I think Simmonds arrived at a heck of a bad time. Erica had just gotten the idea into her head that Russ might have been jealous of Max . . ."

"Because you brought him up."

"Thank you so much for pointing that out, Vicky. A year has passed since Russ was dating Erica. I honestly don't see him getting revenge after all this time."

"Maybe he hoped Erica would come back to him if Max was out of the picture. She *said* she'd only had a glimpse of him. Suppose that's not true. What if they ran into each other and she led Russ to believe she still had feelings for him?"

"Come on, Vicky. Can you really see Russ, our Russ, killing a man for love of Erica Johnstone?"

Vicky pulled up behind the bakery. She switched off the engine and turned to face me, her face dark and serious. "Thing is, Merry, people will do just about anything for love. Throw in Jennifer Johnstone's money, and you have a heady mix of motives."

Chapter 8

"Alan's coming around for dinner," I said to Vicky. "Want to join us?"

"*No!* What's the matter with you? You've been playing hard to get for months. You finally have him coming over, and you want me there?"

"I have not been playing hard to get. I've been sorting out my feelings. And yes, I do want you there. I'm not in the mood for a *date*, Vicky. I just want to spend some time with my friends."

She gave me a smile. "Sorry, sweetie. I understand. Let me go home, change, take Sandbanks for a walk, and I'll pop over."

The police station and the town hall share a complex tucked in behind the library. The bakery is located on the other side of a small walkway that carries on toward the lake. A satellite van pulled into the lot behind us. "Russ said the mayor and the police are having a press conference at seven thirty." I glanced at the clock on the dash. "I wonder if I should go."

"We just saw Simmonds with Erica. She might not be finished in time."

"Sue-Anne would like that better. If Simmonds is late, she can have the microphone all to herself."

"Don't bother with it, Merry. If Sue-Anne gets out of control, your dad will be there to settle her down."

"That's true."

"You need to go home and put your feet up. You've had a heck of an emotional day. Your dad'll tell you anything you need to know."

"You're right." I hopped out of the bakery van.

If Alan was disappointed to see Vicky waving at him from my living room couch when he arrived for dinner, he didn't show it. He handed me a bottle of wine and gave me a peck on the cheek. Mattie then demanded his full attention, so I took the wine into the kitchen and set out a plate of cheese and crackers in the living room.

Alan played tug-of-war with Mattie over a stuffed rabbit missing one ear. By the time the game was over and Mattie was running victory laps around the apartment, the rabbit was missing both ears as well as his tail.

As soon as I got home, I'd tried calling Jackie again. This time, her voice mail informed me that the box was full. I phoned her mother, who hadn't heard from Jackie, but said she was sure she'd show up soon, laughing at everyone's concerns and delighted to have been the center of attention. Not to worry, she said, in a very worried voice that ended in a broken sob.

Being with my friends, casual and comfortable, was exactly what I needed tonight. We ate cheese and crackers, drank wine, ordered in a pizza, and chatted about nothing in particular. By unspoken agreement we didn't discuss Max and Jackie.

Vicky gets up early to get started on the day's baking; by ten o'clock she was yawning heartily. She refused a top-up of her glass and pushed herself to her feet. "I'd better go. We're hoping for another busy day tomorrow with that kids' concert." A popular children's entertainer from TV had been hired to put on a show, and there would be clowns and balloon artists and other kid-friendly festivities at the beach, in the park, and around town. Santa wouldn't put in a formal appearance, but he'd be popping up most of the day. Fortunately, he didn't need the help of Mrs. Claus.

Alan stood also. "I should be off, too." He turned to give Mattie a pat.

"Anyone want to come with me to walk the dog?" I gave Vicky a *get lost* gesture, and she grinned in understanding.

"Not me," she said. "My bed beckons."

The four of us walked downstairs together. I had Mattie on his leash, and when he made a dash for the yard, I called him to heel. He came, reluctantly, and I praised him to the skies. We split up at the end of the street; Vicky headed in the direction of her house, and Alan and I walked with Mattie toward the lake. A full white moon hung in a cloudless sky, and the night air was heavy with humidity. Mattie trotted obediently at my side, only occasionally veering off to sniff at something he found interesting. The moon threw a band of glistening silver across the dark, still waters of the lake.

"His training's coming on well," Alan said.

My chest swelled with pride. "It's been easy. He's very smart."

Mattie woofed in agreement. Alan took my free hand and we walked in companionable silence through the quiet streets. One of the things I like most about Alan is that he never feels he has to fill moments of quiet with meaningless words.

When we got back to my place, Alan pulled the keys to his truck out of his pocket. We stood in the dark shadows of the driveway, the tall house on one side, its old bricks still warm from the heat of the sun, a row of heavy bushes on the other. "That was a nice evening. Thanks, Merry."

"I enjoyed it. It was good to forget about my troubles for a while."

He put his arms around me and pulled me close. He kissed me deeply, and I melted into him. I dropped the leash and Mattie galloped off.

We leapt apart as a burst of bright white light lit up the driveway. "Merry Wilkinson, is that you? What are you doing out there in the dark?"

"Just coming home from a walk, Mrs. D'Angelo," I said. "Don't worry about me." I dropped my voice. "Please, please, don't worry about me."

Alan smothered a laugh.

"I'm glad I caught you. What on earth is this I hear about one of those magazine people being murdered in your very shop? I don't know what this town is coming to. I said to Alison Bracken, Alison, I said, it's those city people. Oh, I know the tourists are good for the town and all, but at the end of the day we're better off without them."

Alan lifted one hand and touched the tip of my nose. I snatched at his fingers with my teeth and he laughed.

"Is someone with you, Merry? I can't see you."

"Just me, Mrs. D'Angelo. Alan Anderson. Good night." Still laughing, he got into his truck and drove away. I walked to the end of the drive and into my own yard, the sound of Mrs. D'Angelo's voice following me. I briefly considered setting the timer on my phone to see how long it would be before she realized no one was there, but decided I had better things to do. Like go to bed. I'd left the gate open and the light above the door on. Mattie was sniffing at the edges of the garden shed, the leash dragging behind him.

I called him to come, and he ignored me. I called again, in my sternest voice. "Mattie! Here!"

He looked over his shoulder at me and whined.

"Mattie! Here!"

He gave the shed one last look and then he came as instructed. I praised him effusively, and we went inside.

* * *

Jackie didn't work every day, of course, but this morning the shop seemed strangely empty without her.

I'd woken early, disturbed by dreams of Max and me in happier days, and had the time to take Mattie for a good long walk. Once again, he seemed interested in the garden shed, and I wondered if a mouse family had taken up residence in there. Get the children's weekend over, and I'd clean out the shed as well as attack the grass, which was growing so fast I could almost see it getting taller in front of my eyes.

I checked in with Diane Simmonds, and she said they were finished with my store and I could have it back. That was certainly a relief. I'd brought in extra stock of children's things for this weekend, and I'd already lost most of a day's business. Although, I could hardly complain after almost selling out the entire store on Friday. Next, I phoned Crystal and asked if she could fill in, "just until Jackie gets back." She agreed, and at ten o'clock I was in the shop.

The door to my office was closed. I stood in the hallway, reluctant to venture in. I looked down at Mattie, sitting calmly by my side. I wondered what he'd make of all the strange and unusual smells in the room. I took a deep breath and threw the door open. Mattie dashed past me. He ran from one spot to the next, nose to the ground. To my feeble human senses, everything was as it had been yesterday morning when I'd left for the boat parade. It might even be neater and tidier than normal. Some thoughtful person had dusted and vacuumed. Not a trace of Max Folger and what had happened here remained.

I left Mattie with a fresh bowl of water and went to the front of the shop.

Business was brisk in the morning. My dad, today dressed in red Bermuda shorts and a green golf shirt with the traditional long-tailed red and white Santa hat on his head, popped in to check if I was okay. We didn't have an opportunity to talk as a pack of wide-eyed and open-mouthed children poured in after him. I gave him a smile and a nod to let him know all was okay. I'd considered handing out the unused candy canes, but decided that might not be a good idea, them spending the day at a crime scene. I'd dumped them into the trash, basket and all.

My mom came in, gorgeous in a blue and white striped jacket with a nautical theme over a plain blue T-shirt worn with white capris and blue and white espadrilles. She pulled me to one side, and we stood in a corner whispering while Crystal waited on customers. "Your father says you want to know if the magazine people were at the beach yesterday."

"I'm just wondering, that's all."

"I can't say where they were all the time, but I did notice them. Two women and a photographer. They spent quite a bit of time photographing our concert. You know how adorable my grade-one class is. Perfect for a magazine feature."

"What time did you start?" I didn't know what time

Max had died, and Simmonds was unlikely to share that detail with me, but it had to be between when I'd left the shop for the boat launch at noon and arrived back to collect the forgotten candy canes around one forty-five.

"The youngest children began at twelve thirty. We broke at one so everyone could watch Santa arrive. Once he docked, the preteens came on, and then Crystal's solo and her age group. The magazine people spent some time watching your father and taking photos of that."

"You should tell the police this."

"Why would I do that?"

"They'll want to know the movements of the people who'd come to town with Max around the time he died."

"Excuse me. I hate to interrupt but . . . ?" a woman asked.

"Can I help you?" I said.

She ignored me. "Are you by any chance Aline Steiner?"

My mom broke into a huge smile. "Why, yes, that is my name."

"Ms. Steiner, I had the great honor of being in the audience at the Met when you sang Annina in *La traviata*, and I have to say it was one of the most memorable performances I have ever seen." Mom beamed, and I knew any talk of the whereabouts of the *Jennifer's Lifestyle* crew at the time in question was finished.

"How kind of you to say so," Mom said modestly.

"At the time, I wondered why you weren't singing Violetta. You have a much stronger stage presence than the woman they gave the main role to."

I walked away as Mom said, "*Everyone* wondered

about that. Now, far be it from me, dear, to cast aspersions on any of my fellow singers, but rumors did say . . ."

Mom was still in the shop, still explaining that she would never say *a word* against *anyone* in the opera world, while implying all sorts of petty jealousies and downright skulduggery, when Willow, Amber, and Jason came in.

"Hi," I said. "I didn't expect to see you guys here today."

"Why not?" Willow said. "We didn't get our shoot done yesterday."

"Uh, because a man died?"

She waved her hand in the air. No one was paying the newcomers any particular attention.

"The police told us we can't leave town," Amber said.

"Erica's holed up at that fancy inn with her lawyer and the Unfriendly Ghost," Willow said. "And we're stuck twiddling our thumbs in that crummy motel."

"We might as well get on with it," Jason said.

"Get on with what?"

"The story about Rudolph, of course," Willow said.

The words "police" and "Erica" had caught people's attention. Whispers began to spread. The woman who'd spoken to Mom left, after buying a Santa's workshop music box, and Mom wandered over to listen.

"Perhaps we should talk in my office," I said. "'Bye, Mom."

She lifted one groomed eyebrow. "Are you going to introduce me to your friends, dear?"

"This is my mother," I said. "Mom, these people are from *Jennifer's Lifestyle*." One of the onlookers squeaked.

Jason held out his hand, and Mom took it. Willow and Amber nodded absentmindedly. "'Bye, Mom," I repeated.

"If you or your friends need anything, dear," Mom said before sailing out the door.

"Okay," Jason said. "Lead the way."

I told Crystal I'd be right back, and we all filed through the curtain. The moment I opened the office door, Mattie leapt up to greet the newcomers. I maintain you can tell a lot about people by how they react to dogs. Jason exclaimed over his size and gave him a hearty rub on the head. Amber knelt down to give and receive sloppy kisses. Willow cringed.

My office was barely large enough for the four of us, not to mention the dog. I shoved boxes into the hallway and ordered Mattie to crawl under my desk. I took a seat behind the desk, more to keep Mattie under control than to be comfortable. Willow took the single visitor's chair.

"You're going to say we're heartless," Willow said. "Carrying on with the story when Max is dead. In the place where, apparently, he died. But we don't see it that way."

"It's kinda like a memorial to Max," Amber said. "We might even dedicate the issue to him."

"Does Erica know about this?"

"I've just come from seeing her," Jason said. "She thinks it's a great idea."

"So it was your idea, not hers?"

"It was my idea, if you must know," Willow said. "Look at it our way, Merry. We're stuck here in your two-bit town, staying at the Flea-Bite Motel, so we might as well make the best of it."

"The Carolers Motel isn't . . ."

"I am exaggerating for emphasis. It's perfectly clean. But it is a *motel*." Willow almost visibly cringed.

"When I traveled with the magazine we all stayed in reasonably nice hotels."

"That was then," Willow said. "This is now. Erica and Max implemented some cost-cutting measures. Cost cutting for us, never for them, of course. I notice they weren't put up in any motel."

"That's not fair," Jason said. "She is the boss. She can spend her money where and how she wants."

"Her grandmother's money, you mean," Amber said.

"What do you want from me?" I said, trying to stop the bickering.

"A photo shoot," Willow said. "Like we planned. We'll do it tonight."

"Tonight?"

"Might as well get it over with," Jason said. "The minute we're free to go, I'm outa here."

"I suppose that would be all right." Mattie tried to push his way out from under my desk. "Stay!" I used my legs to block him.

Jason stepped away from the wall. "I'll leave you two to sort out the details. I want to check out that bakery again. Get a few shots of the place when it's busy. Amber, you can come with me. What time do you close today?"

"Six on Sunday," I said.

"Back at six."

Jason and Amber left. Willow settled into her chair and crossed her legs.

"Jason's new since I worked for the magazine. Is he good?" I asked.

"He's not a regular employee, just a freelancer. He snaps the pics and moves on. He's an okay photographer, but there are a lot better ones out there. Max only hired him because he comes cheap. Can I smoke in here?"

"No. Sounds like things aren't going so well at the magazine." I rubbed the top of Mattie's head.

"It's a mess. Max was promoted way over his head. He could do a fabulous layout. Put him in charge of staff and money. Disaster."

"Did anyone say that to Erica?"

"Are you kidding me? Ted McNamara had some issues with the way Erica was running things. Remember Ted?"

"Yeah. Great guy. Been there forever."

"He came out of her office, packed his things, and walked out."

"He quit?"

"She fired him."

"Wow."

"Yeah, wow. He'd been there long enough that he phoned Jennifer the minute he stepped out of the elevator. She agreed to pay him full salary until his pension kicks in. No one else is going to get that, so no one dares to contradict anything Erica wants. And what Max wanted, Erica wanted."

"How's Max's death going to change things?"

Willow gave me a very long look. Then she said, "Between you and me, Merry, the next boy toy will be in the corner office before Erica dries her fake tears."

"You don't think she loved Max?"

"I'm sure she did. In her way. And her way is love 'em and dump 'em. Max just happened to be the one she was dating when Jennifer decided it was time for a wedding."

"Do you know that, or are you guessing?"

"I'm guessing, Merry, because I know Erica. What, you think it was true love? Those two were the same. Too much head over heels in love with themselves to care for anyone else." She let out a bark of laughter that had Mattie leaping to his feet. I wiggled my legs aside to let him out from under my desk. "Hey, I forgot. You were engaged to him, weren't you? I'd say you had a lucky escape."

Mattie walked over to Willow. He looked into her face, expecting a pat. She pushed him roughly aside.

I didn't know what to believe. I kept in touch with some friends who were still working at the magazine, so I knew much of what Willow was saying was true, but as she talked her spite began to take over. If things were so bad, why didn't she leave? She should be able to get a job at another magazine. Then again, I had no idea what her reputation was in the business. Maybe she didn't fancy trying her chances.

I'd been wondering who would kill Max. Now, I remembered the old mystery novel adage. *Cui bono.* Who benefits? If things were as bad at the magazine as Willow was saying, the employees would be more than happy to see the end of Max's involvement.

Maybe they weren't expecting Erica to find someone to replace Max right away. After all, whether she loved him or not, she had the image of the noble, grieving fiancée to protect. *Jennifer's Lifestyle* was still a major concern. Get a set of steady hands back on the tiller and everything could turn out okay.

"It's an ill wind," Willow said, "as they say. Frankly, it will be nice to have Erica out of the picture for a while. She has not a whit of taste and must be getting her design tips from old issues of *TigerBeat.* You would have thought she'd be busy planning the wedding of the century, wouldn't you, but she hopped down here fast enough to check on what Max was up to. And as for him, sure, he was great at design and layout, but someone had to give him the ideas first. If she got her inspiration from '90s teen magazines, he got his from *Forbes* and *BusinessWeek.*" She grinned at me. "You and me, Merry, we'll create a feature on Rudolph that'll have the New York magazine world talking for months."

"All I'm doing is giving you the space."

"Exactly, you've created a space I can work with. It's about time I got some recognition around that dump."

Judging by the sounds drifting through the curtain into my office, the store was busy. Crystal could use some help. I was torn between getting back to my job and staying here and finding out what else Willow had to say. "Amber seems nice. When I first met her I thought she was a bit of a ditz."

"She seems brain-dead, and she can be a total flake sometimes, but she's incredibly talented. She's massively insecure, that's all. When she gets nervous she can't stop talking. Give her some time and maturity and she'll be fine. She's learning fast. My guess is six more months, twelve tops, and then she'll be out the door."

"Why do you say that?"

"Erica won't pay enough. More of her and Max's cost-cutting measures. They hire kids straight out of college or design school, pay them peanuts, and when they've learned the job and ask for more money, they're told no. So they leave. Amber needs maturing and nurturing, and she's not getting that at *Jennifer's Lifestyle*. I've tried to help her when I can, but we don't often work together. Erica was quite dreadful to her, you know."

"How?"

She shrugged. "Sometimes I wondered if Erica was trying to get her to quit. Always criticizing, always nit-picking. Amber has a lot of talent. Erica has none. She was furiously jealous. She was jealous of anyone who was better than her."

"Has Detective Simmonds spoken to you?"

"I wouldn't want to be under the bright lights with her, I can tell you. She seems as sharp as a tack. She wanted to know where we were around the time Max died. I don't know what Jason and Amber told her; we weren't together until we got down to the park around the time Santa arrived on his boat. I told the detective that. I came into town for a late breakfast at that nice bakery and enjoyed sitting over my coffee for a long time. It was nice to have a break. Then I walked down to the park and met up with the others. I'm sure you're wondering, so let me put your mind at rest. I didn't see Max that day, and I didn't kill him."

"I wasn't . . ." I said.

"I told the detective all that. I also told her that I didn't like Max. I didn't like what he was doing to the magazine. But at least he had some knowledge of how a magazine works. Heaven help us all if Erica drops her next boy toy into the job."

Crystal tapped lightly on the open office door. "Sorry to bother you, Merry, but are we getting any more of those cranberry strings? I've a customer who wants twenty—she and her group have volunteered to decorate their town's official tree this year. I checked the storage room but can't find any more. We've only got nine left."

Willow got to her feet. "I'll let you get back to it. See you at six."

Mattie curled up on his bed, and I followed Willow out. I spoke to the customer, told her I would order as many of the cranberry strings as she needed, and she left happy, promising to return with her tree-decorating committee. I hoped, for the sake of Alan's business as well as mine, that news of the murder weapon didn't get into the press.

As Mattie and I walked to work this morning, I'd deliberately avoided so much as glancing at the newspaper boxes to see the *Gazette* headlines. I didn't want to read anything about the death of Max, and I assumed that if anyone had news of Jackie, I'd hear about it.

Unfortunately, you can't avoid the media forever. Once the regular lunchtime lull descended, Crystal began rearranging some of her beautiful creations. "I don't think I can put in full-time hours over the rest of the summer, Merry. I've got to get ready for school, and I have my jewelry to make."

"No need to worry about it. I'm sure Jackie will be back soon." I was trying to stay optimistic.

"If she's in jail she won't be much help."

"Jail? What makes you think she's going to jail?"

"That's what the paper said this morning. The police say she killed that man."

"What!" I knew Simmonds suspected Jackie, because she'd told me so, but I didn't think she was so convinced that she'd go public with it. I took a handful of quarters out of the cash register and ran for the street. A newspaper box was set up in front of the Gift Nook. The main headline, as I expected, was about the "brutal murder" of Max Folger. I threw quarters into the box and pulled out the paper.

"So sorry to hear about your misfortune," Margie Thatcher said, not sounding the least bit sorry. "I hope you can keep the business going with that girl on death row."

"Don't be ridiculous," I said. "Besides, we don't have the death penalty in New York State."

"Then she might only get life in prison. So sad." Margie shook her head. Her eyes gleamed.

"You'd better not be spreading that nasty rumor around."

"If people come into my shop and ask what's going on, I'm not going to lie to them, am I?"

"You were here on Saturday, weren't you, Margie? I didn't see you down at the parade. The streets were quiet, not many shoppers around. You didn't pop into my store to ask Max to come and visit the Nook, did you? And get into an argument with him?"

"That's a vile accusation. I'll have you know that I was

happy to tell the police my whereabouts at the time in question. I was in the store. I heard nothing. I am not a snoop. I have no interest in what goes on in your place."

"Vile accusations can go both ways," I said. I wasn't going to stand in the street reading the *Gazette* in front of Margie, so I stomped back into my shop.

I opened the paper. It wasn't as bad as I'd feared. Below the fold, there was a nice picture of Jackie, looking young and sweet in her high school graduation photo. The smaller headline read, "Police Concerned for Missing Rudolph Woman." The article had been written by Russ after the police press conference, and it was light on accusations, concentrating on when Jackie had last been seen and giving a description of her. Sue-Anne Morrow was quoted briefly, saying the town of Rudolph had full confidence in the police.

"This isn't so bad," I said to Crystal. "Margie Thatcher made it sound as though a manhunt's raging through the entire state of New York searching for Jackie." I pushed aside an image of barking dogs streaming through the dark woods and uniformed handlers wading through fast-moving creeks as flashlights bobbed.

"That's only the *Gazette*," Crystal said. "My mom was in Muddle Harbor this morning visiting a friend, and her friend gave her a copy of today's *Chronicle*."

The *Muddle Harbor Chronicle*. The nearby town of Muddle Harbor is Rudolph's chief rival, although the rivalry seems to be strictly confined to their imagination. Their local newspaper liked nothing more than to dish the dirt on Rudolph.

"What did they say?" I asked, although I really did not want to know.

"I brought it to show you." Crystal disappeared into the rear of the shop and came back with the scurrilous rag. She handed it to me. The main article was about the murder, emphasis leaning heavily on the fact that the killing happened in Rudolph. The picture was of none other than Candy Campbell guarding the "scene of the shocking crime." Fortunately, the Mrs. Claus's sign didn't appear in the photo. The photographer had been more interested in ensuring that Candy's shoulder patch with the Rudolph police department logo was prominently displayed. They'd also printed a small picture of Jackie, not exactly at her best. The lighting was poor, and it looked as though she was in someone's basement. Her eyes were vacant, staring into the shadows, her mouth slack, and her hair disheveled. I wondered where they found it. If they'd called Jackie's family wanting a picture, no one would have sent them this one. I looked closer. The picture might be as much as five or six years old, taken when Jackie was in high school. It was probably buried somewhere on the Internet, and some keen reporter hunted it down. The headline read, "Missing Rudolph Woman Wanted for Questioning in Brutal Murder." I read the article quickly. It leaned heavily to innuendo, but the point was that the Rudolph police believed Jackie O'Reilly had murdered Max Folger and was now on the run. The byline said Dawn Galloway. I'd run into Ms. Galloway before. "Unscrupulous" and "ambitious" were words that came to mind.

"Oh dear," I said.

"You think she did it?" Crystal asked.

"No," I said firmly. "I do not."

"Then where is she?"

I let out a sigh. *Where indeed.*

The bells over the door chimed, and a group of laughing women poured into the shop, putting an end to that conversation. I shoved the paper behind the counter.

"Can you stay for a while after closing?" I asked Crystal when we again had a lull.

"Sure. Why?"

I explained about the magazine photo shoot. "Some of your jewelry might be of interest to them, and you should be here to talk to them if it is."

"That'd be great."

I wanted to introduce Crystal to Willow and Amber. Max had said no to featuring another jeweler, but Willow might have other ideas. Crystal was so multitalented, I wanted her to get the exposure if it were possible. Not only was she a straight-A student and class valedictorian, she worked part-time at my shop, ran her own small jewelry-making business, and took singing lessons from my mom.

Promptly at six o'clock I flipped the sign on the door to "Closed" while Crystal rang up the purchases of the last customers of the day, two youthful-looking grandmothers loading themselves down with toys for holiday gifts and festive dishes and linens for themselves.

I opened the door for the ladies, and said I hoped they'd be able to bring their families back to Rudolph at Christmastime. I was still holding the door when the team from *Jennifer's Lifestyle* arrived.

Willow came first, then Jason, wrapped in a plethora of camera paraphernalia, followed by Amber, carrying more equipment. I introduced Crystal to Willow and Amber, while Jason began setting up. Amber said she'd love to talk later about what sort of work Crystal did.

I told Willow and Amber they could arrange things any way they wanted and stepped out of the way. As I watched them working, placing everything just so; stepping back to check; rearranging; seeking the exact match of color, shape, and texture; conferring with Jason about angles and lighting, I felt a stirring of regret. I'd loved the magazine world and being immersed in leading-edge design and style. I'd been good at it—everyone said so.

The light on the camera flashed repeatedly, and the steady click of the shutter opening and closing rang through the shop as Jason took some test shots while Willow began arranging items on the jewelry tree. "Most of those pieces," I said, "were made by Crystal. She's going to the School of Visual Arts in the fall to study jewelry and small-metal design. She's got a very bright future."

Crystal blushed furiously.

"Some of these pieces are great," Willow said. "I'm thinking a feature on up-and-coming artists. We'll focus on people under twenty who are already starting to make a splash. The future of American design, if you will. Be sure and give me your number when we're done here."

I gave Crystal a thumbs-up behind Willow's back.

"When you're in New York," Amber said, "maybe we can have a coffee or something. I can tell you what *not* to do in your career."

Willow moved on to study the table-setting display. "The green and red is a mite garish, don't you think, Merry?"

"Red and green means Christmas to a lot of people. These aren't meant to be everyday dishes."

"Still don't like them. But that children's set is charming. Hey! I've had a great idea. What are your favorite pieces, Merry? We can do a sidebar on decorating for the holidays with Merry Wilkinson." She stepped back and studied my knee-length white skirt and blue and white striped blouse. "You look like an Upstate shop clerk, not a doyenne of home decor."

"I am an Upstate shop clerk."

"You'll have to change."

"I'm not set up for photographing people," Jason said.

"Tomorrow, then," Willow said.

She had not asked me what I thought of the idea. Jason growled at me to get out of the way as he had lights to put up. I stepped back.

"Thoroughly unlikable person," Amber was saying to Crystal. "You *do not* want to find your career in the clutches of someone like that."

"Who are you talking about?" I asked.

"No one," Amber said quickly. At that moment our attention was distracted by a loud hammering on the door.

All the blood rushed out of Amber's face, and it was easy to guess who'd been on her mind.

Erica Johnstone was peering into my shop. I threw a quick glance around the room. Willow looked furious, Jason pleased, Amber terrified, Crystal awestruck. I hurried to unlock the door.

Erica fell into the shop, followed, of course, by Muriel and her ever-present giant tote bag and scarf. Lightbulbs popped as the paparazzi jostled each other trying to see inside.

"It's gone!" Erica cried as I slammed the door behind her.

"What's gone?" we chorused.

"My necklace. Call the police." Erica's legs wobbled and she began to sway. Muriel said, "Oh dear." Jason rushed across the room and put his arm around the fainting woman. He led her to the wingback chair. "Water!" he shouted. Crystal dashed for the back rooms.

Once Erica had downed the entire glass of water and Muriel was ineffectively patting her hand, Jason said, "Slowly and calmly tell us what's happened."

Erica took a shuddering breath. "The necklace, the one my darling Max bought me. It's gone. It's been stolen. You"—she pointed to Crystal—"call the police."

Crystal dashed for the shop phone and made the call.

"Are you sure you didn't misplace it?" I said.

Erica glared at me. "Of course I'm sure. Do you think me a fool?"

Behind her back, Willow mouthed "yes." Then she

rounded the chair to face Erica. "That's too bad, but we're kinda busy here, Erica. You know how tight our schedule is and we're already behind."

"Right now I truly do not care about your schedule."

"Why have you come here?" I asked. "If you mean the necklace Max bought on Friday, I saw you leave with it myself. Muriel had it. It wasn't taken from here."

"This is where it came from. I thought the police would want to see something similar."

More chance of drama, I thought but didn't say, with a bigger audience than just the hapless Muriel.

Another rap on the shop door, and Crystal opened it to admit Detective Simmonds. She came in, shouting, "No comment," over her shoulder. "What's this about a theft?"

"That was quick," I said.

"I happened to be passing. Because of what happened here the other day, the dispatcher put the call through to me."

"My necklace has been stolen," Erica said.

"When did you see it last?" Simmonds asked.

"Yesterday. I think."

"Yesterday. Where?"

"In my jewelry case in my hotel room. Max gave it to me. It was his final gift to me," she sobbed. "I was looking at it yesterday."

"Your hotel? What are you doing here, then?"

"It was bought here. I thought you could identify it more easily, seeing the source."

Simmonds looked as though she was thinking the

same thing I was. "Ms. Johnstone, I took this call because I believed it had something to do with the scene of Mr. Folger's death. If not, you need to come to the station and make a statement."

"Oh no," Muriel gasped.

"Come to the police station!" Erica said. "I don't think so!"

Jason stepped forward. "Now, see here. You don't seem to realize to whom you are speaking. Ms. Johnstone has just suffered a traumatic loss."

Erica nodded. "It was a pretty necklace."

"In the murder of her fiancé," Jason continued. "Which you people don't seem to be doing anything about."

"I assure you, Mr. Kerr," Simmonds said, "we are doing a great deal. Which is why I'm not impressed at being called down here on a minor matter that's taking me away from that investigation. I don't see Mr. Claymore. Did he not come with you?"

"He was in his room making calls. I didn't want to disturb him," Erica said.

"You think a crime has been committed but you didn't want to disturb your lawyer?"

"He's very busy," Erica said.

I suspected Erica had snuck out without telling James Claymore what was going on, knowing he wouldn't want her running through town, pursued by the howling mob of the ladies and gentlemen of the press.

"As I am here now," Simmonds said, "what was the value of the item, Ms. Johnstone?"

"Priceless."

"An estimate, please," Simmonds said dryly.

"One hundred and ten dollars," I said.

"One hundred and ten dollars?"

"Plus tax."

"Mustn't forget the tax."

"Mr. Folger bought it for Ms. Johnstone," I said. "The day before he died. She's referring to the sentimental value."

Erica nodded.

"Do you have a picture of the item?" Simmonds asked.

Erica shook her head.

"We might," I said. "Crystal, you photograph everything you bring here for sale, don't you?"

"Yes, I do. It'll be at home."

"E-mail me a copy of the picture, please." Simmonds handed her card to Crystal. "Ms. Johnstone, I can declare your hotel room a crime scene, meaning no one can go in or out until we have finished our investigation. Is that what you want?"

"I can get another room," Erica said.

"Which also means nothing can be removed from the scene until I say so. And some items, such as your jewelry box, might be required as evidence when the case comes to court."

"You can't do that!"

"Up to you."

"Maybe that's not such a good idea," Erica said slowly. "But you will come and fingerprint everything, won't you?"

"Ms. Johnstone, we're talking about a hotel room. Staff are in and out all the time, guests, their visitors. If we are to dust for fingerprints, you'll have to come with me to the station right now so I can take your prints for elimination purposes."

Erica clutched her hands together. "I will not be fingerprinted like some common criminal."

"There you have it," Simmonds said. "Did you report this alleged theft to the hotel management?"

"No," Muriel said. "Erica wanted to come right here."

"I suggest you do so. They'll instruct their staff to be on the lookout for it, in case it was misplaced."

"I'm sure," Jason said, "Ms. Johnstone didn't misplace this item which is so important to her."

"We searched for it," Erica said, "Didn't we, Muriel?"

"Everywhere," Muriel agreed.

Simmonds glanced toward the window. "One more thing, Ms. Johnstone. I'm advising you not to speak to any members of the press about this alleged theft. Doing so might seriously compromise my investigation, as well as exposing you to a lawsuit if you make unsubstantiated accusations. Do you understand?"

Erica nodded.

"Now that that's settled," Willow said, "we have work to do here, people. Muriel, take Erica back to the hotel. She needs to rest. Jason, I'm thinking subdued lighting over the jewelry case. I'd like a mood of . . ."

"I'll stay to help," Erica said.

"Heaven help us," Amber mumbled.

Chapter 9

Erica quickly got bored with the minutiae of arranging a photo shoot, and Willow convinced her to go back to the hotel. Erica said she was considering suing the town of Rudolph and its police department for incompetence, while Muriel fussed over her like a neurotic mother hen. Jason offered to walk them to their car, implying that the streets weren't safe at night. Erica clutched his arm gratefully. At my suggestion, they left through the back door, although most of the paparazzi had taken off in pursuit of Detective Simmonds, shouting questions at her.

"That's going to go over well," I said to Willow. "Let's run a major feature on how great this town is at the same time as we sue them."

"Don't mind her," Willow said. "She's not happy if she's not planning to sue someone. She forgets about it an hour later."

"What do you think happened to the necklace? The Yuletide has a spotless reputation; they're not going to be happy if she starts saying things disappeared from her room."

"She loses stuff all the time," Amber said. "We did a big shoot at her house a couple of months ago for her bridal shower. Worst freakin' week of my life. A pair of earrings went missing and then a ring. The ring was valuable, too, a good-sized emerald. A maid later found it when she was cleaning one of the guest bathrooms. Erica had forgotten she'd nipped in there to wash her hands."

"What about the earrings?"

"When the party and the shoot were over, I left, and never heard anything more about it."

Jason returned and the group went back to work.

It was after ten when they wrapped up and Mattie and I headed home. The streets were dark and quiet, the moon covered by thick clouds. There was no wind, and the air was warm and dense with humidity. I pulled out my phone to place a call while we walked. Helen Pickering and I had been good friends when I lived in Manhattan. She still worked for the magazine, in the accounting department.

"Hey, Merry," she said. "Nice to hear from you. I got the news about Max. We all did, of course. I wanted to call you, but didn't want to look as if I was digging for gossip. Are you okay?"

"I'm fine." I seemed to be saying that a lot lately. "I'm sorry about his death, but we were finished a long time ago."

"Speaking of which, I hear Erica's there. How's she doing?"

"Hard to tell what's genuine and what's playing the prima donna."

"Tell me about it," Helen said.

"Do you know Willow Rasmon and a props assistant named Amber? I don't remember her last name."

"Sure. Why?"

"Tell me about them. How things are going at work, I mean."

"Have you got a couple of hours? Amber's doing good. She's a rising star. She has an amazing eye for finding exactly the right thing at exactly the right time. I've heard she's rising so fast, she's going to be able to write her own ticket soon." That confirmed what Willow had told me. "Different story for Willow. She's done nothing the past year but clash with Max and Erica. We expect you creative types to have your differences, and I know good ideas come out of a back-and-forth, but if Max said he wanted a chair painted white, Willow would tell props to make it black."

"They worked together without a lot of trouble before. Why the change, do you think?"

"Max is the boss now. Sorry, I mean he was the boss. He thought that meant he didn't have to take anyone's advice. Frankly, Merry, it was a case of power corrupting. It didn't help that Erica backed up every decision he made. In most cases, it would have been better if the chair had been black, but everyone soon learned not to argue with

Max. I'm glad I'm an accountant. No one can pick a fight with me or tell me to make a three look more like a five. A lot of people have left over the last year."

"Why didn't Willow?"

"She's managed to get herself a reputation for being difficult. You know how tight that world is, Merry. A bad reputation isn't easy to shake off. Erica isn't popular, but there are one or two folks here who think she should be cut some slack and given a chance. Willow's constant backbiting doesn't endear her to people who are trying to keep their spirits up. The last couple of days have been quite peaceful with Max and Willow both out of town, not to mention Erica. I suppose the project's been canceled because of what happened."

"They've just finished a shoot in my shop. Tomorrow they want me to dress nicely and look like the ultimate source for holiday decorating."

"Seems somewhat tacky, don't you think?"

"I did at first, but I see their point. They're under police orders not to leave town. They have to do something, and work's probably best. I've heard talk of a Max Folger commemorative issue."

Helen snorted. "Spare me."

"Will you keep me posted if you hear anything more?"

"Sure. The office is going to be a hive of rumors tomorrow. I'll try to sort the wheat from the chaff."

"Thanks."

"You take care," she said.

On our way home, rather than go out again to give Mattie a proper walk, I (feeling like a very bad dog owner indeed) took a quick detour into the park so he could tend to his business. We were back on the sidewalk, heading to our house, when a man crossed the street ahead of me, walking rapidly. He was wrapped in shadows, but as he passed under a streetlight I quickened my pace. I'd recognize that slouch and lopsided gait anywhere.

"Kyle," I shouted.

He stopped.

Mattie and I hurried across the street. Mattie sniffed at his pant legs. Kyle gave him a hearty pat.

"I don't suppose you've heard from Jackie?" I asked.

"Nope."

"Do you have any idea where she might be?"

"Nope." He grabbed Mattie's face between his hands and shook. Mattie's rear end wiggled in delight. "He's getting real strong, Merry. Are you going to send him out in the winter with a barrel of whiskey under his chin?"

"Brandy."

"Huh?"

"The monks in the Alps, who used Saint Bernards to rescue people lost in the snow, supposedly filled the flasks with brandy. Not whiskey."

Mattie pulled his head free. Kyle lunged for him and Mattie danced out of the way. "I might head out for a walk in the snow and get lost. I'd like to be rescued by this guy. Just remember, I like whiskey better. Catch you later, Merry."

"If you hear from Jackie, will you tell her to call me right away?"

"Yeah. Sure." Kyle sauntered away.

I watched him go. I'd always thought Kyle was shallow and not terribly smart, but that really took the cake. Then again, who am I to judge anyone else? Kyle played the tough and macho part to the hilt. I guess appearing to worry about another human being, even his girlfriend, didn't fit the persona. Poor guy.

I was attempting to sneak around the house and not get waylaid by Mrs. D'Angelo, when my phone beeped with an incoming text.

Vicky: *How was the shoot?*

Me: *Exhausting.*

Vicky: *Up to a phone chat?*

Me: *Call you in ten.*

I pushed open the gate to the backyard and the leash almost jerked out of my hand as Mattie made a dash for freedom. This time I was ready for him. "Inside," I said. "Dinnertime. You must be starving." He hadn't had his dinner (come to think of it, neither had I), although I kept a tin of dog biscuits at work for times when I'd been working late. Thoughts of chasing rabbits around the yard disappeared at the word "dinner" and he ran up the stairs the moment the door was unlocked. I did not run. I dragged myself up.

I kicked off my shoes, fed Mattie, put the kettle on for hot tea, popped a packaged meal into the microwave, and called Vicky.

"My spies tell me there was a lot of activity outside the shop around six."

"Erica Johnstone showed up, followed by a stream of reporters. I can't imagine living like that. Hordes of people watching your every move so if you make a mistake they can put it on the Internet for the world to see."

"She doesn't have to encourage it," Vicky said.

"That's true. Jennifer lives pretty much under the radar. She could, and usually did, walk down the streets of Manhattan without anyone recognizing her. She loved to try new restaurants, with just a friend or two, and then return a couple of weeks later having had her secretary make a reservation in her name. If the food and service were remarkably better the second time, she never went back."

"You liked her," Vicky said. It was not a question.

"I did. I do. Very much. But she's over eighty, and she's entitled to enjoy her retirement. Erica didn't come in to watch the photo shoot though." I told Vicky about the necklace.

"It was taken at the Yuletide?"

"It went missing at the Yuletide. I can't imagine for a minute that one of the chambermaids stole it. Besides, Erica's scarcely been out of the cabin. Hey, there's a thought. I should check if she left the inn at any time on Saturday morning."

"Merry, why are you getting involved?" Vicky asked.

"I am involved, Vicky, whether I like it or not. Max was killed in my shop."

"Let the police handle it. You know Simmonds is perfectly capable. It's not up to you to be checking the movements of Erica Johnstone or anyone else."

I thought about that. I thought for so long, Vicky said, "Merry, are you still there?"

"Yes, I'm here. I'm thinking. Right now, it seems as though Jackie is the police's main suspect. I am absolutely positive that Jackie didn't kill Max. I'm probably not the world's best judge of character—I was going to marry Max Folger, after all—but I know Jackie and I know she simply doesn't have it in her. It's a good thing the police are looking for her, but if they're focused on her as the killer, then they are not looking in the right places. I know these people, Vicky. The magazine people, Max's colleagues, even Erica. I know them far better than Detective Simmonds does or ever will." I was thinking of the staff gossip about Erica and Max. No one would come right out and tell the police what they really thought of Erica, or what they thought of Max when power began to go to his head. Not if there was any risk of what they'd said getting back to Erica. "Don't worry, I'm not getting *involved*. I'm interested in what's going on, that's all."

"Yeah, right. I know you. If you need backup when you're being interested, you know I'm here."

"I know."

"Do you think the theft of the necklace has anything to do with Max's murder?"

"What, the secret launch codes to America's nuclear arsenal are hidden in the rings of the necklace, and a master criminal killed Max in an attempt to get it? This isn't a movie, Vicky."

"Put that way, it does sound silly. But I can't help but notice the coincidence."

"I don't think it's a coincidence at all. Apparently Erica is always misplacing stuff. Valuable things, too. She makes a big scene, throws a temper tantrum. And then, lo and behold, it turns up." Although, I had to admit, it would be hard to lose a shiny gold necklace in a two-bedroom cabin.

Mattie yawned and stretched. I yawned in sympathy. "It's late. I should go. Another busy day tomorrow."

"Are the magazine people coming back?"

"After closing. They want me to dress like I'm some doyenne of seasonal fashion. I forgot to ask—did they take many pictures in the bakery?"

"Lots and lots. In the front they snapped happy people enjoying their freshly prepared lunches, and in the back, stacks of loaves and homemade baked goods cooling on racks. The photographer, what's his name?"

"Jason."

"He said the food editors at the magazine might be asking for my spice cookie recipe to accompany the article. I'm not sure if I want to hand it over. He didn't take any shots with me in them, though. Perhaps I don't look like a doyenne of Christmas baking."

I laughed. "That you don't."

We exchanged good-nights and hung up. I let Mattie into the backyard one last time, but I didn't go outside with him. Instead I got ready for bed. I hadn't heard from Alan today, and I shoved aside a prickle of disappointment. He knew I was busy with the magazine people. That was all.

I went back downstairs, and called Mattie to come in.

Chapter 10

The next morning we were once again up before the birds. Monday was normally a quiet day in the shop, but it was July and the town was full of vacationers. When I lived in Manhattan I'd done yoga three times a week and went to a gym another two or three days, as well as heading out for the occasional run in Central Park. All that healthful activity had fallen by the wayside once I opened my own business. I'd started running again in the spring, during the quiet season, but I hadn't been out for weeks now.

As I did several times a week, I vowed that I'd go for a run. Tomorrow.

At least I had the dog, and a good walk was a great way to start the day. Saint Bernards aren't big on vigorous exercise, and they don't make good running companions. I found that out quickly enough the couple of times I tried to take Mattie along. But he did love his walks, and the longer the better. In the summer months, the morning was definitely the best time for that. By midday he was too hot to want to do much at all.

I pulled on shorts and a T-shirt and sneakers and we headed out. The sun was an orange streak in the eastern sky, and the streetlights were still on. We walked away from town, toward the lake. A handful of cars passed us, headlights breaking the gloom. Inside houses lining the shore, lights were being switched on as people began their day. The boat launch, where we'd assembled the marine parade on Saturday, has a nice stretch of empty, rocky shoreline, where I can let Mattie off the leash so he can explore to his big heart's content. He usually ends up in the water, having waded in up to his stomach, and then simply sits down. He doesn't try to swim, but he seems to like being in the water. Maybe it's cool and refreshing on his heavy fur, designed for high mountain passes and fierce winter blizzards rather than New York heat and humidity.

Today we didn't make it as far as the waterline.

A battered and rusty pickup truck was parked near the dock. The headlights were off, but the shape of a single person inside was outlined by the rising sun. I knew that truck. It belonged to Kyle Lambert. The truck was facing away from me, and judging by the shape of the back of the head of the man inside, it was Kyle himself. What on earth was Kyle doing here, at this time of day, alone?

Nothing good, I was sure.

It had to have something to do with Jackie. Was he

meeting Jackie? Good heavens, was he arranging to pay ransom to her kidnappers? Or, was he the kidnapper himself and here to get paid off by Jackie's family? Had Jackie staged her own disappearance in the wake of Max's death and plotted to get out of town with Kyle and her family's ransom money? Scenarios tumbled all over themselves in my head.

"Shush," I said to Mattie. I reeled the leash in so he was brushing up against my legs and, trying to make as little noise as possible, we crept behind a clump of thick bushes. We didn't have long to wait. Almost immediately, I heard a well-tuned engine approaching. It slowed as the vehicle turned onto the dirt path leading to the dock. A silver Lexus SUV, polished to a high shine, pulled up beside Kyle's truck. I couldn't believe that any of Kyle's friends owned a car like that, or kept it that clean. Where had I last seen a vehicle like that? Outside Cabin C at the Yuletide Inn. It had to be here for the exchange. Had Erica kidnapped Jackie after all? I found it hard to believe, but the death of Max in my shop was hard to believe. I stroked Mattie's back, whispering for him to be quiet. He gave my face a quick lick before returning to an intensive examination of the ground beneath a sumac.

I pulled out my phone, snapped a couple of pictures of the two vehicles, and sent them to my mom. Mom doesn't usually get out of bed for hours yet. If this turned out to be nothing, I'd phone her and tell her to delete them. If not . . . she could take the pictures to the cops.

The door of the pickup opened, and Kyle Lambert stepped out.

The door of the SUV opened, and Muriel Fraser stepped out.

I sucked in a breath.

They eyed each other warily as they drew closer. Kyle carried an envelope, Muriel a plain paper bag. Mattie let out a bark of greeting, and they both jumped.

I snapped a couple more pictures and then clicked "send." As Mattie was struggling against the leash to reach his friend, I had little choice but to step out of the bushes. "What on earth do you two think you're doing?"

Mattie's tail wagged happily. Kyle relaxed but Muriel did not. Eyes wide with fear, she swung around and moved toward her car.

"Hold it right there," I said. "If you take another step, I'll set the dog on you."

As if Mattie would do anything but lick her to death. She didn't know that, so she froze in place. She stared at the giant dog, clearly terrified.

"What's in the bag?" I asked.

She whimpered. I growled. Mattie barked. Kyle chuckled.

"Nothing! Really, it's nothing." Muriel started to cry.

Kyle stuffed the envelope into his jeans pocket and clapped his hands. Mattie leapt forward and I let go of the leash. "You going to tell me what's going on here, Kyle?"

"Nothing to do with you, Merry," he said as he and Mattie romped.

"Please," Muriel said through her tears. "Don't let the dog hurt him. He hasn't done anything wrong. I'm sorry."

If Muriel had kidnapped Jackie and was holding her for ransom, she made a mighty poor master criminal.

I snatched the bag out of her hand. I pulled a chain out of the bag. The chain was made of interlocked gold rings, with a second smaller chain inside the circle, displaying a wreath of green and red glass beads at the throat. The design was unique, the craftsmanship individual. This could only be the piece of jewelry made by Crystal Wong, bought by Max Folger at Mrs. Claus's Treasures, and later stolen from Erica Johnstone's hotel room. "What's the meaning of this?" I said in my sternest voice. Muriel was crying so hard now she couldn't get any words out.

"Kyle," I said. "Want to tell me what's going on here?"

"It's just a necklace, Merry. Chill. Jackie's birthday's coming up and I want to get her something nice. She likes pretty jewelry, but the good stuff's kinda expensive. So when I heard that this lady was selling, I figured I'd buy."

"How did you hear that?"

He shrugged. "My cousin Lenny keeps his ear to the ground."

"You know this is stolen, right?"

"No way." Kyle lifted his hands and glared at Muriel. "You said your boss gives you her leftover stuff."

"She doesn't need it." Muriel sobbed. "She doesn't even know what she has most of the time."

"How much are you paying for this?" I asked Kyle.

"Fifty bucks. She said it's worth a hundred and ten. She has the receipt."

What a couple of incompetent crooks these two were.

"Kyle, if this is for Jackie's birthday . . . Do you know where she is?"

He tapped the side of his nose and gave me a wink. "No need to worry, Merry."

"If you're in contact with her, you have to tell her the police are looking for her. Everyone's looking for her. Her mother's worried sick. I'm worried sick."

"She's okay, Merry. She's waiting, that's all."

"Waiting for what?"

"For you to sort everything out."

I almost shrieked. "What does any of this have to do with me?"

He didn't answer. Instead, he said to Muriel, "If this is stolen I want nothing to do with it. I gotta go. Don't know why we had to meet this early anyway."

"It's the only time I can find a minute to myself," Muriel mumbled through her tears. She pulled a tissue out of her pocket and gave her nose a blow like a trumpet. "*She* doesn't usually get up before noon."

Kyle gave Mattie a hearty slap on the rump and headed back to his truck.

Still sobbing, Muriel began to head to the Lexus. I grabbed her arm. "Not so fast." Mattie, forgetting his hard-learned manners, jumped on her. She screamed and flung her arms up to protect her face.

"Down!" I grabbed at Mattie's leash "You'd better tell me what's going on here, Muriel. Or else." I clung to the leash, as though it was taking all my strength to keep the giant slobbering beast from tearing her throat out.

Kyle tooted his horn and gave us a cheerful wave as he drove away.

"Why?" I said to Muriel once Kyle and his truck had disappeared around the bend.

"Keep the dog away from me, and I'll tell you."

"Okay. But remember, I have the necklace."

I tied Mattie to a tree. A small bench sits close to the ramp leading into the water where boat owners slide their craft in. Muriel took a seat and I joined her. We sat in silence for a few moments, watching the small waves lapping against the rocky shore. Farther out, a handful of fishing boats were trying their luck.

"She has so much." Muriel wiped at her eyes. "She doesn't need any of it. She doesn't wear most of what she buys, not even once. She throws it into a drawer and there it sits, forgotten."

"That doesn't mean you can just help yourself," I said.

"How was I supposed to know she'd go looking for that ugly necklace?"

"That's hardly the point, Muriel."

Mattie whined and strained at the leash. I shouted at him to stay.

Muriel let out a long, shuddering breath. "My mother's in a nursing home. It's expensive, but she loves it there. The fees are going up—again—and I simply can't manage any more. My brother used to help out, but he lost his job, and he's got kids still in college. If I don't find some money somewhere, Mom will have to move. It's her home. All her friends are there. It'll break her heart."

"Have you asked Erica for a raise? Maybe she can give you a no-interest loan?"

Muriel snorted. "Oh yes, I asked. I explained that the money isn't for me, but for my mom. She said she doesn't believe in charity. People have to make it on their own, pull themselves up by their bootstraps. I've been working for her for eighteen months, which I gather is about a year longer than any other PA she's ever had. She said we'll reevaluate my salary at the two-year mark. I can't . . . Mom can't wait that long." She broke into deep racking sobs.

I let her cry for a while. "You've been stealing from her?"

"I've been putting her unwanted things to good use, yes. I've never taken anything really valuable. Once in a while I'll hide the expensive stuff, things she'll notice missing. She'll make a big fuss about it being stolen, and it'll turn up under a bed or in the glove compartment of her car. Everyone knows she's a total flake, so they figure she misplaces things. That way, no one pays much attention when the small stuff goes missing. That necklace." Muriel nodded to the bag I was still holding. "She'll never wear anything that cheap. She just wanted to make a big show in front of everyone of Max treating her. If he hadn't died, she never would have given it another thought."

I wasn't entirely sure I believed her. Muriel was asking fifty dollars for the necklace. How many fifty-buck deals would be needed to pay the fees at a good nursing home? "How'd you get in touch with Kyle?"

"Over the past year I've made a few contacts in the

slightly shadier parts of New York City. I was planning to take the necklace back to the city, but as we've been told we can't leave, I needed to get rid of it. So I asked my friend if he knew anyone in Rudolph." As she talked, Muriel stopped crying. She blew her nose with vigor and wiped her eyes with a tissue.

The mother story may or may not have been true, and the necklace wasn't worth all that much. And, I have to confess, I didn't much care if spoiled Erica got her property back or not. But I was getting the feeling that timid, mild-mannered Muriel was starting to get a little too comfortable in the shady world of fencing goods, and no doubt also enjoying the sensation of putting something over on her hated boss. If this didn't end now, it would not end well.

I handed her the bag. "I don't care what story you come up with, but see that Erica gets this back."

She looked at me through puffy red eyes. "You're not going to call the police?"

"Not if you return it. Take my advice, Muriel. Give this up. You will get caught, sooner or later, and next time it might not be by someone willing to give you a break. How's your mom going to manage if you're in prison. Have you thought about that?"

She had the grace to lower her head. "You're right, Merry," she mumbled into her tissue. "I've had enough of this petty thieving."

The sun was fully up now, and the day was getting warm. As we talked, a fishing boat pulled up to the dock. A man leapt out and ran for his car. He backed the car slowly down the ramp and into the shallow water, while his friend guided the boat into position. They paid no attention to the two women sitting on the bench or the big dog watching.

I stood up. "I'm going home, and then into work. I expect to hear that the lost item has been found before noon."

"Thank you. You're nicer than I expected you to be."

"Gee, thanks."

"No, I mean it. You were engaged to Max, so I thought you'd be as mean as Erica is. As mean as he was. I'm not sorry he's dead, you know. He was starting to ask questions about all the things Erica kept losing."

Chapter 11

I stared after the Lexus as it turned onto the street and headed back toward Rudolph.

Muriel had just handed me a motive for the killing of Max.

If Max was beginning to suspect Muriel was stealing from Erica, he wouldn't let it be. He'd set out to prove it. I had no doubt, and I'm sure Muriel didn't, either, that if he did, he'd report her to the police. Even in the best-case scenario, Muriel would be out of a job and probably unemployable once word got around that she was a thief.

Muriel was Erica's alibi for the death of Max. I'd dismissed that on the grounds that Muriel would say anything Erica told her to. That meant, of course, that Erica was Muriel's alibi.

Erica would have no reason, that I could see, to lie for Muriel. But they might have agreed, perhaps even without saying the words, to avoid pesky police questions by saying they'd been together at the time Max died.

I untied Mattie and we headed home.

If Muriel had murdered Max—and it was a heck of a big if—because he knew she was stealing, then might she now think she had to get rid of me for the same reason? What if she didn't trust me not to tell what I'd learned? I eyed the big dog trotting happily beside me. I was glad he was there.

With all I'd just found out about Muriel and the necklace, I'd almost forgotten about Jackie. Kyle wasn't the brightest bulb on our town Christmas tree, but he wasn't a total idiot. I tried to remember what he'd said. Jackie was waiting for me to do something. What on earth could that possibly mean? Did Kyle know that for a fact, or had he decided it was probably the case? Was he communicating with Jackie? I should have pressed him harder, but I couldn't handle both Kyle and Muriel at the same time and talk about two different topics. Now that I knew, or suspected, Kyle was aware of Jackie's whereabouts, or at least that he was in touch with her, I should tell Detective Simmonds. But then I'd feel like a snitch. Surely Simmonds had asked him. She might even be keeping him under observation. I stopped in the middle of the sidewalk so suddenly, Mattie jerked on the leash. He glanced back at me with a questioning look.

Was Kyle under observation? I hadn't seen any sign of police activity at the boat launch, but that was sorta the point of surveillance, wasn't it, to keep out of sight. Had the police filmed me handling stolen goods? I tried to remember what had happened. I had the necklace in my hands. I took it out of the bag, saw what it was, and then gave it back to Muriel. Even if they weren't able to get close enough to see or hear what had happened, had they seen me going to the boat launch, shortly after Kyle and only moments prior to Muriel arriving?

The day was hot, but despite the fact that I was lightly dressed, a trickle of sweat ran down my back. Were the police even now sitting around a table in a room lit by only a single bare lightbulb, swigging lukewarm coffee, munching on doughnuts, and deciding whether or not to bring me in?

I looked up and down the street. No one was paying the slightest bit of attention to me.

I gave my head a mental shake and continued walking. I hadn't done anything wrong, and if Simmonds asked me about it, I'd simply tell her what happened and what I'd been told. I was letting my imagination run away with itself.

As for whether or not I should phone her and tell her about Kyle and Jackie, I decided not to. Not right now anyway. It was all nothing but speculation. Kyle might be as much in the dark as me or anyone else.

Murder, theft, kidnapping, betrayal. Everything stops for garbage. Monday is garbage pickup for our street. When we got home, I took the leash off Mattie and left him to play in the yard while I went upstairs for my trash. I bagged it, tossed it into the bin I share with Steve and Wendy, and dragged it around to the front. On the way back, Mrs. D'Angelo waylaid me, demanding to know how the police investigation was going. Why she thought I would know (and tell her if I did) I didn't know. Until now, no one in Rudolph had ever had a bad word to say about Jackie O'Reilly. Suddenly it seemed as though everyone in town, Mrs. D'Angelo's vast network of gossips anyway, had always known there was "something bad about that girl." She had been spotted, I was informed, heading for the Canadian border. I should know better, but I forgot, and I pointed out that that would not be wise. First, there were guards at the border, and second, we had an extradition treaty with that country. Jackie would be arrested and returned to face American justice.

"Sources also tell me she caught a flight to Brazil," Mrs. D'Angelo said smugly. "It's much harder to bring a fugitive back from Brazil. Don't you read the newspapers, Merry?"

"Obviously not enough," I said, admitting defeat. I left her making a call and breathlessly saying to someone, "Merry Wilkinson told me . . ."

As soon as I walked into our fenced backyard, I could tell something was wrong with Mattie. He limped (did not run or jump) toward me. His expressive liquid brown eyes were full of pain, and he let out a plaintive whimper.

I dropped to the grass and let him crawl onto my lap. The part of him that would fit, anyway. He'd been holding his right front paw off the ground. I checked it, and found several thorns embedded in the soft flesh of the pad. "You poor thing. Wait right here." I got to my feet. "Stay!"

I ran upstairs for tweezers. When I returned, he was chewing at the paw. Very carefully, hoping not to break them, I pulled the thorns out. They came easily, releasing no more than a few drops of blood. I prodded gently, searching for any that might be imbedded too deeply for me to see, but I felt nothing. I left Mattie cleaning his wounds and went to look for the source of the thorns. It was not hard to find. The yard was getting so badly overgrown that in the far corner a batch of bramble, including blackberry bushes, was running away from the fence to crawl across the ground. I'd cut the worst of them back now and take care of cleaning up the rest of the yard after work. I went to the shed for the garden shears.

For a minute I wondered why Steve and Wendy, my neighbors, had dumped their camping gear in the garden shed. Then I remembered. They were camping. They'd gone to a reunion at Steve's grandparents' cottage on Lake Muskoka in Ontario. They told me the historic old building was no longer big enough for the rapidly growing family, so Steve and the male cousins would camp on the property, while Wendy and little Tina shared the bedrooms with the old folks and the young mothers and their children.

This wasn't their stuff.

All the clutter of our garden shed had been pushed to one side. A sleeping bag and pillow were neatly laid out on a thin camping mattress. A single set of plastic picnic dishes sat on an overturned box, along with cutlery, a can opener, a large unopened bag of salt-and-vinegar chips, a box of crackers and a jar of peanut butter, a couple of cans of soup and one of Chef Boyardee ravioli. A romance novel with a lurid purple cover featuring a bare-chested pirate and an almost-bare-chested woman fainting into his manly arms rested on top of the sleeping bag.

Someone had taken up residence in my garden shed. As it was unlikely to be a passing hobo, it could be only one person.

Jackie.

No doubt aided and abetted by Kyle, who kept her supplied with reading material and food. Foot forgotten, Mattie had wandered over to sniff around in the shed. "That's what you've been so interested in," I said to him. "Next time, I'll pay more attention to you. Not that there's going to be a next time."

Jackie's stuff was here, but Jackie was not. It did look, however, as though she was planning to return. She probably snuck off in the mornings when I'd be up and about with Mattie, getting ready for work, and returned when I'd gone.

This morning, work would have to wait. I glanced around the yard, looking for something to put in front of the door to tell me when she was once again in residence. A ball would do it. The door opened outward and would push the ball out of the way.

I backed out, calling Mattie to follow, and found one of his balls. After the tenth attempt to get him to leave the ball in place, I had to take him into the house first. Obviously more training was required.

Finally, the trap was set to my satisfaction, and I went inside. I spread antibiotic ointment on Mattie's paw, and then I distracted him from licking it off before it soaked into the skin by serving his breakfast. I made coffee and prepared a meal of muesli and yogurt with fresh raspberries for myself. My bedroom overlooks the backyard, and the walls are thick in this old house. A comfortable window seat is set into a cheerful alcove, painted fresh white and piled with yellow and sage green pillows. Over the winter, I love to curl up there to read and watch the falling snow. Now, feeling like Sherlock Holmes in "The Adventure of the Empty House," I set up surveillance. If Jackie was hidden someplace, watching for me to leave, then my plan was doomed. I thought that unlikely. This was a neighborhood of comfortable homes and well-maintained gardens on a street that led directly to the main stretch of our busy town. It would be hard for her to watch my house while keeping herself concealed. The store opened at ten. Jackie would know that I'd leave by nine forty-five at the latest, as she wasn't there to open up for me. Therefore, I expected Jackie to return to her lair around ten. I'd brought a book with me and settled down to pass the time. Mattie curled up in his dog bed for a nap.

Jackie must have moved quietly, because when I next glanced out the window, the ball had rolled to the other side of the lawn. "Showtime," I said to Mattie.

We went downstairs and across the yard. I didn't want to give her a fright, so I made a lot of noise. Mattie ran on ahead of me, tail wagging. He woofed a greeting and scratched at the door of the shed. Someone was in there, all right.

"Come out, come out, wherever you are." I rapped on the door. "Jackie, I know you're in there."

The door opened a crack. One eye peeked out. "Are you alone?"

"Yes."

The eye moved away, and I pulled the door fully open and walked in. She was still in the clothes she'd been wearing on Saturday. She needed a bath and her hair could use a wash.

"What do you think you're doing?" I said.

"Nothing."

"Jackie, the police are looking for you. Heavens, the whole town's looking for you. Your picture has been in the *Gazette*."

"I saw it. I saw the *Chronicle*, too. When I get my hands on Madison Morrison, I'll kill her."

"Who the heck is Madison Morrison?"

"A friend." Jackie made quotes in the air. "From high school. She must have given them that picture. I recognize her basement. She used to have the best parties, 'cause her parents went away a lot and trusted her to behave. Bad idea."

"Jackie! I couldn't care less about your high school parties or the picture. Let's go."

"Where?"

"Where? To the police, of course. You were witness to a murder." I was suddenly aware that I was alone in a backyard shed with a suspected killer. We were surrounded by garden implements, sharp secateurs, long-bladed shears, even a small saw. As no one was paying him his due attention, Mattie had wandered off. "That is all you are, right? A witness."

Jackie hung her head. *For heaven's sake, what was I thinking?* This was my shop assistant, not a cold-blooded killer. "Jackie, why are you hiding here?"

"Because I couldn't think of anyplace else to go. Steve and Wendy are away, and I know you're not exactly into gardening."

"Weren't you afraid of Mrs. D'Angelo spotting you? She's always standing at the window."

"There's a loose board in the fence, so I can come in through the yard next door. They're on vacation."

"How do you know there's a loose board in my fence when I don't even know it?"

"Kyle said."

How Kyle knew about modes of illicit ingress into my yard was something I'd worry about later.

"Kyle's been great, Merry. He's been bringing me supplies and food and everything."

"You can't stay here, Jackie. I'll take you to the police station. You have to tell them what you saw."

"I didn't see anything."

"What do you mean, you didn't see anything? What's all this hiding about then?"

"I'd just about kill for a cup of coffee. I wanted Kyle to bring me a kettle, but you don't have any electricity in this shed, Merry, and I was afraid if I built a fire you'd see it."

I didn't know which was worse, that Jackie was reprimanding me for not having electricity run into the garden shed, or that she even considered building a bonfire. I pushed aside dual images of my backyard in flames and the police raiding it as a suspected cannabis-growing operation.

"Come inside and I'll make coffee," I said. "While I'm doing that, you can tell me what's going on, and then I'll take you to the police station. If you don't come with me, Jackie, I have to tell them I found you. You can't hide forever."

"Okay. I don't want you to get in trouble on my account, Merry."

She sat on one of the barstools at the kitchen counter while I made coffee. Aside from the dirty clothes and unkempt appearance, she looked totally dejected. "I really like working for you, Merry. The store's a fun place and you're a good boss. Well, you're better than other bosses I've had."

"Thanks. I guess. But I don't see what your employment has to do with anything." I put the sugar bowl on the counter and dug in the fridge for the cream.

She took a breath. Water hissed and the coffeepot began to fill. "I didn't see anything when that guy died because I wasn't there."

"You weren't in the office?"

"I wasn't in the store."

"Did you run for help?" I poured a cup before it finished brewing and slid it across the counter to her. She added a slug of cream and two heaped spoons of sugar. "Not exactly. You were helping your dad, and I knew you'd be down at the park for a couple of hours. I left."

"What!"

"I'm sorry, Merry. But everyone was at the park having fun. Kyle was wearing his cute ice cream seller outfit, and my friend Kate had a stall to sell her mom's stained glass ornaments. I wanted to see them. I thought I'd be back before you and you'd never know. It's not as though we were going to have any customers anyway." She pouted.

"That's hardly the point. Why didn't you lock the door? Anyone could have walked in off the street. Come to think of it, anyone did!"

"I forgot my key at home. You were at the shop before me, remember."

"We'll talk about that later. If you weren't there when Max was killed, why have you been hiding?"

She twisted the mug in her hands and stared into its depths. "When I got back, police cars were everywhere, cops going into your store. Candy Campbell was standing outside not letting anyone in. I thought there'd been a theft. I'd left the door unlocked, so someone had come in and cleaned the place out. I couldn't walk in and tell you I'd been there all the time, could I? I thought, well, I guess I thought if I hid for a while, you'd get over being mad."

I was speechless. She had left my shop unattended, the door unlocked, and gone to the park like some grounded preteen kid climbing out the bedroom window to get to the party.

"When I heard someone had been killed in the store, I was afraid the cops would think I'd done it. And they did, didn't they? That's what the *Chronicle* said."

"I don't know what the police are thinking, but they're looking at many possible suspects."

"Kyle said I should lay low for a while and let you figure out what happened. Then I'd be in the clear, and you'd have gotten over being mad."

"Me! Why would I figure anything out?"

"You did those other times, Merry," she said.

I studied Jackie's face. She trusted me. Those other times she referred to, I'd pretty much stumbled onto the solution to a murder. But Jackie thought I was some great private detective. Sherlock Holmes himself, maybe.

"Why my shed?" was all I could say.

"Kyle said the cops might be watching his place. If I went home, my mom would call the police. Anyone would call the police, once they heard about the murder. Remember that time in the spring when you were sick and I brought some of the vendor catalogs around for you to look at? I noticed the shed then. You're always complaining about having a yard and not having any time to look after it, and with it being the Christmas in July weekend and all." She shrugged. "It seemed like a good idea. It was a good idea. How'd you find me anyway?"

"I was possessed by a sudden, overwhelming desire to trim bushes."

"Really?"

"We'll take my car," I said. "Better not walk into town or we'll have everyone we pass calling 911 to report seeing you. All you have to do is tell Detective Simmonds what you told me, and everything will be all right."

She lifted her head and gave me a tight smile. I refrained from rolling my eyes.

I thought it best to call Diane Simmonds ahead of time

and give her some warning that we were coming. All she said was, "I'll be waiting for you."

"Do you think she's going to be mad at me?" Jackie asked when I put away the phone.

"I think," I said, "she's going to be absolutely furious. They've been wasting valuable time searching for you, time they could have spent trying to find Max's killer."

"I'll say I didn't know about any of that. I was only hiding from you."

"Hiding from me in my own backyard? Jackie, tell them the truth. Okay? Nothing but the truth. Anything else is going to make this much worse, believe me."

Chapter 12

I told Mattie I'd be back for him soon and drove Jackie to the police station. Detective Simmonds, looking as though a thunderstorm was brewing behind her green eyes, met us at the front door. She instructed a colleague to escort Jackie to an interview room.

The moment they were gone, she turned to me and said, almost biting off the words, "You expect me to believe she was hiding in your backyard for two days."

"Yes, I expect you to believe it. Because it's the truth."

"And you didn't notice."

"I didn't have reason to go into my shed, and I don't sit at my bedroom window at night with a pair of binoculars in case someone happens to break into my property, no."

"I have a BOLO out for her. The border guards have

been notified. The coast guard. Police forces all over New York and into neighboring states."

"That is not exactly my problem." When Diane Simmonds came into Mrs. Claus's Treasures with her mother or daughter, we laughed and chatted and were almost like friends. When she was in cop mode, she intimidated the heck out of me. Now I was just mad. Jackie had played me for a fool, first by sneaking out of the store, and then by hiding in my backyard. I was the aggrieved party here, not the police. "I could have just shooed her away, you know. Or told her to go and hide someplace else. But I convinced her to come here and tell you her story. And I brought her myself. So there. Now, if you don't need me anymore, I have a business to run." I marched out the door, head high, steps firm. I almost expected Simmonds to call me back and tell me I was under arrest. But she didn't.

I headed straight to Victoria's Bake Shoppe, which happens to be almost next door to the police station. The breakfast and bread-buying rush was over and the lunch one yet to begin, so Vicky came out of the back to say hi. I pulled her to one side and told her about Jackie.

Vicky let out a bark of a laugh. "Wish I'd been there to see Simmonds's face."

"It was a sight to frighten small children, I can tell you." My sense of righteous indignation was fading rapidly. I was starting to feel bad about yelling at Simmonds. She had a tough job to do and Jackie O'Reilly had not made it any easier.

"Let's hope it frightens Jackie into getting some common sense," Vicky said. "She didn't see Max at all that morning? No mysterious person hanging around waiting for him?"

"That's what she says." I debated with myself whether or not to say anything to Vicky about Muriel. Not about the theft, because I'd decided to keep that to myself, but about my suspicions that Erica's PA had reason to kill Max. Of course, I couldn't say anything about that without revealing what I knew about the missing necklace. I was still undecided when Marjorie yelled, "Vicky, phone call."

"Take a message."

"It's the chef at the Yuletide wondering when he can expect his next delivery." Marjorie, who was also Vicky's dad's sister, shouted much louder than she needed to. The waitress, one of Vicky's numerous cousins, paused from laying out sandwich ingredients. "I'm sure bread's the only thing on his mind."

Vicky was a great blusher. She always had been. These days it was not a good match to her lock of purple hair. "I should probably take that," she said. She grabbed the phone out of Marjorie's hand and went into the back. Marjorie wiggled her eyebrows at me.

Everyone, Vicky most of all, had been telling me not to get involved in the police investigation. The harder I tried not to be involved, the deeper I seemed to sink, through no fault of my own. In that case, I thought, might as well be hung for a sheep as for a lamb. "I'll have two coffees to go, please. And two of the blueberry muffins."

Marjorie selected the muffins and put them into a bag.

"Blueberries come straight from Uncle Bobby's place. Picked yesterday."

"Which," I said, "is why they're so yummy."

It was almost eleven o'clock. I should have opened the shop long ago. However, instead of turning left, back to Mrs. Claus's Treasures, or even going home to drop off my car and pick up Mattie, I turned right. The offices of the *Rudolph Gazette* are on the other side of the street and only a few doors down from the bakery.

Once upon a time, the *Gazette* had been a bustling, thriving concern. Now, like small-town newspapers everywhere, it was barely holding on. Most of the building had been sold off as staff was cut back and their offices no longer needed. Russ, the editor in chief, didn't even have an office. Just a battered desk at the back of a warm, musty, overcrowded room. Russ was from Louisiana by way of New York City. He'd arrived in Rudolph about a year ago, around the same time I came back. The paper he'd worked for, he told me, had been sold, and he'd decided to seek fresh pastures in a small Upstate town. I'd thought nothing of that story: everyone knew the owner of the *Gazette* wanted to retire, and he was searching for someone to take over the day-to-day running of the paper.

This morning, in light of what I'd recently learned, I wondered if there was another reason Russ left New York City.

"Hi," I said to the woman behind the reception desk. "Is Russ in?" I could see him at his desk, hammering away at his computer, but I thought it polite to ask.

"I'll check," she said, picking up her phone. I watched

as Russ answered the phone on his desk. He looked over and saw me. His handsome face broke into a huge smile. I lifted the cardboard tray with the mugs.

"You can go on in, Merry," the receptionist said.

Russ got to his feet as I approached. I put the coffees and the bag of muffins on his desk.

"Not," he said with a grin, "that it isn't a pleasure to see you, Merry, but that looks perilously like a bribe."

"Perhaps it is." I'd decided there was no point beating about the bush. "Tell me about Erica Johnstone."

"Ah, the fair Erica." Russ dropped into his chair. "Take a seat. We were . . . friends once. I'm assuming you know that already. What else do you want to know and why?" He bit into a muffin. He watched me as he chewed. He didn't look like a man with something to hide.

"Curiosity, maybe."

"It's all a matter of public record."

His cell phone was on his desk. It chose that moment to buzz with an incoming text. He glanced at the screen, dropped his muffin, scooped up the phone, and jumped to his feet. "This, whatever this is, will have to wait, Merry. I gotta run."

"What? Why? What's happening?"

"Jackie O'Reilly walked into the police station about fifteen minutes ago. She's talking to Simmonds even as we speak."

"Oh, that," I said.

"I have to get over there and see what's happening." He eyed me. "You don't seem all that surprised to hear the news."

"I'm not." I gave him a smile.

"Want to tell me about it?"

"Nope."

"In that case, this conversation will have to wait. We might do an exchange. Jackie for Erica." He stuffed the phone into his pocket and grabbed his camera. He picked up the muffin and ran out the door, leaving me none the wiser about him and Erica.

Whoever the snitch in the police department was, they'd obviously spread the news far beyond just the newspaper offices. As I walked back to Mrs. Claus's Treasures, heads popped out of shops and businesses to ask if I'd heard that Jackie had been found.

"Arrested for murder," Rachel McIntosh from Candy Cane Sweets said.

I stopped. "Is that true? Or only a rumor?"

"Irene Wozinski told me."

"Jackie has not been arrested. She's answering police questions." I continued on my way.

Margie Thatcher pounced on me the moment I arrived at the door of Mrs. Claus's Treasures. "Witness protection program."

"What?" I said.

"I hear she's going into the witness protection program. She witnessed a mob hit and now they're after her." As the business next door to the scene of the crime (and considering that the owner of the actual scene of the crime—me—wasn't talking), Margie was the center point for gossip these days.

"Whatever." I put my key into the lock.

"Why are you late anyway?" Margie said. "It's after eleven."

"I've been arranging a close protection detail for Jackie."

"Oh," she said.

"Don't tell anyone."

"My lips are sealed." She scurried into the Nook.

My father fell through the door shortly after. His breath was coming in ragged spurts, his hair was wild, his beard unkempt, his shirttails hanging out, and he wore one dark brown sock with beige stripes and one green one with red dots. He also wore sandals, and it was definitely not an attractive look. My heart leapt into my mouth. I could only think that something had happened to Mom or one of my siblings. "What's wrong?" I cried.

"You're alive," he cried back.

"Huh? Of course I'm alive. Why wouldn't I be?"

He lifted one finger telling me to hold on for a moment, pulled out his phone, and pressed buttons. It was obviously answered immediately as he began to talk, gasping for breath all the while. "She's here. At the shop. She appears to be fine. Yes. I'll find out." He hung up and put the phone away.

"What's going on?" we said at the same time.

"Your mother found some pictures on her phone when she turned it on this morning," he said.

"And so? Oh shoot. I forgot all about them." I'd sent Mom pictures of Muriel and Kyle's furtive meeting to do the "exchange" down at the boat launch, intending to tell her to delete them if everything turned out okay. Which it had. But then with the excitement over finding Jackie's hiding place, lying in wait for her to return, pouncing on her, taking her down to the police station, arguing with Simmonds, and then confronting Russ over his relationship with Erica Johnstone, I'd totally forgotten.

It was barely eleven o'clock, and all that had happened today. No wonder I'd forgotten a minor point. "Sorry," I said. "I meant to tell her to ignore them. Why are you in such a tizzy anyway? They're just pictures."

"Where's your phone?"

"Right here." I dug into my pocket and pulled it out. I pushed the button. Nothing happened. "Oops, I must have forgotten to charge it." I found a spare charger in a drawer and plugged it in. Sure enough the box showing the strength of the battery power was an exceedingly thin red line.

"Merry, your mother and I have been frantic. You're not answering the phone at the shop."

"That's 'cause I just got here. Busy morning."

"You're not answering your cell."

"Because it ran out of juice."

"After sending your mother photos saying you need help."

"I didn't mean that. I wanted her to have them in case . . ." In case I'd been kidnapped or murdered and needed her to take the evidence to the police.

"While I went to your house and then came here searching for you, Aline's been on the phone to Eve, Chris, and Carole asking if they've heard from you. Also Vicky and anyone else she could think of."

"But I was in the bakery earlier. Didn't Vicky tell her?"

"Marjorie said Vicky was unavailable. That worried us even more. Your mother tried to remain calm so as not to worry anyone but . . ."

But, my mom the opera diva, didn't *do* calm.

"Sorry," I said. "But it's just a couple of shots of the boat launch." The phone had enough power now that I could use it. I pulled up the photos page. I'd taken the pictures quickly and sent them off without looking at them. I had to admit, they weren't going to be used in Rudolph tourist brochures anytime soon. I'd been facing into the rising sun, so the people and vehicles were nothing but ominous black blobs against the bright light. In the foreground, branches crisscrossed the frame, and my finger could be seen in a couple of the pictures.

Without context (like Mattie happily sniffing under the bushes) they could have been used for publicity stills for *The Nightmare Before Christmas*. (Not that I knew anything about movies of that ilk, of course. They were banned in Rudolph as well as in my family.)

I looked up to see my dad glaring at me. It had been a long time since I'd last seen that look directed my way. "Sorry," I mumbled again.

"Can you explain?"

"I thought I'd stumbled across . . . two people who might have had something to do with the death of Max or the kidnapping of Jackie. In case I was . . . detained . . . I took pics and sent them to Mom so she could go for help. I sorta forgot to tell her all was okay."

His face relaxed fractionally. I gave him a tight grin.

"Don't do that again."

"I won't."

"Now that that's settled, and your mother is no doubt collapsed on her chaise lounge trying to remember to breathe, I heard Jackie has popped up hale and hearty."

"She'd been hiding in my garden shed. Not out of fear of a ruthless killer but an angry boss."

Dad merely shook his head. "I'm sure I'll get the full story later, whether I want to hear it or not. Right now, I could use a few minutes on the chaise lounge myself."

He held out his arms, and I snuggled into him. There's nothing in the world as wonderful as one of my dad's hugs. We stood there for a long time before he patted my back and I pulled away.

"Don't ever frighten us like that again, Merry."

Jackie walked through the doors of the shop a couple of hours later. She didn't exactly look happy, but at least she wasn't in jail.

"Everything okay?" I asked.

"Simmonds said I could be charged with interfering with a police investigation, but I won't be."

The shop was busy at the moment. Ears pricked up, and two women developed a sudden interest in examining the North Pole teacups on the shelf nearest to where Jackie happened to be standing.

"Go home," I said. "You need to clean up and rest. Have something to eat. Have you called your mother?"

"Not yet."

"Well, do that first. I'll expect you here tomorrow at noon, as per the schedule."

"Thanks, Merry." The bells over the door tinkled as she left, and the listening customers went back to what they were doing.

Sometime later two women approached the counter, ready to pay. The larger one had a stack of festive table linens. "You have so many marvelous things, I scarcely knew where to start looking."

"I'm pleased you like them. Much of the stock changes regularly depending on what our local artisans are making, so do check back."

She leaned over the counter. Instinctively, I leaned toward her. "I was, well, I have to confess that I hoped to see Erica Johnstone around town."

"She was in yesterday," I said, "but not since."

"Such a tragedy, isn't it? Her fiancé being struck down mere weeks before their fairy-tale wedding."

"Tragic," I agreed.

"I was *so* looking forward to the wedding issue of *Jennifer's Lifestyle*, wasn't I, Ruth?"

"You sure were, Joanie," her friend replied.

"I was keen to see what Jennifer planned to wear to an outdoor summer wedding. My granddaughter Ashley's getting married, you see, dear, and I was hoping to get a sense of what's appropriate for grandmother of the bride."

"This is Ashley's third marriage," Ruth said. "Or is it her fourth? Hard to keep track. No one else bothers to buy a new outfit for the fourth wedding, Joanie."

"I like to keep up with fashion," Joanie snapped. "Even if some people don't." She snatched her shopping bags and stomped out of the store. A chuckling Ruth followed.

I glanced toward the curtain leading to the back of the building. Anyone who'd been in town on Saturday knew that Max had been found in Mrs. Claus's Treasures, but that detail hadn't, thank heavens, made it to the national press. If word got out, it might help with business, but I didn't need crime scene groupies or the truly ghoulish hanging around.

Speaking of Erica. With a pang, I remembered that the magazine people were due to come in at six to photograph me as the arbiter of all things holiday decorating. With everything that happened today, first discovering that Muriel and Kyle were partners in crime, and then finding Jackie hiding in my backyard, that was another thing I'd totally forgotten. I glanced down at my jeans, T-shirt, and sneakers. I'd thrown on what clothes were at hand to bring Jackie into town. The store had been busy since I opened, and I hadn't had time to get my car from the police station, take it home, and pick up Mattie, never mind change, fix my hair, and put on some makeup.

It was after three now, and the shop was busy. No time to go home to get myself smartened up and ready to be photographed at six. I'd sent Jackie away, but it probably wasn't a good idea to have her working today anyway. Who knows where her mind would be? I could probably call Crystal and find out if she was free, but the last thing I felt like doing was posing for Jason's cameras trying to look fashionable. Willow had given me her number last night, and at the moment no one in the shop needed my help. I dug in my bag and gave her a call.

"Hey, Merry," she said. "What's up?"

"Just checking in. Something's come up and I'm going to have to cancel tonight's shoot. Do you think you'll still be in town tomorrow?"

She groaned. "I'm beginning to think I'll be in this town until I grow old. Which won't be much longer, the way things are going. That cop was here again. She's just left. More questions. Usually it's the same questions over and over, all asking the same thing: who would want Max dead? And every time we give the same lying answer: no one, he was such a sweetie, everyone who knew him loved him to bits. This time the detective wanted to know if we'd met your shop assistant before Saturday. What on earth that meant, I've no idea. I told her she was there on Thursday when we came in to scout things out, but we didn't exactly engage in intelligent conversation. We're still under orders not to leave town. James has been on the phone nonstop, trying to get hold of someone, anyone, who can order Simmonds to let us go. Let Erica go anyway. I doubt he cares much about us, if he even knows we're alive. I hear Erica's climbing the walls. At least they have nice walls at that place. I've memorized the pattern of cracks in the ceiling at this dump."

"You hear? You mean you haven't seen Erica?"

"No, she's all in a snit."

"Willow, her fiancé has just died. She's allowed to be upset."

"Whatever," Willow said. "Jason's been over at the

inn, trying to be all sympathetic. Rather him than me. Oh, she found that necklace she was making such a to-do about."

"Is that so?" I said casually.

"It had fallen onto the floor and somehow got itself under the rug. Muriel found it. How anything that long and bulky could accidentally disappear under a rug is beyond me. But that's Erica. She could lose an elephant in her shoe closet.

"Anyway, it's not going to be a problem, about tonight, I mean. We were going to cancel you anyway."

"Gee, thanks for telling me."

"I would have. We want some pictures of the inn and the grounds in the evening. You know, dusky shadows and the pretty lights coming on. All that romantic hogwash our readers love. I was there earlier, checking it out, and it is a nice place, so we're going to give it a good amount of space in the feature. The weather forecast for tonight is clear with a good-sized moon, and it's supposed to rain tomorrow in the afternoon and evening. The gardens have to be tonight. We can do you tomorrow, because that's indoors."

She hung up without bothering to ask if the change of timing suited me at all.

Shortly before six my dad arrived, followed by Alan carrying a large box containing a new product we were planning to feature in the store. A Santa Claus version of a toy farm. The main house at the North Pole, smaller outbuildings for the workshops and the elves' dorms, the reindeer barn complete with reindeer, one of which had a big, cheerful, red-painted nose, and figures of Santa and Mrs. Claus and the elves. The entire collection was large and expensive—every piece was hand-carved and hand-painted, after all—but Dad and Alan's idea was that proud grandparents could buy a couple of pieces as they could afford them and build the set over the years of their grandchildren's childhood.

I made space for the box on the table next to the live Douglas fir. I was excited about this project although all I knew so far was the concept.

"Where do you want it to go?" Alan asked.

I studied the room. "I'm thinking of moving the angel choir. They need to be more at eye level to emphasize the height differences. We can put the village there."

"Okay," Alan said.

"No," Dad said. "The angels are fine where they are. The village needs to be at a child's eye level. We'll put it here, under the tree."

"We only have one of each piece," I said. "If the pieces start selling individually, it'll leave holes."

"Then you can fill the holes," Dad said firmly. "But not with the angels. Leave them where they are."

Alan shrugged and gave me a grin. *What can you do?*

"Now, that's settled," Dad said. "Go into your office, Merry."

"Why?"

"So you can be surprised when you see the entire set assembled."

I headed to the door to lock it, but before I could do so, Russ came in. "Hi, y'all." He nodded to Dad and Alan. "I thought we might continue our talk, Merry, but it looks like you're busy."

"You can talk later," Dad said. "Give us a hand here, Russell. Shoo, Merry."

"Shooing," I said.

My office is a small, overcrowded, disheveled space, but today I thought how big and empty it was without Mattie snoozing on the floor. I didn't have to wait long before Dad called, "You can come out now."

I smiled to myself. He sounded exactly like he had when we were kids, calling us to come downstairs and see what was under the tree.

The moment I saw what was under the tree in my shop, I did feel exactly like a child on Christmas morning. "It's marvelous!"

Alan beamed, and Dad looked as proud as if he'd made it himself. Russ, who'd had nothing to do with it, was all smiles.

Even on a hot, humid evening in July, there is nothing as wonderful as Christmas magic. Alan's village wove that magic into physical form.

Every miniature building was perfect, every person, reindeer, and elf lovingly carved. The wood gleamed and the paint shone. Alan cleared his throat. "I see this as something kids can play with and when they're past playing, it could be used as a holiday decoration. Placed on the mantel beside the nativity scene, for example."

"How many sets have you made?"

"One finished, so far. This is it. I have one in progress for the toy store, then I'll work up a few more of the main buildings and some of the smaller pieces. I need to see what the market's like, before I invest much more time."

"I'm sure it'll sell like hotcakes," I said.

"I've always wondered," Russ said, "why anyone would want to eat their cake hot."

"I'm off home," Dad said. "I'll leave you young people to do whatever young people do these days."

"In a shop in Rudolph, New York, at six thirty on a Monday night? Not much, Dad."

Dad headed for the exit but stopped abruptly. The small table beside the door is piled with soft toys, stuffed Santas and reindeer. "Hum," he said. He gathered up the toys and carried them into one of the alcoves. He came back with a large crystal vase filled with an assortment of glass balls. The balls ranged from clear to deep red and were about the size of a baseball.

"Dad," I said, "I can't have that sitting so close to the door. They're fragile, as is the vase, and people sometimes barge in with kids or dogs without watching where they're going."

"It makes a statement," Dad said. "Better than the dolls. Night all."

I considered putting the things back once he was gone, but what the heck. It was late and I was tired. "Night, Dad."

Dad waved and left. Russ and Alan eyed each other.

"You have excellent timing, Alan," I said. "The magazine people are coming tomorrow after closing to do more pictures of the shop. I'll make sure the village is front and center."

"My timing isn't an accident. This has been a rush job. But I thought they were coming tonight."

"Change of plans." I turned to Russ. "Erica Johnstone is still in residence at the Yuletide. Are you thinking of going around to see her?"

"I am not."

"Why would you do that?" Alan asked. "I've heard the press are camped out front and not being allowed on the property. Although they say the crowd's rapidly dwindling as nothing more seems to be happening."

"It's a very short story," Russ said. "One better told over a drink at the Holly. Anyone interested?"

"I could use one," I said. "But I can't stay long. Mattie's been home alone all day."

"Great idea," Alan said, not sounding as though he was as wildly enthusiastic as the words implied. I moved closer to him and touched his arm. "Give me a sec, and I'll be right out."

I went into the back for my bag. My phone buzzed.

Vicky: *Photos tonite?*

Me: *Changed to tomorrow. Off to Holly for half an hour. Wanna come?*

Vicky: *I'm in!*

Back in the main room of the shop, the two men were glaring at each other. At the sound of my footsteps on the old wooden floors, they pasted on strained smiles. Nice to be wanted, I thought with a small shiver of pleasure. I gave Alan a private smile, and then turned to Russ with what I hoped was a friendly, not flirtatious, grin. Not that I really know the difference. I hoped I'd gotten it right.

I switched off most of the lights, leaving only the ones in the windows and behind the counter on. The men left first, and I locked the door behind us. I slipped my hand into Alan's. He squeezed it lightly in return, and we ran across the street at a break in traffic.

A Touch of Holly is an upscale restaurant with a comfortable bar and lounge that's perfect for popping in for a quick drink after work. It's a winter place: all dark wood paneling, red carpets, black leather chairs and stools, a long, smooth mahogany bar. In summer the mood is lightened with giant glass vases of fresh flowers in lighter shades of yellow or pink and plenty of white, and the bartenders and waiters wear a more casual uniform with an open yellow shirt over their black pants, rather than the strict black and white and bow tie of the holiday season. Tonight, the room was crowded and every seat taken. Russ spotted a group of guys he knew at the end of the bar. He went over and told two of them to vacate their stools. They hopped off, and Russ made a deep formal bow to indicate I could take a seat.

Chivalry isn't entirely dead. I was glad for the chance to sit down. It had been a heck of an emotional day, not to mention a busy one, and even though I was wearing sneakers, my feet were killing me. I spotted Vicky coming through the door and waved to her. She wore a pretty white summer dress dotted with blue and yellow flowers, with a thin blue belt around her tiny waist. "New dress?"

I said once she'd joined us. "Fabulous. And check out those shoes."

She bent her knee and tilted her leg to show me. Strappy blue sandals with high heels. Russ whistled and Vicky grinned. "Mark has the night off. So I only have time for a quick one."

I ordered a glass of wine and my three friends had beers. When the drinks were in front of us, and the bartender had moved on, Russ and I spoke at once.

"Erica?" I said

"Jackie?" he said.

"What?" Vicky and Alan said.

"Jackie walked into the police station this morning, looking, so my sources said, as though she'd been sleeping rough," Russ said. "She was, again my sources said, brought there by you, Merry. Where'd you find her?"

"She'd been hiding out in my shed, of all places, on the advice of none other than Kyle Lambert. Her criminal instincts are not as highly refined as they might be. What did Simmonds have to say?"

"Not a lot," Russ said. "I hung around for an awful long time, and when they finally came out, Simmonds told me Jackie was facing no charges and had been unable to contribute to the investigation into the murder of Max Folger. I took Jackie for a coffee and she told me she'd left the store before Max came in, and she was hiding because she'd skipped off work and was afraid of you, Merry."

I nodded. "That's about it. She came back to the shop to find cops crawling all over the place and assumed we'd had a theft. She was afraid of me being mad at her, so wanted to keep her head down for a few hours. When she heard that a man had been killed and the police were looking for her, she didn't know what to do. When the *Chronicle* article said she was the police's prime suspect, she really panicked."

"What's your story going to be tomorrow, Russ?" Vicky asked. "Police find terrified suspect on run from ogre of a boss?"

"Very funny," I said.

"I was thinking of something along those lines." He took a sip of beer. "But I'll just run a small story saying Jackie turned up unharmed, having not been a witness to the killing. Unless you know something more, Merry."

"Nope. That's it."

"Are you going to keep her on?" Vicky asked.

"Why the heck not?" I said. "I doubt very much she'll ever try to sneak off work again. Ironically, if Max hadn't died, and she hadn't bolted into hiding, I probably would have fired her for skipping out, never mind leaving the shop unlocked. As it was, I'm giving her another chance."

"You're too nice for your own good," Vicky said.

"Who knows, perhaps it turned out for the better. If she'd been in the store when Max and his killer, whoever that might be, came in . . ." I let the words trail off and took a sip of wine. A sudden somber mood settled over our little group. Jackie didn't seem to have realized that she might have had a lucky escape. I wasn't going to enlighten her. Better she not think skipping off work had positive consequences.

Alan put his hand on my shoulder. I rested mine on it and smiled into his blue eyes. Russ looked between the two of us. He took another drink of beer.

"Your turn, Russ," I said. "Erica Johnstone. You dated her. Spill."

"You did?" Alan said. "Wow, that's a shocker. How'd that work out?"

"Not well, as you can see," Russ said. "Me being here and all. I didn't go out with her for long. We met when my paper sent me to cover a story on a charity event her grandmother had been the patron of. I interviewed Erica, and she was somber and serious and sounded very much involved with her grandmother's cause." He shrugged. "On the spur of the moment, I asked her out. She said yes, and the whirlwind began. I won't lie, it was a thrill at first. Walking into restaurants that have reservation lists a year long, weekends in the Hamptons at the sort of houses I've only ever seen in magazines, being admitted to private rooms at the hottest clubs, going to the best parties. Schmoozing with celebrities. I danced with Kim Kardashian once."

"Sounds tough." Alan's fingers lightly stroked my shoulder.

"Believe it or not, it soon was. Tough. My work started suffering. I wasn't a celebrity journalist, and I didn't want to be. The charity event was a last-minute thing because the regular guy got sick. I was supposed to be a crime reporter, but I could scarcely drag myself out of bed in the mornings after those weekends and all those parties. But most of all, Erica was so much *work*. 'Needy's' the word I'd use. She needed attention, all the time. She soaked up attention like other people breathe air. That dance with Kardashian? Erica had a screaming fit on the way home. She'd been left alone when I got up to dance. What would people think, seeing her sitting by herself?"

"Sad," Alan said.

"That's the word I'd use. In hindsight I feel sorry for her. So much money, so many expectations. She just can't cope. Her parents died in a car crash when she was a baby, and she was raised by her grandmother. Raised by a network of servants, more like it. By all accounts her grandmother's a good person, but she had a business empire to build. Erica has no brothers or sisters, not even any cousins. She lived in a big empty house with people paid to love her. All the dolls and toys she could possibly ever want, but no kids to play with other than children of the staff."

Russ sipped at his beer. We said nothing and waited for him to continue. "Our relationship ended at her birthday party. Someone gave her some minor slight, I don't even remember who or what it was, and she had a hissy fit, right there at the table. Which was, of course, in the center of the room. I yelled at her to get herself under control. I'd had enough of it all; I got up and walked out. She phoned me the next morning, full of apologies, but I told her we were finished. Over the next two days, she left about a hundred messages on my phone, tears mixed with threats, but I didn't answer. I never spoke to her again. Next thing I knew, I read she'd taken over her grandmother's magazine and was photographed on the arm of a new guy. This Max Folger. The paper where I worked folded not long after that, and I found myself out of a job. I came here, and never gave Erica Johnstone another thought. It was one heck of a shock, I can tell you, to see her in Rudolph."

"Sounds to me," Vicky said, "that you, like Jackie, might have had a lucky escape. Do you suppose Max was killed because he was engaged to Erica? Or was it for some reason that had nothing to do with her?"

I said nothing. I thought about what Russ had said. His story sounded genuine enough. I could easily imagine what life with Erica must be like. "Tempestuous" would be the word. But I had to wonder if he really regretted breaking up with her. Or did he want her back, whether for love or for money? Had seeing her and Max together brought back those feelings? Russ was working as the editor in chief and general dogsbody at a small-town paper on its dying legs. Living in a town where the highlight of the year was the Santa Claus parade. A far cry from the glamour of Manhattan and the Hamptons and the celebrity party circuit.

"Have you spoken to her?" Vicky asked. "Since what happened, I mean. She's still here. The police won't let her leave town. She's staying at the Yuletide."

Russ shook his head. "I should drop by, I know. Express my sympathies. Regardless of what happened between us, her fiancé died, and that's hard. But I honestly don't think I can bear the drama."

I caught him looking at me, a rueful smile on his face, beer mug in hand.

I felt absolutely dreadful.

Here I was, asking Russ about his relationship with Erica, because I wondered if he'd killed Max so he could get back together with her. As Vicky had said, money makes men do terrible things. Murder makes people do terrible things, too, I realized. And not just the killer. I was questioning one of my friends, thinking he might be a murderer. I gave myself a mental slap. "Gotta run." I hopped off the stool and gave Russ a quick, heartfelt hug.

"Take care, Merry," he whispered in my ear.

Alan finished his beer and said, "I'll walk you home."

"Russ didn't kill Max," Alan said a few minutes later as we strolled past the park.

"I never said he did."

"No, but you were wondering, weren't you?"

It was a perfect summer's evening. Warm, but not as stiflingly hot and humid as it had been. Sailboats dotted the blue waters of the lake, a few hearty swimmers were still in the water, children built sand castles onshore, and families enjoyed picnic suppers on blankets spread out on the grass. The sun cast long shadows through the thick branches of the old trees, turning the light a soft gentle green.

"Yes, I was wondering," I said. "And I feel bad about it. I don't know how Simmonds can do that job. Everyone she meets, she has to look at them and try to come up with reasons they might be a killer."

Alan's rough, scarred, calloused woodworker's hand felt comfortable in mine. As if it belonged there. Did it? Yes, I now knew, it did.

"The difference is, Merry, Simmonds is doing her job. It's nothing personal. Russ is your friend."

"I don't want to be involved in this, Alan, really I don't. I can't forget that Max was once very important in my life, and that he died in my shop. Vicky said earlier Jackie might have had a lucky escape. What about me? Suppose I'd been at work when he came in?"

"But you weren't," he said. "There's no point in worrying about what might have happened." We were walking east, and shadows followed us. I loved Alan's Upstate New York sensibility. Practical and down-to-earth as befitted a man who made his living with his hands, with an artistic touch that turned a piece of wood into art. Capable of whimsy on occasion, as befitted Santa's head toymaker.

"That's true," I admitted. "Care to stay for dinner?"

"Best offer I've had all day."

First things first; we collected Mattie and took him for a long walk. When we got back to my place, I called the Chinese restaurant on the outskirts of town and placed an order. Then I opened a bottle of wine, and we sat at the kitchen counter, drinking wine and eating General Tso's chicken, vegetables with black bean sauce, and fried rice. By unspoken agreement, we didn't talk about the death of Max or who might have wanted him dead.

Eventually, Alan pushed himself off his stool. "I'd better be off. I promised the toy store their delivery tomorrow, and I have some finishing touches to put on."

"Santa's village is going to be a huge hit."

He pulled me close for a long kiss. Eventually, Mattie

got bored of the kissing stuff and announced that it was time to play. He barked and swatted at Alan's legs. We separated, laughing.

"I have my marching orders," Alan said.

Mattie and I walked him downstairs. Alan and I kissed again at the garden gate, and only then did I remember that my car was still at the police station. If I didn't move it, I might find it in the impound lot tomorrow. I groaned.

"What?" Alan said.

"I have to go back to town for my car. I'll walk with you. Wait while I get my bag and the leash."

We retraced our steps back to town. It was fully dark now. The boaters, swimmers, and picnickers had packed up and gone home. Streetlamps cast warm yellow light through the leafy trees to form pools on the sidewalk, and most of the houses had lamps shining behind curtains.

Alan's truck was parked outside Mrs. Claus's Treasures. We kissed good night, and he drove off. Mattie and I walked the half a block to the police station. A happy glow spread throughout my body. Cheap wine and takeout Chinese had made for a perfect evening. I spent the short walk dreamily checking out store windows. The Christmas in July theme was prominent, the accent heavily on family fun at the beach.

My car, I was glad to see, was where I'd left it, and a flapping piece of white paper wasn't stuck under the windshield wiper. I flicked the key fob and the headlights flashed in greeting. At that moment the doors of the police station opened, light spilled out, and Detective Diane

Simmonds trotted down the stairs. She spotted me watching and headed over. Mattie leapt toward her, and she had him sitting down with a single flick of her index finger. She'd once told me her parents trained dogs for movies and TV. It was almost uncanny, the way Mattie reacted to her.

"He's coming on very well," she said. "I'm pleased to see it. The first time we met, I was worried you wouldn't have the patience to train him properly. A dog that size, untrained, soon becomes nothing but a nuisance." She gave him a scratch behind the ears. His whole body wiggled in delight, but he made no move to stand up as she hadn't yet indicated that he could.

"You're working late," I said.

"A murder investigation doesn't stop for time off," she replied.

I didn't want to be involved; all my friends were telling me not to get involved. "How's it going?" I said.

"I won't say an arrest is imminent, but we are working on it."

"I've been wondering if it's possible Max's death didn't have anything to do with Rudolph. With him being here, I mean. Maybe someone followed him from New York, something to do with his past? Have you considered that?"

"Yes, Merry, I have considered that." Her eyes narrowed. "You're from his past, aren't you?"

"Me?" I squeaked.

"Relax. I'm not accusing you of anything. We've been in contact with our colleagues in the city, and they've been very helpful. Everyone at Mr. Folger's place of employment can't say enough good things about him. I'm considering anointing him for sainthood. Do you have a comment on that?"

"I shouldn't speak ill of the dead . . ."

"See, Merry, that's the problem. I think Mr. Folger would prefer I find his killer than preserve his memory, wouldn't you agree?"

"Max wasn't well liked," I admitted. "Not after he took up with Erica and got promoted way over his capabilities. But it was all just business. Feelings run bitter at any company facing big layoffs and staff changes."

"Is there anyone in particular whose feelings might have run especially bitter?"

"Not that I can think of, but remember I haven't been around for a year. If a cabal had formed with the intention of getting rid of Max, I wouldn't have known about it."

"Anything else you think I should know? Closer to home, maybe." She fixed her green eyes on me. I almost felt her digging around in my mind, wondering what secrets were hidden there. Is that what she did to Mattie? He was sitting so quietly between us, I might have to check that he was still breathing.

"There is one thing," I said. "Erica and her personal assistant, Muriel Fraser. I wouldn't count on any alibi they give each other."

"Why is that?"

"Erica's a tyrant, to say the least. I've heard that Muriel has a mother in an expensive nursing home. Muriel needs that job, and if Erica thinks she's talking to the police behind her back, her job will definitely be in danger. As for Erica herself, she's a publicity hound, but in this one instance I'd expect her not to want publicity. Not the sort that involves being brought into the police station for questioning. They have reason to lie for each other. I'm not saying," I hastened to add, "that I suspect they did. I'm pointing it out, that's all."

"Thank you, Merry. That's helpful. Anything else?"

"In the two times they were in my shop, I detected a simmering conflict between Willow and Amber and Max. Willow in particular. But," I hastened to add, "probably nothing worth killing over."

I didn't mention Russ, because I believed him when he said he was happy to be rid of Erica.

"When are you going to let them go home? I'm sure I'm not breaking any confidentiality if I tell you they're not happy being stuck in Rudolph."

Simmonds sighed. "Tomorrow morning, I'm going to talk to them all one more time, and then I'm going to have to let them leave. That lawyer of Erica's is making a lot of noise and pulling a lot of strings. Regarding Erica anyway. He doesn't seem to care one whit if her employees are left swinging in the wind. Not that I much care about him or his strings, but I can't keep them here forever."

When I'd been training Mattie to stay, I'd always laughed at the way he headed for the treat on the floor the second I released him. In the same fashion, I expected the whole gang to stampede for the city the moment they were told they could go. Unlikely they'd hang around long enough to do the photo shoot tomorrow night at Mrs.

Claus's Treasures. No matter. I'd prefer to see the last of them rather than have my picture in their magazine.

Simmonds's cell phone rang. She glanced at the number and her eyebrows rose as she answered it. At that moment, a cruiser tore out of the parking lot, under full lights and sirens. From farther down the street, I heard another.

"On my way." Simmonds shoved her phone into her pocket and dashed for her silver BMW without so much as a good-bye to me. Taking that as the signal he'd been released, Mattie jumped to his feet.

"What's happened?" Mattie and I trotted along behind her.

"There's been a death at the Yuletide. I have to go."

"Who? How?"

Simmonds paused with her hand on the door and turned toward me. "You were telling me about Erica and her PA."

I nodded. Mattie woofed.

"You know these people. You can come with me."

Chapter 13

At a gesture from Simmonds, Mattie leapt into the backseat of her car. I climbed into the passenger seat and we took off at considerable speed. Simmonds said nothing more, and I didn't ask. She switched the police radio on. All I could make out were people shouting numbers amid bursts of static.

The celebrity journalists who'd been lying in wait for Erica outside the Yuletide had very short attention spans. They'd left when nothing more seemed to be happening. Tonight, only a state police cruiser was parked at the entrance. Simmonds slowed, gave him a wave, and drove up the long driveway. More police cars were clustered at the path leading to the gardens, and Candy Campbell was stringing yellow crime scene tape between the trees. Simmonds pulled up and jumped out of the BMW. I followed, telling Mattie to guard the car. When we got to the tape,

Simmonds turned to me. "Wait here. I'll want to talk to you." Candy let her pass, not able to hide her surprise at seeing me in the company of the detective. Simmonds soon turned a corner and disappeared behind a tall, lush, meticulously trimmed hedge of American holly.

I looked around me. People were outlined standing in the windows of the inn, and more were gathered on the steps. I spotted Jack Olsen, the owner of the Yuletide, talking to a man in plain clothes. I went to join them. Jack had suffered a heart attack last December. He'd lost a lot of weight since, and the cheerful ruddy color was gone from his face, but he looked well. My parents were good friends with the Olsens, and I knew Jack's wife, Grace, was not only keeping him on a strict diet, but had taken over most of the day-to-day running of the inn.

"What brings you here, Merry?" he said.

"Detective Simmonds. She thinks I might be able to help."

"Can you?"

"Probably not. Do you, uh, know what's happened?"

"Woman found dead, is all I heard."

Simmonds came out from behind the hedge, stripping blue gloves off her hands. "Mr. Olsen," she said.

"Detective."

"I'm sorry for the inconvenience, sir, but we're going to have to keep this section of the gardens restricted, probably through tomorrow."

"Is it a hotel guest?" he asked.

She nodded. "It would appear so."

Erica, I thought. Simmonds brought me because, as

she said, I know these people. It had to be Erica. Poor little rich girl.

"I need to speak to Ms. Johnstone," Simmonds said. "Merry, you can be there when I break the news."

"What! I mean, who? If not Erica, who's dead?"

Simmonds said nothing more, but spun on her heel and marched across the neatly mowed grass toward Cabin C. I hurried along behind, like Mattie keeping to heel. "Who is it?" I repeated.

"Muriel Fraser."

"It can't be. I saw Muriel this morning."

Lights were on inside Cabin C, but the drapes were closed. Simmonds rapped on the door. Loudly.

"Did she have an accident?" I asked, "A heart attack or something?"

"Murder. No doubt about it." She knocked again. "Police!"

The door opened. James Claymore filled the entrance. He peered down his long nose at Diane Simmonds. "Good evening, Detective. It's late for a social call."

"Not a social call, as you're well aware, I'm sure," she said. "May we come in?"

He stepped back. He kept his eyes fixed on the detective. Me, he ignored. "There seems to be a great deal of police activity outside."

"Is Erica Johnstone here?" Simmonds asked.

"I am." Erica stood in the doorway to one of the bedrooms. Her face was scrubbed clean, her hair tied into a loose ponytail, and she was dressed in a simple pair of yellow cotton summer pajamas. Her feet were bare. She had, I was surprised to notice, particularly unattractive feet, all misshapen lumps and jutting angles. This, I thought, was the real Erica, all her expensive armor removed. "What's happened?" Her voice was low and soft. "I saw the police cars outside, but James said it had nothing to do with us."

"Is Ms. Fraser in?" Simmonds asked.

Erica shook her head. "She went out a while ago, didn't she, James?"

"I wasn't here, Erica. Remember, I only came when the police activity began to ensure you were okay."

"Oh yes, that's right. Muriel went up to the hotel bar for a drink. I didn't notice the time."

"She didn't order room service?"

"No," Erica said. "Sometimes, she drinks more than I think wise. She didn't want me counting her drinks."

"Why are you asking this, Detective?" the lawyer asked.

Simmonds gave me an almost imperceptible nod. I slipped across the room and went to stand by Erica. She blinked at me and I tried to give her a supportive smile. I doubt I succeeded.

"I'm sorry to have to tell you this," Simmonds said, her penetrating green eyes fixed on Erica. "Ms. Fraser was found dead a short while ago. Hotel guests walking in the gardens came across her body."

Erica slumped. I grabbed her and guided her to a wingback chair upholstered in cream and pink chintz next to the window.

Claymore sucked in a breath.

"You're lying," Erica said. "Why are you telling me this? James, make her go away."

"I'm sorry, Ms. Johnstone," Simmonds said. "But it is the truth. What time did Ms. Fraser leave?"

"I don't know. I wasn't paying any attention. She's always flitting about. I'm her employer, not her mother. She's entitled to have time away from me sometimes."

I patted Erica's hand. She gave me a weak smile.

"What did you do this evening, Ms. Johnstone?" Simmonds asked.

Claymore turned to her. "Now, see here . . ."

"Just asking," Simmonds said calmly.

"I stayed in," Erica said. "I ordered room service. You can ask, they'll tell you. I answered the door myself, so the waiter saw me. I don't know what time that was. Then I got ready for bed, and I was watching TV when James came over."

"What about the photo shoot in the garden earlier?" I said.

"I don't think you should be asking the questions here," Claymore said.

"Photo shoot?" Simmonds asked.

"We took some pictures around the hotel," Erica said. "For the magazine."

"Was Ms. Fraser involved in this shoot?"

"Not directly, but she was there, of course, in case I needed anything."

"Who else was there?"

"The people from my magazine. Willow and the girl with the blond hair who's always underfoot. What's her name, Merry?"

"Amber."

"Yes, her. Jason, the photographer. We let the owners of the inn watch us, the old guy and his wife. But no one else. A couple of security guards kept people from getting too close and ruining the pictures. They always do. Some people are just so hungry for attention. That's about it. And James, of course."

"What time did you finish?"

Erica shrugged. "I don't know."

"Was it still daylight, twilight, or full dark?" I asked.

Simmonds couldn't help giving me an approving look. I almost preened.

"Twilight," Erica said. "Until dark. We wanted the romantic atmosphere. The gardens look really nice when the lights first come on."

"What did everyone do when the shoot was over?"

"I don't know what Jason, Amber, and Willow did," Erica said. "As soon as we finished, I came back here. My grandmother had called earlier when everyone was around, so I returned her call when I had time to talk. Then Muriel came in, and I asked her to order room service. She didn't want anything for herself. She said she'd go up to the hotel to get something to eat. That's code for a drink."

"Ms. Fraser came back to the cabin after you. How long were you here alone?"

"Ten, fifteen minutes, maybe. I'd just hung up the phone when I heard the door open."

"Ms. Johnstone needs to rest," Claymore said. "She's had a terrible shock. She and Muriel were extremely close." How he could say that with a straight face, I didn't know. "And following so closely on the death of Max. What a tragedy."

I glanced at Erica. She looked very small in the depths of the wingback chair. She was staring out the window, but I didn't think she was seeing anything. Her eyes were blank, her expression dull and lifeless.

"What did you do after the photo shoot, Mr. Claymore?" Simmonds asked.

"I watched Erica cross the lawn, heading back here, but I didn't see what anyone else did. They packed up and melted into the shadows. I went straight to my room. I'm not staying here, but in the main building. I poured a glass of scotch and made some phone calls. You can check on that."

"Thank you. I will. Did you use your cell phone or the hotel landline?"

"My cell, of course."

"I'm finished here for now," Simmonds said. "I have to ask that Ms. Johnstone and her party remain in Rudolph for a while longer."

Claymore huffed and puffed and protested, but his heart didn't seem to be in it. He had to know Simmonds wasn't about to let the people closest to a second murder victim scatter across the country.

"Are you going to be okay?" I asked Erica. "I can stay with you if you'd like."

She gave me a sad smile. "Thank you for caring, Merry. I'll be fine."

"Yes, she will," Claymore said. "I'm sending for my things. I'm moving into Muriel's room, Erica. No arguments. You can't be here alone."

"Probably wise," Simmonds said. "But first, I'll have to ask you to stay out of there until my people have given it a going-over."

"Understood," Claymore said.

We left.

Once we were outside, I took a deep breath. The night air was heavy with the scent of flowers and freshly mowed grass. All the garden lights had been switched on, and the shadows of men and women moved in the shelter of the hedge. "There's something I have to tell you."

"What?" Simmonds said.

"Muriel was stealing from Erica. Small things mostly, things that wouldn't be missed. Erica has a reputation as a scatterbrain, a reputation Muriel was happy to cultivate. I told you she has a mother in an expensive nursing home. She asked Erica for help with the fees and Erica said no."

"How do you know this?"

"I caught her trying to sell the necklace Erica reported missing. You remember, you were called to Mrs. Claus's Treasures when Erica had histrionics about it. I recognized the necklace because Max bought it in my shop." I held my breath, hoping she wouldn't ask for any more details. I didn't want to drag Kyle into this.

"I will momentarily refrain from asking why you didn't tell me about this earlier, and instead ask when you saw Muriel with it."

"This morning."

"And less than twenty-four hours later she turns up dead. Did you tell Erica that Muriel was the thief?"

"No. I didn't tell anyone. I felt sorry for her. I didn't tell you because I didn't want to get her in trouble. I warned her that if she didn't quit stealing she'd find herself in real trouble. I heard a while later that the necklace had been found, and Erica was happy again. I thought Muriel had understood me. She said, 'I've had enough of this petty thieving.' I thought that meant she was finished stealing, because it wasn't worth it. But now I wonder."

"You wonder if she decided to move on to bigger game."

I nodded. "Erica has some extremely valuable things. But much of it isn't even her own, it belongs to her grandmother. Art and antiques and stuff like that. People would notice if they went missing."

"Did Erica find out Muriel had been stealing from her, do you think? Perhaps she tried to take something else this afternoon, and Erica caught her."

"And then Erica killed her?" I shook my head. "I don't buy it. You brought me along tonight because I know these people. I'm beginning to wonder if Erica is quite the empty-headed drama queen she pretends to be. Regardless, she wouldn't kill anyone because they stole something. She'd call the police and have the criminal tossed in jail. But . . ."

"Go ahead, Merry."

"Suppose Muriel didn't mean she was moving on to

taking more valuable things? She needs money, and she lives among people who have more money than she can dream of. People to whom the cost of her mother's care is a drop in the bucket. People she doesn't like or respect."

"Blackmail."

"Yes. She was Erica's personal assistant. That's a close relationship. I don't think Erica has many secrets worth protecting; her life's pretty much an open book. We can't forget that Erica's fiancé was murdered only a few days ago."

"I'm not forgetting," Simmonds said. "You're saying Muriel tried to blackmail the person who killed Max?"

I nodded. "I am. I'd considered the possibility that Muriel herself murdered Max. She said he was getting suspicious of her. If Max told Erica that Muriel was stealing, she'd be out on the street without a penny."

"You should have told me this, Merry."

I hung my head. "Sorry. I didn't want to get anyone in trouble because of my suppositions and guesses." I tried not to think that getting Muriel into trouble for stealing a hundred-dollar necklace would have probably saved her life. "It's still possible she killed Max, but I'm more inclined to think she considered herself terribly clever and tried to blackmail the killer."

"And got herself killed for her pains. It makes sense, Merry. Erica?"

"Try as I might, I don't see her as a cold-blooded killer. Either of Max or of Muriel. How did Muriel die, by the way?"

"Strangled by her own scarf. I recognized the scarf as

one she'd been wearing when we met earlier. That's confidential."

"If Erica had killed Max, I'd expect her to collapse into tears of remorse, genuine or not, confess to the crime, and immediately lawyer up. Erica may not be stupid, which was my first impression of her, but she is spoiled. She doesn't think the rules of life apply to her. She would want everyone to know she was a woman scorned, and she'd killed in a mad dramatic fit of jealous passion. Or something." My voice trailed off. "Then again, I could be totally wrong."

"I don't think you are," Simmonds said. "So we're back to square one. Find out who killed Max Folger, and we'll get the killer of Muriel Fraser also."

"Unless . . ."

"Unless what?"

"That lawyer arrived on the scene mighty fast. Erica's grandmother sent him here to protect Erica's interests."

"That's normal enough for people of that income level."

"I suppose it is. We've always assumed he arrived after Max died, but suppose he was already here? Suppose he snuck into town without anyone noticing? Maybe he decided that for some reason, no doubt financial, Max shouldn't marry Erica after all, and he had to go." I absolutely refused to believe Jennifer would put a hit out on anyone. Was Claymore acting on his own? Had Jennifer said, in a tragic re-creation of Henry II, "Will no one rid me of this meddlesome fiancé?" Had Claymore, loyal servant, done precisely that? "Does he have an alibi for the time of Max's death?"

"I never asked. But I will now. His alibi for tonight isn't much of one."

"How far would he go to protect Erica's interests? Jennifer's interests, I should say. What if Muriel came to him and told him she could prove Erica had killed Max? Suppose she threatened to go to the police. Or, even worse, the press. It didn't have to be true. Maybe Muriel believed no such thing, but figured the lawyer would pay up to prevent her talking. Instead . . ."

"I'm going around to the Carolers Motel next," Simmonds said. "I was going to have someone drive you back to town, but I've changed my mind. You can come with me. Wait in the car, please. I have one more thing to do first."

Mattie and I waited, if not patiently, in the car. From my vantage point I had a perfect view of the police activity. Vans pulled up, men and women in white suits disembarked. Not many hotel guests tried to get past the police barrier, but a few did, and Candy turned them away. I could tell she was dying to know what I was doing being so chummy with Simmonds. Once, I caught her looking my way, and I gave her a cheerful wave. She pretended not to see me, but the speed with which she swung her head back to front and center threatened to give her whiplash.

The car door opened and Simmonds got in. Mattie leaned his big head over her shoulder in greeting and she gave him a pat. After he spent any time in my car I had to hose the drool off the seats, as well as out of my hair, but he left Diane Simmonds and her sleek BMW perfectly clean and dry. I wondered, again, how she did that.

"Muriel didn't go into the bar tonight," Simmonds said. "The bartender knew her; she'd been in other nights. She always came alone. Ordered a glass of red wine, from the higher end of the price scale, and sat at a table by herself with a book. He was on duty tonight during the time in question."

"She lied to Erica about where she was going."

"Or she intended to go to the bar but didn't make it as far as the main building. The receptionist didn't see her come in, either. She did see Mr. Claymore in the lobby—apparently she thinks he's most attractive—but she can't say what time that was. He later left the hotel in a great hurry, and she does remember that time, because it was only a few minutes after the first cruiser had arrived."

"He said he was in his room when he heard the activity and went to check on Erica."

"I asked if Mr. Claymore had ordered a drink from room service—he had not—but I was told that each room has a fully stocked minibar. If Mr. Claymore wanted a scotch, he wouldn't have had to phone down for it." She switched the BMW's engine on and we left the Yuletide Inn.

The news traveled faster than we did, and by the time we got to the Carolers Motel the magazine crew—Willow, Amber, and Jason—were gathered in Willow's room having a drink.

They expressed shock at Muriel's death, but said they

knew nothing about it. They said they'd seen her at the photo shoot, standing silently in the shadows, but they hadn't paid her any attention. They'd broken up about nine and returned to the motel.

"Did you travel to the Yuletide and back together?" Simmonds asked.

"No," Amber said. "We came from different directions so we each had our own car." They all claimed to have returned to the motel immediately after the shoot was finished, but none of them could say what time the others arrived. As this was not a hotel, with a lobby, elevator, and central interior corridor, but a motel where cars parked outside the individual rooms, their comings and goings wouldn't have been seen by anyone in reception.

Willow's room was small and crowded and smelled of cleaning fluid and air freshener. The furniture consisted of one double bed, a small dresser with a flat-screen TV and a coffeepot, and a cheap desk with a single chair. Willow and Amber sat on the bed. Jason had the chair. Simmonds and I stood. When Simmonds asked them about their relationship with Muriel, Willow answered.

"We didn't actually *know* her, Detective. At least I didn't." The others nodded in agreement. "She followed Erica around, but never spoke to the likes of us. We didn't even have much to do with Erica herself in the normal course of our work. Unless she was the main feature, with her wedding stuff, she didn't have much interest in individual stories or locations. She only came here this time because she heard Max was stepping out of line."

"Stepping out of line? How so?"

"Seeing old girlfriends," Jason said, pointedly looking at me.

"Once she realized Merry was involved in the story," Willow said, "then Erica had to be involved, too."

"You don't like her very much," Simmonds said.

Willow raised one eyebrow. "Frankly, Detective, I can't stand her. If she turns up dead, I'll be the first in line as a suspect."

"You don't mean that," Amber said.

"Sure I do. But Erica hasn't been murdered, has she? It's time someone came out and said it. She thinks she can play at doing the jobs we depend on for our livelihoods. Well, my job is not a rich girl's game. Let her take up championship checkers if she's bored, and leave me alone."

"Has anyone ever given her a chance?" I said. "Tried to teach her some of the ropes maybe?"

Willow snorted. "I've got better things to do with my time. As for Muriel, I didn't have an opinion of her one way or the other. She didn't care about the running of the magazine, that wasn't her job."

"Willow's right," Jason said. "About Muriel anyway, although she's too hard on Erica. Erica just wants some respect from the people she employs, and all she gets is smiles to her face and backbiting the minute she leaves the room. You people want her to fail."

"I don't care . . ." Willow began.

"You keep saying that," Jason said. "You keep saying you don't care so much, but it's obvious that you do."

Willow's eyes blazed, but before she could retaliate, Simmonds lifted a hand. "As interesting as this is, I am asking about Muriel Fraser. Jason, what were you going to say?"

He turned away from Willow. "Muriel didn't have much to do with any of us, ever. Tonight, she kept to one side and never said a word. That was normal."

"Did you see her leave the group at any time?"

"Detective, I was kinda busy," Jason said. "It was a difficult shoot, trying to capture the light precisely the way I wanted it. If Muriel had dressed in a Santa Claus costume and arrived in a sleigh pulled by eight tiny reindeer, I wouldn't have noticed her."

"Same," Willow said.

"She stood in the shadows with that lawyer guy most of the time," Amber said. "Seems to me she spent her life in the shadows. Poor Muriel."

"Don't give me 'poor Muriel,'" Willow said. "If she spent her life in the shadows it was all the better to try and get the gossip. Remember how Samantha Crawford got fired right out of the blue, and everyone was totally shocked? I heard that Muriel overheard Samantha dissing the outfit Erica wore to the shower Max's mom put on for her, and ran squealing to Erica."

"I heard it was Max who fired Samantha for disloyalty. But you have to admit," Amber said, "the dress was totally hideous."

"I'm going back to the Yuletide to talk to the forensics people," Simmonds said "You've been a help, Merry. Thank you. I'll drop you off at home."

"My car's still at the police station."

"I'll take you there, then. I should probably speak to Muriel's next of kin. You said she had a brother?"

"Yes."

"Erica should have that information, but I don't want to disturb her if she's sleeping. I never mind disturbing a lawyer." She dug in her pocket and made the call. We were still standing outside the motel. A car drove slowly through the lot, and moths fluttered around the lights over the doors. Mattie grinned at us from the backseat of the BMW. I got into the car and gave him a hearty pat on the head. "Bed sounds pretty nice about now, don't you think?" He whimpered in reply.

The driver's door opened and Simmonds got in. She didn't switch the engine on, but turned to me, and I knew right away she'd learned something interesting.

"What?" I said.

"Claymore is still with Erica. She didn't want to go to bed, and she didn't want to be alone, so they're watching a movie. He passed the phone to her, and I asked if she had Muriel's brother's number. She said not with her. She'll call the office in the morning and get it. She then said that she should probably give Mrs. Fraser a call. But she's on a cruise right now so might be hard to reach."

"Muriel's mom's on a cruise?"

"Apparently she's in the Mediterranean. She goes cruising two or three times a year. I confirmed that Mrs. Fraser means Muriel's mother, and that she didn't have two mothers. Not as far as Erica knows, at any rate. Mrs.

Fraser lives in Palm Beach, Florida, where she's active in her local gardening club."

"Oh," was all I could say.

"So I then asked Erica if Muriel had ever approached her for money to help her mother out of financial difficulty. Whereupon Erica said, and I quote, 'I didn't know her mother was having financial troubles. I thought she was quite comfortable.' You're sure Muriel told you she needed money for her mother's care?"

"Positive. Obviously, Muriel lied to me. She was nothing but a common thief. Pure and simple."

"So it would seem."

"And a snoop. I bet she was poking around where she shouldn't and discovered something, so the killer decided they had to get rid of her. Which brings us back once again to the question. What did she know and who killed her because of it?"

It was long past midnight when Simmonds dropped me off at the police station. I said good night, and Mattie and I got into my car and drove home.

Poor Muriel, indeed. Did greed do her in? I couldn't help but think so. There might be another reason someone would have killed her, nothing to do with Max or Erica or the magazine, but it didn't seem likely, not so soon after Max's death.

My phone had been buzzing all evening with incoming texts. I ignored the ones from Russ Durham and called my mom as soon as I got home.

"Grace phoned earlier," she said. "One of the magazine people was found dead at the inn?"

"Yup," I said. "Muriel Fraser, Erica's PA."

"Do the police think it's related to what happened to Max?"

"They don't see how it could not be."

"Grace said you were with the police. Why?"

I explained about being with Simmonds when she got the call and going along for the ride.

"I don't like this, dear. That brings it too close to home."

"I know, Mom."

"Let me know if you hear anything more," she said.

We hung up. I wanted to call someone, someone I could talk to about my feelings, but Vicky and Alan both got up very early in the morning, so they'd be sound asleep by now. Russ Durham was obviously still up, but he wouldn't want to talk to me as a friend. He'd want to find out what I knew about the killings. Simmonds had asked me to keep everything we'd talked about to myself.

I figured she didn't mean Vicky or Alan.

I was far too restless and disturbed to sleep, so I plugged in the kettle and made myself a pot of tea. I found a pad of paper and a pen and sat at the kitchen table. I sipped hot sweet milky tea and doodled on the page. I had planned to write up a list of suspects, possible motives, and my observations, in an attempt to put my jumbled thoughts in some sort of order, but I got no further than writing down names. Erica. Willow. Amber. Jason. James

Claymore. And POPU, meaning person or persons unknown. Reluctantly, I added Russ Durham.

I studied the list for a long time. No brilliant insights came to me, so eventually I sighed and put down my pen. "Come on," I said to Mattie. "Let's go to bed. Everything will be clearer in the morning."

Chapter 14

I dreamt that I was trapped in a maze of tall American holly. I ran and ran in ever-decreasing circles as sharp thorns reached toward me. Whenever I managed to break through the hedge, I fell into another, more confusing, section of the maze. Mattie also tossed and turned all night, and when I got up for a glass of water I saw that his legs were moving in his sleep as though he dreamt he was running.

In the morning, I glanced at the list of names on the kitchen table as Mattie and I got ready to head out for our walk. I turned away. Nothing was clearer in the light of day. If anything, it was jumbled even more.

Russ was standing by the front door of Mrs. Claus's Treasures when I arrived for work with Mattie and a large latte.

"Another killing." His voice was grim as he gave Mattie a rub behind the ears.

"Yup."

"I saw you last night at the Yuletide. With Simmonds." He took the cup out of my hand while I fumbled with my key.

"She wanted someone with her when she told Erica what had happened."

"How did Erica react?"

"I'm not going to tell you, Russ. That wouldn't be nice."

He gave me a rueful grin. "Fair enough. Simmonds has, once again, ordered Erica and the people from *Jennifer's Lifestyle* not to leave town. I doubt that order can stick for much longer. Erica's lawyer issued a statement this morning to the effect that she should be permitted to grieve in the comfort of her home, surrounded by her loved ones."

"Did he say anything else?"

"Other than Muriel was a valued, trusted, even loved employee? That she and Erica were more like best friends than personal assistant and employer? Nope."

"I have no comment about that. Are the vultures of the press, present company excepted, gathering once again?"

"Some. But there's unlikely to be the mass onslaught we had last time. You heard about that senator?"

"What senator?"

"Never mind. You'll be hearing more about it soon enough. The press pack has gone to hound him and his wife. What's a little murder when there's a juicy political scandal to report? You'll let me know if you hear anything?"

"About the senator?"

"Very funny."

"If I hear anything about Erica and her group that is suitable for the press, I will let you know, Russell."

"Fair enough." Russ gave me a quick peck on the cheek and a light hug. I hugged him back. "I don't like you being involved in this, Merry. Look after yourself."

"Don't I always?"

"No, you do not."

I'd kept a firm grip on Mattie's collar while Russ and I talked. A young frisky Saint Bernard and my delicate ornaments are not a good combination. Once Russ left, I took Mattie into the back, settled him down for the day, and opened the shop for business.

The morning passed swiftly, and I was starting to think about lunch, when a text arrived.

Willow: *We'll be there at six as planned. Remember: dress for pix.*

Me: *What*?

Willow: *Photo shoot in your shop tonight. Not as though we've got anything else to do in this miserable town.*

Me: *Ok.*

One of the first customers of the day had scooped up Alan's entire Santa's village, right down to the little wooden trees. My next text was to him.

Me: *Magazine people coming at six. Village sold already. Can you bring another?*

Alan: *It'll be tight.*

Me: *Hold off toy store.*

Alan: *Already gone. I'll try. Paint might be wet.*

Jackie arrived for work a few minutes early. That was so unusual it deserved to be written down in the record books. I suspected she'd be on her best behavior for a few days, not wanting to remind me of how she'd skipped off work on Saturday, leaving the shop deserted for a man and his killer to walk in unobserved. I doubted the good behavior would last any longer than a day or two, but I was determined to enjoy it while it did.

I didn't want to say anything to her about tonight's shoot, but I didn't see how I couldn't. I had to go home and put on my decorating-diva clothes, and she'd certainly ask why. It would no doubt be a major battle to get her out of the shop before the crew arrived.

"You okay?" I asked. "Suffering no aftereffects from hiding out in my shed?"

"I'm fine. Your accommodations leave something to be desired, Merry."

"You're lucky it was summer. You would have frozen to death in there in the winter. I would have found your desiccated body in the spring when I decided to cut the lawn for the first time."

She shivered. "Don't even joke about it."

"The magazine people are coming in at closing. You don't have to stay."

Her eyes lit up. "They're going to take more pictures, you mean?"

"They might."

"Great. Is this outfit okay or should I go home and change?"

"You won't be in the pictures, Jackie."

She pouted. I was starting to get very tired of that pout. I considered telling her it made her look like the next kid in line for Santa after the candy canes ran out. But I didn't. "The store will be crowded with all their equipment, so you can leave fifteen minutes early today. Are you seeing Kyle after work?"

"Nope. He's gone away for a couple days."

"What!"

She eyed me. "What do you care, Merry? He's been under a lot of pressure lately. His art's not going well, and he needs to spend some time alone in the woods. Getting his soul back to center. His cousin has a cabin on Lake Oneida, so he's gone there for some private time."

"When did he decide to do this?"

"This morning. He's very spontaneous. It's the artistic spirit. He has to respond when it speaks."

Of all the stupid moves. I hadn't told Simmonds Kyle was the one buying stolen jewelry off Muriel, because she hadn't asked. If she did ask, I wasn't going to lie. And if Simmonds did then want to question Kyle, she'd find he'd skipped out of town right after the woman's murder. He might as well have hung a guilty sign around his neck.

The bells tinkled, customers came in, and we talked no more about either Kyle or the magazine shoot.

I went home in the middle of the afternoon to get changed. I'm not entirely sure what a doyenne of holiday decorating wears, and after all that had happened, by now the magazine article seemed so minor that my heart wasn't in it. It was hard for me to maintain even a shred of enthusiasm for this project in the face of two deaths.

Willow and the crew might as well be working as hanging around their motel grumbling, but I couldn't help thinking it was somewhat disrespectful.

On the bright side, Mattie enjoyed the unexpected afternoon walk.

Mrs. D'Angelo was on her knees weeding a weedless flower bed when we came around the bend in the road. The moment she spotted me, she leapt to her feet with an agility that belied her years. "Terrible goings-on at the Yuletide, I hear. Still, what do you expect from those city people, bringing trouble everywhere they go? I hear you were there last night, Merry, dear. Did you see . . . ?"

Mattie would have been happy to stop to chat, but I simply said, "Can't talk, big hurry," and carried on as Mrs. D'Angelo's voice trailed behind me.

I took off my multi-pocketed khaki capris and loose-fitting navy blue blouse and pulled on a knee-length white skirt, a lacy white camisole, and a turquoise jacket that was cropped at the waist and had three-quarter-length sleeves. I added blue glass earrings and a long string of chunky blue and silver beads. I freshened my makeup and forced my unruly black curls into some semblance of order, and then I studied myself in the mirror while Mattie watched. I stuck my tongue out at my reflection. In this humidity, by the time I made it back to town, my hair would be a frizzy mop once again. I slipped my feet into a pair of turquoise suede ballet flats, and we headed out one more time.

To my infinite relief Mrs. D'Angelo was nowhere to be seen. I called Vicky as Mattie and I walked back to town. "Feel like coming to the shop tonight to watch the photo shoot?"

"They're going ahead with it?"

"Apparently."

"You heard that Erica's PA was found dead last night at the Yuletide?"

"Yeah, I heard."

"Mark says police are crawling across every inch of the gardens and have been questioning all the staff. Erica's holed up in her cabin, and the press are howling at the gates. Figuratively speaking, although Mark said they found one guy creeping through the shrubbery searching for Erica's cabin. To his intense disappointment they didn't have a sign over the door directing him to the correct one, so he got some nice shots of a honeymooning couple enjoying an intimate moment. They're threatening to sue, not only the photographer, but also the hotel. Mark doesn't think they have much of a case. If they wanted privacy they should have closed their drapes."

I didn't even laugh. "I just want them all gone."

"It doesn't seem to be affecting business though. Mark says the inn and the restaurant are going to be full again tonight, and I've been rushed off my feet all day. Do you need me to come, Merry?"

"I don't need you, no. I thought you might like to."

"In that case, I'll bow out. Just think about all the marvelous publicity you'll get."

"They might decide to throw out the entire Rudolph feature. I think it's tasteless in the extreme, and Jennifer will probably agree if she hears about it."

"Every cloud has a silver lining. In that case I won't have to give up my spice cookie recipe. I forgot to tell you that I got a call from none other than the editorial director of food at the magazine begging me for it. Can you imagine? I'm thinking of changing my own title. Director of Eating. *Chief* Director of Eating. Has a nice ring, don't you think? Catch you later, sweetie."

"Bye," I said.

Once again business was steady all afternoon. The beach tourists were still in town, and a fresh batch of *Jennifer's Lifestyle* groupies had arrived now that Erica, and her continued presence in Rudolph, was back on the online gossip feeds. News trickled in throughout the day. The police had sealed off the Yuletide gardens. Reporters were clamoring for an interview with Erica. The mayor and the police issued a statement that an arrest was "imminent." Sue-Anne Morrow added that Rudolph remained a safe, family-friendly town, and Santa Claus had decided to extend his vacation one more week because he was having such a great time.

When I heard that, I called my dad. "You're going to do another public appearance?"

"Sue-Anne and the council think it's a good idea in light of this most recent murder. Unlike those," he cleared his throat, "other times, these killings don't seem to be having any effect on the town's reputation. Still, they want to remind everyone that Rudolph is about more than visiting celebrities and their crimes and scandals."

"Are you okay with that?"

"Honeybunch, I don't know. There's a sentiment in

town, not openly expressed, that all this attention is good for Rudolph. I'm a team player, and they've asked me to do my bit on the weekend. It won't be a big production this time. I'll set myself up down at the beach under an umbrella and talk to kids. You don't have to help, and I'm not going to ask Alan, he's busy enough. I'll get a couple of the high school students to put on their elf hats."

Sue-Anne herself popped in shortly after five. Her Honor stood in the doorway, checking out all the corners of the shop. Jackie was busy ringing up purchases. "Can I help you, Sue-Anne?" I asked.

She lowered her voice. "Those magazine people are still in town."

"So I heard."

"Do you know what their plans might be?"

"Why?"

"As disruptive as these murders have been, it's nicc that we're getting so much attention from such a popular magazine. I went around to the Yuletide earlier, to ask Erica Johnstone if she needed anything while in Rudolph, but she was"—Sue-Anne searched for a suitable word—"indisposed."

Which I interpreted to mean that she was not interested in taking part in a photo op with a small-town mayor. I said nothing. I waited for Sue-Anne to get to the point.

She cleared her throat. "Her lawyer—such a handsome man, isn't he?—mentioned that Erica's staff plan to continue working, and I thought they might be coming back here." She smiled at me. I didn't smile in return. I tried to remind myself that Sue-Anne truly did have the welfare of the town of Rudolph at heart. And if she got her picture in a major national magazine, so much the better. I could see it appearing on her campaign literature when the next election rolled around.

"It's going to be a closed-door shoot. Sorry." Meaning, I would close the door on anyone who tried to come in uninvited.

She tried not to look too disappointed, and left.

At five forty-five I told Jackie she could leave. At five fifty I ordered her to leave. At five fifty-five I went into the back, got her purse, shoved it at her, and marched her to the door. I flipped the sign to "Closed," but left the door unlocked for my expected visitors. I ran to the back, checked my hair in the restroom mirror, decided I couldn't do much about it, and popped my head into the office. Mattie jumped up to greet me. Fortunately, I read his intentions in time and managed to scramble out of the way as he leapt. "Down! No jumping!" I wagged my finger at him and he let out a whimper. With a pang of guilt I remembered what our obedience school teacher had said. At ten months, he's still a puppy and it's vital that training be constantly reinforced. I'd slipped badly this past week with all that was happening. I took the dog biscuit tin out of the drawer. I didn't even have to say the word "sit" before his big furry rump hit the floor and his tongue lolled out of his mouth in eager anticipation. I laughed and gave him the treat. It disappeared in an instant.

"You are a good dog. Yes, you are." I scratched at his favorite spot behind his ears. "But you still have to stay in here for a while yet. Hopefully, I can get this over and done with before too long."

I went back to the main room and studied the shop. Everything looked lovely. Silver and glass sparkled, the lights of the tree glowed, the dolls stood in neat rows, the tableware and linens were so inviting it made me wonder what was in my fridge that I could prepare for dinner. I hadn't heard from Alan, but I still hoped he'd be able to bring me a sample of the village in time. I wanted it to be prominently displayed. I'd cleared space for it under the Douglas fir, but I'd have to put something else there if he didn't get here soon.

Jason arrived at quarter after six, laden with camera and lighting equipment. "Willow and Amber not here?"

"No."

"I wonder what's keeping them? Willow's famous for her punctuality." He cleared some room on the counter, near the curtain leading to the back and thus out of the way of anything he might want in the pictures. He zipped open his bags and laid out a series of black lenses, each one larger than the other. He studied the room, adjusted the flash, and took sample pictures, checking angles and lighting.

I watched, still fascinated by the process. At the magazine, I'd loved this part of my job, when we worked to make everything look absolutely perfect. I'd tried to bring some of that eye for detail with me when setting up my shop.

At six thirty, when I'd decided I couldn't wait for Alan any longer and I'd have to put the vases containing the glass balls onto the table by the tree, my phone rang. I'd put it on the counter, not wanting a bump in my skirt pocket showing in the pictures. I crossed the room and scooped it up.

Willow. "Sorry to be late. Is Jason there?"

"Yes. We're ready and waiting. Where are you?"

"Amber had a bad fall and I'm going to have to take her to the hospital."

"Oh no," I said. I mouthed, "Willow," to Jason. "What happened?"

"As far as I could tell she tripped over a crack in the sidewalk outside her room. She fell badly and seems to have twisted her ankle. I tried propping it up and got some ice out of the machine in the hallway, but I'm worried it might be more than sprained. It's swelling up like a balloon. She has to go to the hospital. Jason knows what I'm looking for. You and he can arrange things, and he can get set up. I'll be there as soon as I can. I'll have to manage without Amber."

She hung up, and I told Jason what had happened.

"I'm almost ready. Why don't you take a pose over there by the tree, and I can check the lighting?"

I put the phone back on the counter and did as instructed. I then posed in the alcoves, by the jewelry display, next to the dishes and linens. I considered suggesting bringing Mattie out for a couple of pictures, but I still wasn't too sure of letting him wander about my shop. Having him on the leash would be worse. I didn't dare think of it bringing down the tree, decorations and all, or getting tangled around the legs of the table displaying wineglasses and crystal candlesticks.

"How's everything been going?" I asked. "Shooting at the other places in town, I mean."

"Pretty good. This town of yours is perfect for a photo spread."

"Can I see?"

"Sure." He pushed a couple of buttons and handed me his camera.

The first pictures I saw were of me, taken a few minutes ago. They were just practice shots, to check lighting and placement, so I hadn't bothered to pose or even to smile. I went through them quickly. The next bunch had probably been taken last night. Most were of Erica in the gardens at the Yuletide. The light of a summer evening was soft, and she looked, I thought, genuinely lovely. Pictures of Erica admiring the fountains, leaning over to smell the flowers, sitting on the grass, her legs tucked demurely behind her. I continued clicking, moving backward in time. Erica around town, peeking into storefronts and studying the displays. In one shot, she'd been captured looking back over her shoulder, her hair loose, her eyes shining, laughing. Then Erica at Victoria's Bake Shoppe, nibbling on a croissant and sipping tea out of a china teacup with a pattern of red roses. Erica admiring the two (two!) best-in-show Santa Claus parade trophies in a display case above the rows of bread. She grinned at the camera, her relaxed smile making her look fresh and pretty. Some pictures had been taken in my shop, but in every one of them the object of the photo wasn't me or the customers or even the goods for sale, but Erica. More shots of Erica at the inn, around town, curled up in a big chair, relaxing in her hotel room.

A bad feeling started climbing up my spine. Every one of these pictures was of Erica. They were all carefully, dare I say lovingly, shot. The feature was supposed to be about Rudolph, the year-round Christmas destination. I clicked rapidly back and forth through the pictures. None of Dad as Santa, of the boat parade, of kids lining up to sit on Santa's knee, or my mom's children's concert.

Erica. All of Erica. Many were close-ups of her face.

The gardens at the Yuletide again. These photos had been taken at night. Erica was walking through the grounds, but she wasn't alone. A man walked with her. He had his arm around her waist, and their heads were close, as though they were talking. These pictures looked as though the photographer was taking shots while he remained unseen, even hidden. Many had branches in the foreground. The couple were not looking at the camera, and they didn't seem to be aware it was there. The man was obviously Max.

I clicked backward. I'd skipped over one group of pictures, because they were dark and blurry, as if the photographer had been disturbed and the camera had moved. I had to see them again.

Max. Still in the gardens, still night. No sign of Erica. Max was walking toward the person with the camera. His face was twisted in rage, his hand was lifted, his mouth open in an angry shout.

And I knew.

I felt as much as heard Jason walk toward me. He lifted the camera out of my hands. "Wrong memory card. I was looking at this one earlier and forgot to put the working one back in. Did you like the photos?"

"Very nice." I stood up. I tried to control the trembling in my legs. "I'm going for a coffee. Want one?"

"No."

I'd been told Jason was a freelancer, hired only for this job. The machinations at the magazine would have been of no interest to him, nor the future of the business. Thus, I'd concluded that he'd have no reason to kill Max.

I'd been wrong.

Jason stood between me and the front door. The back of my legs pressed against the center table, the one with the fresh rosemary bush. I might be able to get through the curtain, into the back, and out the door to the alley. Mattie. If I could get to Mattie, his size alone might stop Jason.

I slid along the table, edging toward the curtain.

"Won't be a sec," I said. "Coffee shop's right next door. I'll go out the back."

"I don't want a coffee."

"I do." I tried to smile. I failed.

He took a step toward me. His eyes were dark, empty pools.

"There you are," I shouted. "I was wondering what was taking you so long."

Jason half turned toward the front door. I darted past him, but he was too quick. I tried to shove him aside, but as soon as he realized no one was coming in, he grabbed my arm and twisted. "Sorry, Merry. But you don't need any coffee, either."

He held my arm and pulled me toward the back. I stumbled, lost my balance, and fell against him. There are no curtains on the windows, and the lights were on inside the shop. It was early in the evening. People had to be walking past, tourists heading for restaurants and shop owners going home after a long day. Surely someone would look in. Someone would see what was happening.

I screamed. With one swift movement Jason jerked me around, so my back was pressed against his chest. He put one hand over my mouth, holding me against him. His other hand found my necklace, and his fingers wound themselves around it. He jerked it tight. I felt the silver and turquoise beads dig into the tender flesh of my throat. I kicked out but connected with nothing. He began pushing me toward the back while twisting the necklace harder, so it dug in deeper. I gasped, trying to find air. My fingers fumbled for the necklace, but I couldn't get a grip on it to break it or loosen it. My vision swam. I couldn't breathe.

Mattie began to bark, the sound rising as his panic increased.

Bells rang in my ears. Was I dead already? Mom. Dad. Vicky. I'd miss them all so much. Alan. I'd miss what we never had.

"What on earth is going on here?" a woman's voice demanded.

Help. Help had arrived. I almost collapsed in gratitude,

but I quickly realized something was wrong. Jason's grip lessened slightly, but he didn't let go, of me or of my necklace. I clawed at my throat.

"Get out of here, Erica," Jason said. "This is none of your business."

With enormous effort I was able to turn my head slightly. Erica Johnstone stood in the doorway. I tried to signal with my eyes. *Don't leave me.*

"Let go of her, Jason," she said.

"I can't do that, Erica. She knows too much. Go back to the hotel. I'll clean everything up when I'm done here and then we can talk."

"Clean up?" Her voice was surprisingly steady. "You mean you won't let her be found? Like the other times? Muriel? Max?"

"I'm glad you understand. He wasn't the right man for you. He wouldn't have made you happy. He couldn't give you what you deserve."

"That's all right then," she said.

I continued to struggle. While he talked to Erica, Jason had relaxed his grip on the necklace fractionally, and I was able to suck in a few desperate breaths. He pulled it tight again and shoved me toward the curtain.

Erica turned around. I couldn't believe it. She was leaving me to die. I let out a sob and gave her one last imploring look.

As she passed the table by the door, her hand shot out. She grabbed one of the glass balls piled in a crystal vase. The ball was about the size of a baseball. She pivoted on her four-inch heels, turning back to face into the room, and she threw the ball with a powerful overhand, straight at Jason's head. It connected, getting him smack in the center of his forehead. The glass shattered. "What the . . ." Shocked, he relaxed his grip on the necklace and lifted his hands to protect his face. She threw another, and then another. Balls pelted Jason in a barrage of red, green, and clear glass. Some broke on impact and some bounced off him to hit the floor and shatter into a hundred pieces.

My throat was on fire, my legs felt like rubber, and I was desperate for breath but I couldn't pass out. I had to help Erica.

When the vase was empty, Erica leapt onto Jason with enough force to knock him off-balance. He crashed into the table. The rosemary bush and the decorations fell to the floor. More glass ornaments shattered in a shower of color. She fell on him like a woman possessed. She pummeled him with her fists, scraped his face with her long nails. She screamed, "You killed him. You killed Max. I'll kill you." She kept on screaming. Shut in the office, Mattie howled. My adorable pet sounded like the Hound of the Baskervilles loose on the moors. I scrambled across the room to get to the counter and my phone. I grabbed it in shaking hands. I swiped the screen. Nothing happened. I swiped again and the emergency button appeared. I fumbled to press 911. "Help. Help," I shouted. "He killed Max. He tried to kill me."

I shoved the phone into my pocket. Only later did I realize I hadn't told the operator where I was. Jason was fighting back now. He hit Erica on the side of the head. She recoiled and he hit her again. She fell to the floor. I looked frantically around the room. The row of singing angels filled the shelf near the counter. They'd been made by Alan, carved out of hardwood and carefully painted, arranged in a row according to size, from about three inches tall to two and a half feet. I grabbed the tallest and ran to help Erica. Jason was standing over her now. He lifted his foot to kick her. I held the singing, white-robed, and winged angel in both hands. Between the glass balls and the angel bat, Erica and I made a formidable ball team. Jason heard me coming and swiveled to face me. I shifted the bat. Erica crawled across the floor, the broken glass tearing at her hands and knees.

"Game's over," I said. "The police are on their way." From outside came the sound of . . . nothing. No sirens. No flashing blue and red lights washing the front of the shop.

I had my back to the front door. Jason saw it move first, and his eyes widened. The cheerful bells tinkled and Alan said, "I hope I'm in time. What the . . ." A crash as whatever he was carrying fell to the floor.

Jason ran. He leapt over the broken rosemary bush and shattered ornaments. Alan filled the main entrance, so Jason headed for the back. He pushed aside the curtain and was gone.

"Merry," Alan yelled. "Stay here. Call the police." He took off after Jason.

"Erica," I yelled. "Stay here. Call the police." I ran after them, still gripping the singing figure, now turned into an avenging angel.

The curtain opens into a small, windowless hallway.

A couple of doors lead off it. To the outside, the staff restroom, the storage room, and my office. The light was off and the hall was almost completely dark. In his panic and confusion Jason threw open the office door.

I arrived in time to see a hundred and twenty pounds of furious canine hit him full on. Jason went down with a terrified scream. Mattie planted his front paws on the man's chest and peered into his face. His teeth were bared and he growled, low in his throat. I had never heard him do that before.

Finally, I heard the oh-so-welcome sound of police cars screeching to a halt outside Mrs. Claus's Treasures.

Chapter 15

Diane Simmonds was the first through the curtain, gun drawn, a uniformed officer hot on her heels. She took one look at the sight in front of her and let out a bark of laughter. Mattie stepped off Jason and gave Simmonds a woof of greeting. "Nice to see you, too, Matterhorn," she said.

She slipped her gun into the holster at her hip and said to the officer with her, "Cuff him."

The officer also put his gun away, grabbed Jason's arm, and pulled him to his feet.

"That dog attacked me. I was trying to do my job, and she"—Jason jerked his head toward me, spittle flying—"set it on me. If you hadn't arrived in time, Officer, it would have killed me."

"Save it for your lawyer," Simmonds said. "Get him out of here."

Mattie woofed in agreement. I dropped to my knees and gathered the dog into my arms. I buried my head in the soft warm fur. I felt Alan crouch beside me. He put his arms around me, and I gave into my tears.

"Erica!" I heard Jason yell as he was led through the shop. "I did it for you. Tell them. It was all for you. He didn't love you. I'm the only one who can love you. Erica!"

I let go of Mattie and struggled to my feet. "I want," I croaked. My throat burned. "Erica," I managed to say.

Alan nodded. He kept an arm around me and we went into the shop. Shards of colorful glass covered the floor. The box Alan had been carrying lay on its side, and I had the presence of mind to be glad he worked with wood, not glass. Erica stood in the center of the room, her hand over her mouth, her eyes wide with shock. Her lip was cut where Jason had tried to force her off him, and a thin line of blood dribbled down her chin. The knees of her pants were torn and her hands bloody. The trickle of blood dripping down her face gave her the appearance of a frightened vampire. I held out my arms and she fell into them with a sob.

We cried together, while Alan patted my back and Mattie sniffed in the forbidden corners of the shop.

Simmonds waited patiently until we pulled apart. I wiped my nose on the sleeve of my turquoise jacket.

"I'm sorry, ladies," Simmonds said, "but I'm going to need a couple of pictures of your injuries before you clean up." We kept our faces impassive while she used her phone. "I promise you, Erica, these will never be released to the public."

While that was happening, Alan went into the back, and returned with a pile of wet paper towels. He handed them to Erica, who wiped at her face and hands, and he then brought out the box of tissues I keep under the counter.

"You're both going to the hospital," Simmonds said. "I'll question you there."

"No," Erica said. "I'm fine."

I nodded. I couldn't speak.

"You don't look fine to me," Simmonds said.

Alan picked up the little mirror on the jewelry table. He handed it to me. An angry red line streaked across my throat. The skin was raw and puffy. "Close one," I croaked.

He offered the mirror to Erica. She waved it away. "I can't possibly look worse than I feel."

Simmonds directed Erica to the chair, and Alan went behind the counter to get the stool for me. I dropped onto it gratefully. He stood behind it, so I could rest my back against him. I felt his warmth creep into my very bones.

"Matterhorn," Simmonds said without turning around. "You shouldn't be in that. Sit with Merry." He trotted across the room, a stuffed Santa doll in his mouth. He put the doll on my lap and sat proudly beside me.

"I'm assuming he's the hero of the hour," she said.

I nodded. "A big soup bone from the butcher tonight."

"Don't talk, Merry," Simmonds said. "It's only going to get worse. Mr. Anderson, want to tell me what went down here?"

"I don't really know. I walked in on total chaos." He

indicated the entirety of the room. "Table overturned, ornaments broken, women cut and bleeding. I could hear the dog from the street. When I came in he, that photographer, ran for the back, so I followed. Mattie did the rest."

"Ms. Johnstone?"

Erica's eyes were wet, but she'd stopped crying. "Jason killed Max. My darling Max. He was going to kill Merry. Willow told me they were going to do the photo shoot here tonight. James said he had calls to make. Muriel was"—she paused and swallowed—"dead. I was alone up there at the hotel. I didn't want to be alone, so I came to see if I could help. No one believes me, but I do want to help sometimes. When I have an idea, everyone says it's the best idea ever, then they do something else as soon as I leave. They never try to help me to make my ideas work. But"—she gave me a sad smile—"that's neither here nor there." Quickly but efficiently, Erica told Simmonds what had happened once she arrived. I nodded in agreement.

"Do you have something you can write on, Merry?" Simmonds asked.

I pointed to the counter, and Alan brought me my iPad. He handed it to me.

"Why did he attack you, Merry?" the detective asked.

I typed on the iPad, and Alan, looking over my shoulder, read it out. "Check out his camera. All the photos are of Erica. It's obvious by looking at them that he loves her. Is obsessed with her, I'd say. There's one of Max, looking furious, probably chasing him away."

"He was in love with me?" Erica said. "I didn't know.

I truly didn't know. It gets difficult sometimes, believe it or not, having people always hanging around wanting to flatter you, get your attention. I thought nothing of it when Jason was always taking my picture. Max said Jason was out of line. But"—her voice broke—"I dismissed it as the same old thing. Max told me he was going to tell Jason to respect my privacy. I forgot all about it when Max died. I never thought for a minute that might be what got him killed."

"More than that, I'd suspect," Alan said. "I heard what Jason said on the way out. He loves you, Erica, in some twisted way."

I typed, *He said Max wasn't good enough for Erica.*

Erica's eyes filled with tears. She twisted the engagement ring on her left hand. "Max loved you more than he ever loved me, Merry. I knew that. I knew he was only marrying me for my money. I knew he'd rather be with you. I'm sorry about the way I behaved when I first came here, but I really believed—I tried to make myself believe—that in time he'd come to love me the most."

I was also crying. Alan's hand was against my back. Solid, warm, loving. I typed, *You didn't have an arrangement, you and Max?*

She looked blank. "An arrangement? You mean other than our wedding plans? We had a prenup of course. Grandma insisted on that. Why do you ask?"

No reason. I was sorry Max had died, and Erica had a lot of grieving ahead of her, but I couldn't help thinking she was better off. Marriage to Max would have brought her nothing but heartache.

As we'd talked, people had been coming in and out of the shop, climbing over Alan's box, stepping over broken glass. Now a man said, "You going to be much longer, Detective? We need to get into this room."

"I'm done here for now. I'm sorry, Merry, but we'll have to treat this entire place as a crime scene. Again."

"I'll take Merry home," Alan said. "And we'll see that Erica gets back to the hotel."

"There's a lawyer outside," the officer said. "Wanting to see Ms. Johnstone."

"Do you mind, Merry," Erica said, "if I come to your house with you? I don't want to be alone, not right now. And being with James is much the same as being alone."

I nodded.

"Go out the back," Simmonds said. "It sounds as though the ladies and gentlemen of the press are gathering."

Chapter 16

As Alan's truck was parked out front, surrounded by the frenzied, braying pack of reporters and photographers, we left through the back and walked to my house. Totally unaffected by the trauma he'd just witnessed, Mattie sniffed under bushes and used his nose to follow invisible trails along the sidewalk. Alan and I put Erica between us, and I slipped my arm around her thin shoulders. Her whole body trembled. Or that might have been me.

We said nothing, each of us wrapped in our thoughts, trying to absorb all that had happened.

Eventually Erica broke the silence. "I'd say that I'd kill for a cigarette, but I think that would be an inappropriate metaphor."

Simmonds had told us we could take nothing out of

the shop, not even our own bags. Fortunately, I'd slipped my cell phone into my pocket after using it to call the police.

"It'll get you started on quitting," Alan said.

"I've been wanting to do that," she replied.

"Where'd you . . . throw . . . ball?" I croaked.

"Where did I learn to throw a baseball, you mean? I was the pitcher for the team all through high school. I was pretty good, if I do say so myself."

As we turned into the driveway of my house, a curtain at the front window twitched, but Mrs. D'Angelo did not leap out to verbally accost me. Perhaps she had the sense, this one time, to read the expression on my face.

"This is so charming," Erica said the moment I opened the door to my apartment. Not expecting company, I hadn't cleaned up this morning, but it didn't look too bad.

"Small but comfy," I croaked.

"No talking, Merry," Alan said.

"I absolutely adore it," Erica said. "You must be so comfortable here. The privacy you have!"

I'd never before thought that I had all that much privacy, not with Mrs. D'Angelo downstairs charting my every move (and reporting it to her network of snoops), or sharing the staircase and backyard with Steve and Wendy and their rapidly growing baby. But, compared to how Erica must live, I suppose I did.

I pointed to Erica and then to the bathroom.

"She's telling you to freshen up first," Alan said. "The bathroom's through there."

I imitated taking a drink.

"While you're doing that," Alan said, "would you like a glass of wine?"

"I'd love one," Erica said.

"You sit down, Merry. I'll get it," Alan said.

When Erica came out of the bathroom, I went in. I turned the water to hot hot hot and washed my face and hands thoroughly. My throat felt as though I'd swallowed a bucket of flaming coals, but it looked worse. I changed out of my designer diva duds and put on tracksuit pants, T-shirt, and a heavy sweater. It was a warm evening, but I was chilled to the depths of my bones. Guessing that Erica would be feeling the same, I took a wrap out of the back of the closet where the winter clothes were stored.

She was sitting on the couch, with her legs curled up beneath her, cradling a glass of white wine. She'd scrubbed her face and twisted her hair into a high ponytail. I draped the wrap over her shoulders and she gave me a grateful smile. I settled next to her on the couch. Mattie found a favorite toy and dropped it in Erica's lap. She looked at it.

"He wants . . ." I said, ". . . throw it."

"How sweet," she said. "I've never had a dog."

Poor little rich girl.

I leaned over and gave her a hug. She threw the toy and Mattie scampered after it.

"Once only," Alan said. "He needs to learn that we don't throw things in the house." Alan handed me a glass of wine. When Mattie brought the toy back to Erica, Alan snatched it up and they engaged in a fierce tug-of-war.

Erica watched them, sipping her wine, a small smile on her face.

The doorbell rang.

Alan gave me a look.

I shook my head firmly.

"I'll take care of it," he said.

He didn't take care of it very well, because when he came back he was followed by my parents. Mom let out a long screech when she caught sight of my bruised and swollen throat. She swept across the room and enveloped me in her arms. Dad's face was set into tight lines, making him look nothing at all like Santa Claus tonight.

"You heard what happened," Alan said.

"Police activity at Mrs. Claus's Treasures, again," Dad said. "Sue-Anne phoned me. She had no details, but looking at Merry, I'll assume she was in the thick of it."

"That she was," Alan said. "You can thank Matterhorn here. He was tonight's hero."

Dad gave the dog a hearty pat, and Mattie preened.

Alan introduced Erica to Mom and Dad.

"I believe we've met before," Mom said.

Erica's smile faded slightly. She was getting comfortable pretending to be a normal person relaxing with friends.

"I performed once at your grandmother's home in Westchester," Mom said. "It was a fund-raiser for Doctors Without Borders. I never do private concerts, but darling Jennifer was such a true fan, and she begged and begged me, so how could I say no? Such a wonderful organization as well. You were maybe thirteen years old. You were allowed to join us, and I must say I don't think I've ever seen such a vivid expression of total boredom in all my life."

Erica laughed. "I remember that. What can I say? I was thirteen."

"Didn't know . . ." I said, ". . . knew Jennifer."

Mom waved her hand. "I know a lot of people. I don't think you should be talking, dear. Tomorrow I'm calling my doctor in the city for an appointment. He'll check for damage."

"Not a singer . . ." I croaked. Which was true. I inherited all of my musical talent from my dad. Meaning I had none. To my mother's continual disappointment.

Mom didn't hear me. Either that or she chose to ignore me. "I'll have a glass of wine. Alan, be a dear."

The door opened and Vicky and Mark Grosse came in. "Sounds like a party to me," Vicky said. "Although I'm guessing it has something to do with the crush outside your shop. Wow, that looks nasty. What on earth happened to you?"

"Come on in," Alan said.

I got to my feet to give Vicky a hug and managed to whisper in her ear, "Tell Mark not to say anything too rude about recent guests at the inn."

"Gotcha," she said.

My little apartment was getting seriously overcrowded. Mom joined Erica on the couch, I sat next to her, and Vicky took the chair. Alan turned the barstools around to face into the living room, and Dad and Mark sat there. Mattie ran from one person to another in sheer delight.

"Spill, Alan," Vicky said.

"What happened?" Mom said.

"Unless you'd rather not talk about it," Dad said.

"No reason not to," Alan said. "It'll be in all the papers in the morning." He was interrupted by another ring of the doorbell. "Be right back."

This time he was followed by Jackie, Willow, and, of all people, Mrs. D'Angelo. Mark hopped off the stool to give the seat to my landlady.

"Wow, Merry, you look awful. Does that hurt?" Jackie said.

"Only when . . . talk . . ."

"I told you not to attempt to speak," Mom said. "You need to keep that warm. Noel, find a scarf for Merry."

"Any beer in the fridge?" Jackie said.

"Help yourself," Alan said.

"That wine looks lovely," Mrs. D'Angelo said, making herself comfortable. "I don't normally indulge after dinner, but as this is a special occasion . . . I was on the phone to Rosemary Cooperman, when I saw Jackie and her friend coming up the drive. What's this about a gun battle raging on Jingle Bell Lane?" I didn't think she recognized Erica, small and quiet in a corner of the couch.

"I heard the cops and went to see what was happing," Jackie said, twisting the top off a bottle of beer. "I told them I worked at the shop, but they wouldn't let me in. I didn't see any bodies on the street or bullet holes in the windows though."

"No bodies," I said. "This time."

"Don't talk." Mom accepted a scarf from Dad and wrapped it tightly around my throat. It did feel good, lovely and warm. She put her hand lightly on my shoulder, and I smiled at her.

"They wouldn't tell me anything, either," Willow said. "So I asked Jackie what was going on, and she suggested we come here to try to find out."

"Amber?" I said.

"Still at the hospital. A bad break to her ankle. I left her there and hurried into town so we could continue with the shoot, and I arrived to find the place locked down." She studied the faces in the room. "So, what is going on? I note that Jason isn't here, and no one is weeping."

I'd taken my phone out of my pocket and put it on the kitchen counter when we came in. It rang, and Dad grabbed it. "Noel Wilkinson speaking." His eyes flicked toward me. "She is. That would be fine." He hung up.

Another rap at the door. This time I could tell who it was before they came in by the way Mattie, who'd been running from one guest to another, dropped immediately into the sit position. Diane Simmonds was followed by Russell Durham.

Her eyes widened as she saw the size of the crowd staring at her.

"Join the party, Detective," Mark said.

"I can't stay, but I thought Merry and Erica deserved to know what's happened."

"And I," Russ said, "just happened to follow her." He spotted Erica. "Nice to see you, honey. You okay?"

She nodded. He bent over and gave her a hug. They held each other for a long time. When they separated, Erica's eyes were wet. Russ went into the kitchen and found himself a beer.

"Would you like a drink?" Dad asked the detective.

"A glass of water would be welcome, thank you." Mattie sat on the floor at her feet. His whole body vibrated but he didn't move. "Matterhorn," she said, "sit by Merry."

He trotted across the room, to the amazement of everyone present. He sat, and I gave him an appreciative pat.

Simmonds spoke to Erica and me. "Do you want to talk in private?"

I glanced at Erica and shook my head. Erica nodded. "It'll be common knowledge soon enough," Alan said. "Noel, pass me Merry's phone. If she has anything to say, she can type and I'll read."

Simmonds turned to Russ. "I'll be making an official statement in the morning. This is all off the record, and if I see anything in print before that time, you will be in a mountain of trouble."

"Perish the thought," he said.

"Mrs. D'Angelo," Simmonds said, "you are not to use your phone until tomorrow at noon."

"What!"

"Police orders. I can access your cell phone records, you know."

Mrs. D'Angelo sputtered.

"Jason Kerr has been arrested for the murders of Max Folger and Muriel Fraser. He is, as they say in the movies, singing like a canary. He seems to be under the impression that I am interested in his sob story, and I'll set him free if only I understand his motivations.

"I'm sorry, Ms. Johnstone," Simmonds said to Erica. Mrs. D'Angelo and Jackie let out a collective gasp as they realized who was sitting among them. "But it would appear that Jason killed Mr. Folger because he wanted to be with you."

Silent tears ran down Erica's face. Mom put her arms around her shoulders and gathered her close. Russ watched them, a soft expression on his face, but he made no move to comfort his ex-girlfriend.

"Jason overheard Max and Merry talking on Friday afternoon," Simmonds said. I remembered the noises I'd heard in the alley when Max made that ridiculous proposal to me. Fortunately, the detective didn't tell the group precisely what Jason had overheard. "He decided that Mr. Folger would not be a suitable husband for you."

"I barely knew the man," Erica said. "Max hired him a couple of months ago to take photos of me and my bridesmaids shopping for dresses. He did a good job, so Max invited him on this trip. He was always watching me, always taking pictures, but that's normal behavior for a photographer. Isn't it?"

"No," Russ said. "It's not. Not when it becomes obsessive and intrusive."

"I remember one time in Milan," Mom said. "Early in my career. We were singing *Tosca*, I believe, or perhaps *Madama Butterfly*. A nasty, rat-faced Italian and his camera followed me everywhere. It was . . ."

"You can tell us that story another time, Aline," Dad said. "Please continue, Detective."

"Not without me!" came a cry from the door. Sue-Anne Morrow burst into the room. "I've been looking all over for you, Detective Simmonds. My phone has been ringing nonstop. It's my job to comfort and reassure the citizens of this town. How can I do that if I don't know what's going on?"

I typed a message on my phone for Alan. *Maybe you should go down and lock the door?*

"Be right back," he said. "Don't start without me."

Simmonds took a sip of her water and then repeated her warning about off the record. I stroked the top of Mattie's head. He looked as interested in what was being said as any of us. When Alan returned, Simmonds cleared her throat.

"Jason decided Max wasn't suitable for Erica, and he planned to tell her so. But before doing that, he wanted proof to take to her. So he set about following Max, hoping to find him in a compromising position. On Saturday afternoon, Max came into town, saying he was going to the park to watch the boat parade along with his colleagues. Jason followed him. Instead of going to the park, Max went to Mrs. Claus's Treasures. I can only assume he did so because he wanted to speak to Merry and wasn't aware she'd left. The door to the shop was open, and Max walked in. Jason followed, no doubt trying to be unobserved. He found the shop empty."

Simmonds and I couldn't help looking at Jackie. She took a deep swallow of her beer. "He heard a noise from the back, went through, and found Max opening the door to the office. Again, I can only assume that Max thought Merry was in her office, having sent her salesclerk down to the park. Max turned around and saw Jason standing there. He told Jason to get lost, and the men argued."

Simmonds shrugged. "Jason says it was an accident. That Max struck him, he pushed back, and Max fell."

"No!" I croaked. My throat seized up and I was left sputtering.

"Type, Merry," Alan said.

The cranberry string.

Simmonds grinned. "Precisely. As it's highly improbable that Jason just happened to be admiring one of the ornaments and forgot to return it to its place, we will attempt to prove he picked it up with the intention of using it when he passed through the shop."

"What cranberry string?" Mom, Jackie, and Willow chorused.

"You can't put that in the paper!" Sue-Anne shrieked. "Russell, don't you dare."

"I'll say 'rope,'" he said.

And Muriel? I typed. *She was blackmailing Jason. She was with Erica much of the time; she would have noticed Jason's behavior.*

"You're right, Merry," Simmonds said. "Muriel was Erica's personal assistant. That means Muriel and Erica spent a great deal of time together. Am I right, Ms. Johnstone?"

Erica nodded.

"Sharp-eyed Muriel had noticed that Jason was acting almost obsessively around Erica. Muriel overheard Max and Jason arguing on Friday night in the Yuletide gardens, when Max confronted Jason about hiding in the bushes and taking photos of Erica. Max threatened to fire

Jason. When Max died, she put two and two together, came up with four, and confronted Jason. Blackmailed him, if you will. He agreed to pay her off and arranged to hand over a considerable sum of money in the gardens once everyone had left after the Monday-night photo shoot.

Muriel was crafty, but not very smart. Greed did her in.

"Exactly," Simmonds said. "Jason's defense is that she deserved what she got. What else was he supposed to do but get rid of her?"

"Gee, Merry," Jackie said. "If I'd been at the store when Max and Jason came in, I would have been killed. Good thing I'd gone out."

You might be killed yet . . . I began typing. Alan took the phone out of my hands and erased the line.

My mom stood up and smoothed her skirt. "As tragic as all that is, my daughter needs to rest. Time for everyone to be leaving." She made shooing gestures. A stampede for the door did not begin.

"What I want to know . . ." Mark said.

Simmonds's phone buzzed and she checked the display. "Mr. Claymore is at the police station and threatening to have me fired if I don't produce you, Erica."

Erica took out her own phone. "Silly me, I accidentally switched it off after I sent a text to Grandma telling her not to worry about me."

"You can . . ." I began. Alan tapped my phone to remind me to type, not speak. *Spend the night here if you want. The couch pulls out to make a bed.*

Erica smiled at me. "That would be nice, but I'd better

go. If James loses track of me, Grandma'll fire him. Another time?"

I nodded. Then I typed a message for Alan only. *Get rid of them all. Erica last.*

He got to his feet. "You all heard Mrs. Wilkinson. Time to go. Besides, we've run out of drinks."

Vicky gave me a hug. "We'll communicate by smoke signals tomorrow."

"Chicken soup," Mark said. "I'll send you my special secret recipe. Guaranteed to work."

"Night, Merry," Russ said. "Take care, Erica. If you're staying in town, let me know and we can go out for a drink or something." He gave her a smile. "It would be nice to catch up."

"It would," she said. "But I don't think I'll be staying."

"Let me walk you to your car, Detective," he said. "Any word yet on unsolved cases from other placcs Jason Kerr worked?"

"No comment."

"Do you think she'll really check my phone records?" Mrs. D'Angelo said.

"Oh yes," Dad replied. "They call it interfering with a police investigation. It can result in a stiff fine as well as a considerable jail sentence. You'd better not chance it, Mable."

"I'm always one to do my civic duty. You know me, Noel."

"I guess that means the shoot's canceled," Willow said. "At least until we can find another photographer. I'll call Amber and let her know."

"I coulda been killed," Jackie said. "I'm thinking of applying for danger pay, Merry."

Just try it. Alan did not read my words aloud.

"I'll call you as soon as I've made an appointment with Dr. Decker, dear," Mom said. "All the top singers go to him. He's terribly busy, but he'll fit me in." She brushed my cheek.

One question, Dad, I typed, and Alan said, "Hold up a minute, Noel, Merry wants to ask you something."

I thought back to Monday evening, in the shop at closing time. I'd been about to rearrange the angel choir and had objected to Dad putting the vase of glass balls so close to the door. Dad told me to leave things where they were.

The angels. The big balls. How did you . . . ?

Alan and I exchanged a glance. I erased the line with a single tap on the screen. Some things are better not understood.

Dad gave me a grin and followed my mother out.

Erica, Alan, and I were left. Released from what I could only assume was a magic spell Diane Simmonds laid on him, Mattie leapt to his feet and charged through the apartment, checking every inch in case anyone had dropped a crumb or moved one of his toys.

I took my car keys off the hook by the door and handed them to Alan.

"She's telling me to take you to the inn," Alan said. "Is that where you want to go?"

"Yes. I've got a lot of thinking to do tonight. I'll phone

James and tell him I'm okay and he can call the attack dogs off. Thank you, Merry. Thank you for everything."

"You saved me. I didn't . . ."

She drew me into a hug and whispered something in my ear. It was so low I barely caught it, but I think she said, "Now I know why Max loved you so much more than he loved me." She pulled away and gave me a smile. "Sounds like your mom'll get your throat all sorted. Good night."

"Good night."

She left the apartment. Alan leaned over and gave me a quick but deep kiss. "Thanks . . . care . . . her," I said.

"We'll talk tomorrow, Merry." He grinned. "I'll talk. You can make hand gestures. Night, Mattie."

Mattie woofed. I shut the door.

Chapter 17

I slept surprisingly well, although when I looked in the mirror the next morning, I let out a strangled gasp of dismay.

I hadn't known skin could turn those colors.

I wrapped a heavy scarf around my neck to keep it warm and then made coffee and took Mattie into the yard. I sat at the picnic table, sipped my coffee, and watched him play. I didn't phone Simmonds to ask if I could open the shop. Today was a day to stay in my pajamas, play with my dog, and spend time by myself. I had a new mystery novel waiting until I had the time to dive into it. I knew that as soon as I got back to work, everyone in town would come in demanding to know what had happened.

My phone buzzed. I had no intention of talking to anyone today. Not that I was capable of talking, in any event. When I'd tried to speak to my reflection in the mirror, all that I'd managed was a strangled squawk. I glanced at the display.

My granddaughter says you are unable to speak. Is that correct? J.

Jennifer Johnstone.

I texted back: *Still a bit sore.*

Jennifer: *I will call. You don't have to talk if unable.*

Me: *Okay.*

The phone rang. "Uh," I said.

"Good morning, Merry," the deep husky voice of the most famous woman in American design said. "I heard you had quite the exciting night."

"Uh," I said.

"Erica and I talked for a long time last night. We've decided that she's not entirely suited to management of the magazine. I've been contemplating for some time beginning a charitable foundation in honor of the memory of my daughter Karen, Erica's mother. The foundation will raise money to help with thc cducation of motherless, underprivileged girls in this country and around the world."

"Good," I said.

"Erica will be in charge of the foundation, with me serving as the figurehead. I think she'll be better suited to working with well-heeled donors in pursuit of a good cause than managing a fractious, opinionated, highly talented staff."

I nodded. Realizing that even Jennifer Johnstone couldn't telepathically understand me, I grunted, "Goo . . ."

"As the magazine needs reorganization, top to bottom, I want you to come back, Merry."

"I . . ."

"Hear me out. I need you. If I'm going to get the best editor in chief I can find, I need to be able to offer him or her the best staff possible. I want you as chief editorial director of style."

"Uh . . ."

"A salary to match, of course."

"N . . ."

"You didn't save my granddaughter's life physically, Merry. But you saved her in other ways. Erica means everything in the world to me. She's been indulged for too long, and last night we both came to realize that. Thank heavens it wasn't too late. Will you come back to me, Merry?"

"Text," I managed to say.

She hung up.

Me: *Thank you so much, Jennifer. I'd love to work for you again, but I've moved on. I have my life here, in Rudolph, and it's where I'm happy.*

Jennifer: *If you change your mind . . .*

Me: *I won't. Love to Erica.*

Jennifer: *Love to you!*

High over my head, a squirrel sat in the big branch of a maple, laughing at Mattie, who hadn't yet realized he couldn't jump sixty feet in the air.

I studied my phone. And then I started another text.

Me: *Breakfast at my place?*

Alan: *You're on.*

Me: *You'll have to stop at the bakery first.*